Caroline Overington is a bestselling Australian author and the Associate Editor of *The Australian* newspaper. She has been a foreign correspondent in New York and in Hollywood; she has previously worked for *The Age*, the *Sydney Morning Herald* and the *Australian Women's Weekly*; and she has written eleven books, including some prize winners. Caroline lives in Sydney with her family, including twins, and an adored blue dog.

The One Who Got Away

CAROLINE OVERINGTON

HarperCollins*Publishers*

HarperCollins*Publishers*

First published in Australia in 2016
This edition published in 2017
by HarperCollins*Publishers* Australia Pty Limited
ABN 36 009 913 517
harpercollins.com.au

HarperCollins*Publishers*
Level 13, 201 Elizabeth Street, Sydney NSW 2000, Australia
Unit D1, 63 Apollo Drive, Rosedale, Auckland 0632, New Zealand
A 53, Sector 57, Noida, UP, India
1 London Bridge Street, London, SE1 9GF, United Kingdom
2 Bloor Street East, 20th floor, Toronto, Ontario M4W 1A8, Canada
195 Broadway, New York, NY 10007, USA

National Library of Australia Cataloguing-in-Publication entry:

Overington, Caroline, author.
The one who got away / Caroline Overington.
ISBN: 978 0 7322 9975 0 (paperback)
ISBN: 978 1 4607 0365 6 (ebook)
Detective and mystery stories.
Suspense fiction.
Psychological fiction.
A823.4

Cover design by HarperCollins Design Studio
Typeset in Sabon LT by Kirby Jones
Author photograph: *Australian Women's Weekly*
Printed and bound in Australia by Griffin Press
The papers used by HarperCollins in the manufacture of this book are a natural,
recyclable product made from wood grown in sustainable plantation forests.
The fibre source and manufacturing processes meet recognised international
environmental standards, and carry certification.

Molly Franklin

'If you love something, set it free.
If it doesn't come back, hunt it down
and kill it – ha-ha, that is so true!'

Tweet posted by Loren Wynne-Estes

I was sitting on the balcony of my little apartment with my iPad on my lap and my bare feet up on the rails, when my dad called to say: 'Molly? Can you come over?'

I said: 'Sure, what's up?'

'Come,' he said. 'Just come.'

'Is it Mom?' I asked, as I made my way to the bedroom to find a dress to pull over my bikini.

'Your mom's fine. Just please hurry.'

'Well, is it Gran?' I said, because Gran had senile dementia and we were all waiting – we were all ready – for something to happen to Gran, but then it couldn't be Gran because Dad would just have said, 'It's Gran'.

So I tried again: 'Please, Dad, just tell me. What's happened?'

'Just hurry, Molly,' said Dad, his voice tense. 'Please. Just come now.'

'Okay, I'm coming,' I said, but Dad had already hung up.

My apartment building is pretty old, and the elevator can be oh-so-slow and temperamental, so I had to press and press the button to get the thing to come, and then when it finally did, I had to press and press the inside buttons to get down and out and into the garage and into my car and on the road to Dad's place. It's not far. We both lived on the Low Side of Bienveneda, a town on the Californian coast.

What did I see when I got to Dad's?

A police car, parked right out the front. Also two kids, legs straddling their bikes, stopped dead in the street, staring.

I swerved my car into the driveway and bolted up the path. I grew up in this house, and still have keys, but I banged on the door, expecting Dad to come and open it. But the person who came to the door wasn't Dad: it was a female police officer who introduced herself as Officer Callie Croft of the Bienveneda Sheriff's Office.

Dad was standing in the sitting room with a second police officer whose name I did not catch but who was sitting next to Mom's kooky lamp that looks like a lady's leg in a fishnet stocking.

'Where's Mom?' I said.

'Your mom's out, seeing Gran,' said Dad.

I felt sick. 'Dad, why are the police here? What's happened?'

'We've had some bad news. It's Loren.'

Loren is my big sister. Technically, she's my *step*sister, since she is Dad's daughter from his first marriage, but that's not important.

'What's happened to her?'

'You tell her,' said Dad, addressing the police officers.

Callie cleared her throat. 'Well, she's missing.'

'Missing?'

'Off the boat,' said Dad.

He was standing with his meaty, freckled arms folded across his chest, his expression all defiant, like he was being asked to swallow something fishy.

'No, that can't be right,' I said.

'Of course it can't,' said Dad.

I moved a pile of newspapers off the sofa and sat down.

'Loren's on a cruise,' I said. 'I made the booking. It's like a second honeymoon for her, with her husband, David. They're aboard the *Silver Lining*, off the coast of Mexico ...'

The two-way radio on Callie's shoulder crackled. She reached up to silence it. 'I understand that,' she said, 'and we got a call this morning to say a US citizen was missing, off a cruise ship off the coast of Mexico. And the name we were given was Loren Wynne-Estes, and I understand that your father is next of kin?'

'This is crazy,' I said. 'Loren's missing? But where is David?'

'David is fine,' said Callie, as if that might be a relief to us. 'He raised the alarm. As I understand it, he woke this morning to find Loren gone.'

'But how can that be?' I said.

Callie reached into her top pocket, and withdrew a business card.

'You've probably got a lot of questions,' she said, handing the card to me. 'The lady who called us this morning, her name is Gail Perlot. She's with the US embassy in Mexico. Here's her number. You can call her, and she'll be able to help with things like how to handle the media attention.'

'Media attention?' said Dad. 'What do you mean, media attention?'

'With a case like this – when you've got somebody missing off a cruise ship – there's often media interest,' said Callie, 'and Loren ... doesn't she have young twins here in Bienveneda? David's worried about them being mobbed by the media when the story leaks out.'

I was agog. 'That's what he said? That he's concerned about the media, not about Loren?'

'That's the message we were given,' Callie said apologetically. 'He wants his girls taken somewhere safe before the media turns up. And he wanted us to tell you what's going on so you can get out of town, too.'

That was too much for Dad. 'In case we want to get out of town? My daughter's missing off a ship and her husband thinks we might want to get out of town? I don't get it. Why would we want to get out of town?'

Callie looked like she didn't get it either. 'I wish I could answer these questions, Mr Franklin, but what you really need to do is call the lady whose details are on that card. She's the one who can help.'

*　*　*

'This number doesn't look right to me,' said Dad, as soon as the police left.

He had taken Callie's card and was examining the writing on the back.

'Show me,' I said, taking the card from him. 'That's a Mexican cell-phone number. It's okay. I know how to do it.'

We went out to the patio, where the cell-phone signal was strongest. I put the phone on speaker and placed it on the patio table. It hesitated, like phones do when you're dialling abroad, but then a woman picked up, saying: 'Gail Perlot.'

I nudged Dad to talk. He shook his head, like *No, you talk*, so I said: 'Hello, Ms Perlot. My name is Molly Franklin. I'm Loren Franklin's ... I mean, I'm Loren Wynne-Estes' sister. I'm here with our dad. We were given your number ... The police are telling us that Loren is missing.'

Gail's voice came back crackly. The line was terrible.

'Yes, and I'm sorry,' she said, 'the information you have is correct. We do have information that Loren is missing off the cruise ship the *Silver Lining* ...'

'But how can that be?' Dad said angrily.

There was a pause on the line. We couldn't tell if that was because of the bad line or because Gail was choosing her words carefully. Eventually she said: 'We're not entirely sure what's happened but I've spoken to David. It seems they attended the Captain's Dinner last night and then returned to their cabin, and when David woke at around five this morning, Loren wasn't there. He went looking for her but couldn't find her. He called her cell phone but it didn't respond. He tried the dining room, where the breakfast is served. At some point, he expressed concern to a member of the crew, who put a call out over the loudspeaker but there was no response.'

'And what happened then? Did they stop the ship?' I asked.

'They did,' said Gail. 'You probably know, it takes some time to stop a cruise ship but they did stop and a head count was done, and that's when I suppose they confirmed it, that Loren was definitely not on board.'

I waited for more but it seemed that Gail was finished.

In the vacuum, I said: 'Gail, sorry, this is Molly again. It was me who booked Loren onto that ship ... it's not a huge ship, is it? I mean, how far did she fall? Maybe she's still out there, in the water?'

Gail's voice crackled back. 'No, it's not a huge ship and we – or rather, the authorities here in Mexico – have been out searching the water for Loren but ...' Gail had paused a second time.

'But?'

'But to be honest, the likelihood of somebody surviving such a fall and especially when we don't really know when she fell ...'

'You don't know when? But how can that be?' I said. 'Don't they have any surveillance?'

'They do,' said Gail. 'But not a Man Overboard system. This particular ship – most ships, in fact – don't have them. They aren't foolproof. They can be set off by birds – it's really expensive if you have to stop a ship every time there's a false alarm, so most ships, they don't have them.'

'Okay, but surely they have cameras,' I said.

'They do have cameras,' said Gail, 'although my understanding – and I'm not an expert – is that the cameras don't cover the whole ship. I mean, how could you do that? You just can't. But yes, there are some cameras, but at this stage, we – or rather they, meaning the representatives of the company that owns the *Silver Lining* – are still going through the footage and, as of half an hour ago, there was no sign of Loren.'

This was more than Dad could take. He pushed his chair back, strode away from the patio table and let out a wild cry.

'I am so sorry,' said Gail. 'This is terrible news to have to pass on. And I know that David wants to speak to you as soon as he lands back in the US ...'

'Wait,' I said. 'He's coming *home*?'

'I believe so,' said Gail.

'But doesn't he think there might be a *chance* that she's alive? And don't the police need to speak to him?'

'Well, there are a number of different types of police down here. There's the *Federales* – that's the federal police – and there's the *Policia Turistica* – that's the tourist police – and they've spoken to David ...'

'Spoken to him!' said Dad, slamming a fist down on the table, making the phone jump. 'This is just crazy. They have to do more than speak to him. You can't let him leave. You have to arrest him.'

The phone sat silently on the little table between us. Had Gail hung up? No. She was still there, and her tone remained sympathetic. 'I can hear how upset you are, but please understand, Mr Franklin, we are not the police. We are the embassy. We don't conduct investigations. This is not the United States. This is Mexico ... and if police here don't feel they have a reason to hold David, there isn't much we can do.'

* * *

Dad and I had finished our call with Gail and were sitting on opposite sides of the patio table, trying to get our heads around the things she had said.

'We have to go to Mexico,' said Dad. 'We have to get down there.'

'What are we going to do in Mexico?' I said. 'David's already talking about coming back.'

'I don't care about David,' cried Dad. 'Can't you see what's happened? David's not like us, Molly. He's got money. Money means power. He's already off the boat. He'll be on his way home soon. He's going to hire a fancy lawyer, and pay who he needs to pay to sweep this under the carpet. We can't let that happen. We have to go there. We have to talk to the other passengers. We have to find out what the search crews are doing. Maybe we can even get one of those high-speed power boats like the lifesavers use ...'

'Right,' I said, 'but how quickly could we even get there? And what about the girls?' I added, meaning Loren's girls. The twins. Peyton and Hannah. Hannah and Peyton. They hadn't been on the cruise with Loren, because it's not really a second honeymoon when two five-year-olds come along for the ride, is it? So the girls had stayed behind, in Bienveneda, with David's sister, Janet.

Why with Janet, and not with me?

That had been Loren's idea.

'Janet has offered to move in while we're away, to take care of them,' she'd said.

'But she doesn't even like kids,' I'd said. 'Why don't you let them stay with me? There's a pool in my building. They've got a whole box of those foam noodle things. I'd love to have them.'

But Loren had said: 'No, no. It's nice of you, Molly, but ...'

'But?'

'But going to and from school, the traffic on the bridge, Low Side to High Side and back again, is just awful ...'

It wasn't the traffic.

Loren didn't want the girls to stay with me because I lived on the wrong side of town. I'd been upset about it, but that was no longer important.

'I can't even imagine what he's going to tell them,' I said.

'We can't worry about that. We have to start making plans to get to Mexico as fast as we can.'

'Okay, Dad. Let me think. Even if we leave now, by the time we get to the airport ... I mean, there's just no way to get there before tomorrow.'

'Then we go tomorrow,' cried Dad, 'and for now, let's think of who else to call to make sure they're searching properly. The police? There must be police we can talk to there?'

'Okay,' I said. 'Okay. We'll go. But right now, I want to go to Loren's house. I want to go and see if I can catch those girls before Janet takes them God knows where and tells them God knows what. You call Mom. Tell her what's happened. I'll go now and then I'll race by my flat to get some stuff together, and we'll go tomorrow.'

Dad nodded. I got up, kissed his forehead, and went out the front door, to get into my car. The boys on their bikes had gone, but I was fairly sure I saw the curtains in a window across the street move.

Stickybeak neighbours. You can't blame them, I suppose.

* * *

I got across the bridge as quickly as I could, but if I'd been thinking that I could pull up outside Loren's house without anyone noticing, I was mistaken.

The media had set up camp outside her front gate. Among the vehicles were two satellite trucks. I recognised one woman – white blazer, pink lips, coiffed hair – from the local news.

The story was out. But were the twins still home? I didn't know. Loren's garage requires a clicker and I didn't have one, so I parked on the street, and began walking towards the tall, stone gate pillars.

The journalists in the media pack couldn't possibly have known who I was but as soon as I stopped by one of the pillars and began punching the code – the twins' birthday – into the security pad, they pounced.

'Are you family? Are you a friend? Do you know Loren Wynne-Estes?'

My hands were shaking and I must have punched the numbers incorrectly. I tried again.

A reporter said: 'Loren who is missing from the cruise ship? Do you know her? Is that why you're here?'

The gates were taking their sweet time to swing open. A fluffy TV mic was hovering over my head and an iPhone with a recorder app was under my face.

'Do you know what happened? Did she fall?'

Did she fall?

I turned as if to say: do you really want me to answer that? Because what was the alternative? She either fell or she jumped? She either fell, or she was pushed. Those were the only options.

* * *

It was completely quiet inside Loren's house. I can't tell you how unusual that was. Loren was a proper High Side mom. She employed a team of nannies. She had a housekeeper who hummed and clattered about. She liked to have music playing, and she had the girls. So Loren's house was a noisy house.

I thought back to one of the last times I'd been there. Loren had invited me over. My business, before all this started, was cosmetic surgery. I'm not a doctor, obviously, but I used to work in a cosmetic-surgery office, and I got to know what people want, as well as how much they had to pay. That's where I came up with the idea of starting a business doing cosmetic-surgery vacations down to Mexico. New boobs. New butts. Mommy makeovers. They're all much cheaper in Mexico, provided you know what you're doing. So I set out on my own, and three or four times a year, I'd take clients down there for a nip and tuck, with a luxury vacation tacked on the end. And because I was in that business, I sometimes used to get freebies in the mail from cosmetic companies. And on this occasion, I'd received a basket of face-cream samples, and I'd texted Loren, who'd texted back: **Ooh ... bring them over!**

It wasn't like she couldn't afford her own fancy skin-creams, but who doesn't like a freebie?

I'd arrived to find Peyton and Hannah dressed as Elsa, from *Frozen*. They're both blonde. Loren had plaited their hair and gone crazy with the costumes. They were belting the theme song into a set of those comedy-sized, plastic microphones.

'Sing with us,' Hannah cried, 'we can upload it to iTunes!'

I'd gone along with it, singing loudly into one of the microphones, doing my best to keep up while one of the nannies hovered with a video recorder. It had been so much fun, and now the house just seemed so quiet.

I went down the corridor and into the kitchen. Loren's kitchen normally gleams, yet it was a mess. The juicer was still out on the bench, with a stick of celery jutting out.

Whoever was last in there – the girls, Janet and at least one nanny – had obviously left in a hurry. The image of Loren's children being bundled into an SUV, being told to hurry, hurry, hurry, made my heart hurt.

Had the media already arrived by then? How awful. Imagine being five years old, still with a teddy or a doll under your arm, having to dodge a TV camera. Imagine being seated in the SUV, with the cameras coming up close to the tinted windows.

I left the mess in the kitchen and headed down the hall, my footsteps echoing on the parquetry floor. I don't know if you've ever been in somebody's house when they aren't home, but it's nerve-racking, which is weird because it wasn't like I had broken in. This was my sister's house. I had the code.

I poked my head into the girls' bedroom. Hannah and Peyton were old enough to have their own rooms, and the house was certainly big enough to accommodate them, but they are twins and they love to be together. Maybe that comes from when they were babies. One of Loren's first helpers – the baby whisperer, she'd called her – taught Loren how to swaddle each of her infants, and then place them together in one cot. Being together seemed to soothe them.

Now they were bigger they had their own canopy beds, but they still shared a room. The bed curtains were supposed to be tied back with bows, but they were loose – more evidence of how quickly everyone had left? – and the sheets were messed up and jumped on. The rocking horse was wearing a hat. The kid-sized table was set for a mini-tea party, with one American Girl doll, one Talking Dora, and a matching set of teddy bears sitting in little chairs, waiting expectantly.

I continued down the hall, towards Loren's bedroom. My heart was beating like a bird under a blanket. It wasn't often that I was in my sister's house, and rarely did I venture into what she grandly called the 'parents' retreat'. Fair enough, too, because Loren's bedroom was more like a suite: there was the bedroom, a dressing room, a walk-in robe, and then the bathroom, with double sinks, a double shower and double mirrors.

I opened the door. Unlike the girls' room, this was immaculate. The bed was beautifully made. The cover – it's Scandinavian wool, I remember Loren telling me that – was stretched and tucked around the mattress, and the pillows were smooth. The housekeeper had set out felt slippers on each side of the bed, ready for when the occupants returned.

I looked around. I knew what I was looking for. My sister has always kept a journal, and wherever she's lived, it's always been hidden in the same place: under the bottom drawer of her dresser.

I removed the bottom drawer. There was a leather-bound notebook in the cavity. It wasn't old – on the contrary, it was new – and it wasn't even all that thick, and the way the writing all ran together, I could just tell that Loren had been pouring her heart into it.

I sat down on my butt on the floor by her bed, with knees up under my chin, and started to read.

Loren Wynne-Estes

'Love is blind, and marriage is the
eye-opener. That's a classic!'

Tweet posted by Loren Wynne-Estes

We met by the fridge. That was twelve years ago. I was twenty-three and straight out of college.

Thinking about it now, a fridge probably wasn't the best omen. Fridges are cold and hard and full of dead things, ha-ha, but who was looking for an omen?

Not me. I was looking for a tub of strawberry-flavoured yoghurt I'd left in the fridge earlier that day. Where the hell was it? There was a big note: IF IT'S NOT YOURS DON'T TAKE IT, but this being an office full of unpaid interns, people took things anyway.

A voice behind me said: 'Lost something?'

I turned and straightened and, wow. There stood a guy who I was going to say was at least as good-looking as George Clooney, but forget George Clooney. There stood a guy who was just hellishly handsome.

This guy was tall and strong and lean and tanned. Dark hair, blue eyes.

So, who was he? Besides being Captain Handsome? I had no idea. I'd only been working for Book-IT for ... well, certainly for less than six weeks. The company doesn't exist anymore, but Book-IT was basically a Brooklyn-based start-up.

Our founders were two guys – they weren't related, yet both had these curiously long white eyelashes – who had devised a computer program that was going to let people choose their own hotel rooms, and their own flights. I was one of twenty marketing graduates they had hired to help get the concept off the ground. If you're wondering whether that meant people sat on balance balls at their desks and brought their dogs to work, then yes, they did.

If you're wondering whether we had all been promised big bonuses if the whole idea took off, then yes, of course we had.

Anyway, I looked at this guy and said: 'Somebody stole my yoghurt.'

David – for that was Captain Handsome's name – tilted his head and said: 'Right,' and then, in a kind of quizzical way he added: 'Hang on ... don't I know you?'

Don't I know you?

That's a line, right? To this day, I can remember thinking: *Oh, come on, that is a line.*

It may not be the lamest line ever – 'I have a rare tropical disease that will kill me if I don't have sex in the next half-hour' is the lamest line ever – but it was a line nonetheless, and if there was one thing I really wasn't in the mood for that day, it was being fed a line, but then, just as I was about to shut the fridge and say, 'Excuse me,' and make my way back to my desk, David clicked his fingers and said: 'No, wait, we do know each other! You're from Bienveneda.'

That floored me because, as it happens, I was – and I am – from Bienveneda.

Could this guy also be from Bienveneda? The odds were against it. Bienveneda is a town on the Californian coast road, too far from LA to make a day trip of it, and the nice parts are too filled with gated estates to be the kind of place that anyone would go to for a vacation. The chances of meeting somebody else from Bienveneda in Brooklyn, let alone at Book-IT?

Surely nil.

'No way,' I said, startled. 'Why, are you?'

'I am,' he said. 'Maybe we've met?'

Maybe we had, but then again how? Looking at him, I could see that he was at least eight or maybe even ten years older than me, which wasn't necessarily a problem, except that he had probably abandoned Bienveneda for college before I had even started high school.

'I don't know,' I said doubtfully. 'Which side were you on?'

Which side were you on? It sounds like a sporting question, but it's not a sporting question. It's actually a question that only a fellow Bienvonite will understand.

Which side you were on refers to the Bienveneda River – the lovely, muddy, rocky Bienveneda River – which runs right through the middle of town.

When that river rises, one side of the town floods. Which side? The Low Side. Where was David raised? The High Side. And never the twain shall meet.

'Well, that can't be it,' I said.

'Well, who cares anyway?' he said. 'We're here now. We should have a drink.'

Ah, but should we?

David might have thought so, but I had my reservations. It wasn't so much that he wasn't cute. Oh my goodness, he was cute. It wasn't that he was married. He definitely wasn't married. No, for me the problem was that David was obviously quite a bit older than I was – I was twenty-three; he was thirty-two – and much more senior at Book-IT.

Was falling into bed with somebody who may well turn out to be one of my bosses really what I wanted to do in my first few weeks on the job?

I wasn't sure.

'Oh come on,' said David, sensing my hesitation, 'we're only talking about one drink.'

'Well, alright,' I said, although I think I knew even then that we weren't. 'I'm Loren, by the way.'

David grinned and stuck out his hand. 'Well, how do you do, Loren By-the-Way,' he said, 'I'm David Wynne-Estes.'

* * *

We went to Hudson on the West Side. Being new to New York City, I'd never heard of Hudson and yet it was standing room only on the green glass floor.

'Are those antlers?' I asked, as David led me through the buzzing crowd, past a chair made from what seemed to be bits of deer.

'I believe so,' said David, 'they had an artist come in. I read about it in the *Times*. He was big on natural materials.'

'Including animals?'

'Yes,' said David, laughing, 'including animals!'

It was late Autumn, and cold and grey outside. We stripped out of our layers and handed them in at coat check. The main bar was completely full of women with stick legs and high heels and with men holding beer bottles from the neck, but there were a few empty nooks and crannies in the cramped library bar, so we squeezed ourselves into one of them. The table was the size of a steering wheel, on a high pole. The chairs were cracked leather. There were bookshelves to the ceiling on three of four walls, and they had one of those library ladders on a rail.

'What can I get you folks?'

The waiter looked like a young Bruce Springsteen in faded denim with a stars-and-stripes hankie in his back pocket. David did the ordering, for which I was grateful. Being new to town, I wouldn't have known what to order. This was to be my first ever lychee martini, and my first ever wasabi peas.

We sipped, we nibbled, we ended up staying five hours.

'You're fun,' I said at one point.

'And you're pretty,' he said, touching my nose.

I blushed. Was I pretty? I don't know. I guess so. Who isn't at twenty-three?

Anyway, eventually, David said: 'So ... shall we find a quieter place to eat properly?'

'Yes,' I said, 'I think we should.'

The alcohol had loosened me up. We gathered our things from coat check – David tipped five dollars, which I remember thinking was quite a lot – and stepped onto a near-vertical escalator for the ride out to the street, and guess what? It was snowing.

'It's beautiful,' I said, putting out my mittens to catch some flakes.

'Today it's beautiful,' said David, 'tomorrow it's dirty slush on the sidewalk.'

'Can we walk around in it?'

David looked down at me – he's a good foot taller than I am – to see if I was serious.

'I keep forgetting you're new here,' he said.

'Well, I am.'

'Then let's go.'

He took my arm, and we began walking – slowly, since I didn't have quite the right boots on – down to the corner of Central Park South.

'Would you like a ride?' said David.

'You mean in a carriage?'

Yes, he meant in a carriage. The driver helped me up. I settled back into the bench seat. David got in beside me, and put a blanket over my knees.

'This is like something from a movie,' I said.

'Which movie?' said David.

'All of them!'

We went once around the bottom end of the park, which was just long enough for David to get his hands under the blanket, and then under my skirt.

Cheeky monkey was already taking liberties, and for all my earlier hesitation, I found I didn't mind.

* * *

'So, how did you know that I was from Bienveneda?'

We were lying naked in David's bed on the ninth floor of a cast-iron building on Mercer.

'Easy,' he said. 'I took a peek into your personnel file.'

I sat bolt upright, not easy given I was tangled in sheets at the time. 'You did what?'

'Hey, don't be like that,' said David, propping himself onto an elbow, 'it's not like I was stalking.'

'Except that you have been poking around in my personnel file!'

'Well, sure. You were sitting at your desk on, what? Day one or two of the new job, and I thought, *Wow, who is that?* So I asked my PA to bring me your file. That's not stalking. That is due diligence.'

'Oh, come on. That's stalking!'

'Hey, don't be like that. Imagine if I hadn't had that peek?' he protested, 'we might not be here now, and how bad would that be?'

Bad. Very bad, because honestly, there was nowhere in those days that I wanted to be, other than in David's bed.

It seems ridiculous now, but I can still remember how nervous I was during my first sleepover at his place. All the gossip at Book-IT was that he only ever dated models, and I wasn't a model – not even close – but I knew where to find Victoria's Secret.

Don't spend a fortune, I told myself.

I spent a fortune and honestly? I shouldn't have bothered, because men don't care. They want you naked.

'You are gorgeous,' David said. He was pretty hot himself.

Do I have to describe the sex? Well, it probably goes without saying that David was more experienced than me in that regard, too. I'm not saying that I hadn't had any kind of sex life before I met him – of course I had – but it had been vanilla. My greatest skill was faking orgasms, or so I thought until I fell back against the pillow – this was after one of my better *When Harry Met Sally* performances – and he said: 'So ... do you always fake?'

How had he known? Because guys do. They pretend they don't, but they do.

Part of me wanted to splutter: 'Oh no, I wasn't faking ...' but it wasn't like David was smirking. He seemed really interested to know.

'I'm not sure how to answer that,' I said.

'Well, faking is stupid,' he said, 'and it has to stop.'

With that, he got up and took his firm ass into his en suite.

'What are you doing in there?' I said.

'Picking up this.' David was holding an electric toothbrush. 'Do you know what this is?'

'A toothbrush?'

'No. It's a pleasure machine,' he said, and honestly, I had no idea what was coming, except that I soon was.

'How did you even know how to do that?' I said, afterwards. 'Who even taught you that?'

Thinking back now, I guess that was a stupid question, because did I really want to know the answer? No. All that mattered was that David seemed keen on giving me an education in the bedroom – and we all know what happens when we come across one of those guys, right?

We become enthusiastic students!

It wasn't long before we were doing everything. Alright, maybe not everything. I've seen on the internet what some people get up to and I'm not doing any of that, but I can't be the only girl to have figured out that the more sex we had, the more I wanted; and the more things we tried, the braver I became.

One day, I brought chocolate sauce into David's apartment. Another time it was candles (I'm laughing now, remembering how he yelped when I dripped the wax on him).

Given how I was raised – pretty conservatively, and mostly by Mom, after Dad walked out – this was all a big deal for me, but I don't want anyone to think that my relationship with David was all about sex.

We talked.

No, I promise, we did.

Lying in David's bed – he had a leather-bound bed in those days, with very manly Calvin Klein sheets – we shared stories about our friends, our schools, our childhoods. I'd taken it for granted that he had had an easier time growing up than me – basically because his parents were still together, and because he was High Side – but he didn't see it that way.

'It wasn't fun being sent to boarding school,' he said, as the New York taxis honked outside and the coffee went cold in our cups. 'It wasn't fun being told over the phone that my dog had died.'

I had been running my bare feet up David's naked legs in that sexy way you do when you're young and in love, but now I stopped.

'How did they break it to you?' I asked.

'We used to get weekly phone calls, and Mom just said: "Oh, and we had to put Lucy down. She'd gotten incontinent." And then, you know, "So, that was sad. But listen, we have to go. Talk to you next week."'

I placed a hand on David's chest. 'That's awful.'

'They're British. They don't show emotion,' said David. He had removed one hand from behind his head and he was stroking my hair.

'But enough about me,' he said. 'What did your parents do to you?'

'Well, they certainly never had my dog put down.'

'No, but I'm sure they did something. Parents can't help themselves.'

The worst thing my father did to me was leave my mother for a woman with a kid about the same age as me. And the worst thing my mother did to me was die of a stroke, in my last year of college – but that was too hard to talk about.

'I wasn't that happy when my parents split up,' I said.

'Why did they split?'

'Why? I guess because Dad met somebody he liked more than Mom.' I was talking about Val, who is Molly's mom. 'Dad left when I was eight. Molly was six. There was a time when I couldn't stand to look at her,' I told David. 'We're still not that close.'

We were cuddled as close to each other as two people can get.

'You held it against her?'

'Maybe, which is stupid. It's hardly her fault. But I guess there were a few years after that where it was pretty ugly, and maybe I didn't behave all that well, but it was hard, knowing that Dad preferred living with Molly to living with me.'

David kissed the top of my head. 'You know that's not right. He left your mom, not you.'

'But that's not how it feels when you're a kid. It felt like he was choosing Molly.'

'Right, but it's all good now. Because now you have me.'

* * *

'He's The One.'

'Who is?'

'David. He's The One.'

I was sitting near the window in my Brooklyn apartment with Nadine Perez. Yes, yes, with *that* Nadine Perez. Nobody believes me when I tell them this but, two weeks after I moved to New York, Nadine Perez placed an ad for a roommate on Craigslist, and I answered it. This was back before *Crank Girl*, obviously. This was back when Nadine was still one of a million girls waiting tables and taking acting lessons and hoping for a break.

I'm off-topic, but whenever people find out that I used to room with Nadine, they ask me: could you tell, even then, what was going to happen for her? Honestly? Yes. She had that ... that thing that some people have. Don't even ask me to try to describe it, but Nadine Perez had it.

For the record, it wasn't just the two of us living together. We had another roommate, a girl who moved in at the same time as me, a girl called Emma ...

Emma ...?

Emma-what?

Emma-something. Oh come on, Loren, she must have had a surname?

Emma, Emma ... jeepers, all I can remember is that she was British and thank God she was living with us, because she paid her share of the rent, which is more than I can say for Nadine, which is hilarious when you think about it because I mean, I haven't seen Nadine for years, but when I do see her – in magazines and on the TV – she's on the red carpet, dripping Harry Winston diamonds and rocking Gucci couture, whereas when I knew her, she had money for cigarettes and black toenail polish, and that was about it.

Nadine Perez, twelve years ago, was broke.

Anyway, the point is that Nadine Perez was the first person I confided in about David and she was ... well, let's say sceptical.

'This man, David Wynne-Estes, I know this man,' she said, tapping the ash from her cigarette into the brick courtyard four floors below. 'You be careful, Loren.'

'You know David?' I said, surprised. 'How do you know him?'

'Not him. I know a man like him,' she said impatiently. 'A man like him, I've met before. These men, they're bachelors. You must watch yourself, Loren. You're going to get hurt.'

Did I listen?

No.

Do we ever?

No.

Would Nadine be proven right? Yes, because just six months into what I considered our relationship – our wild, funny, mutually supportive, madly sexy relationship – David ended it.

Didn't expect that, did you?

No. Me either. But that's what happened. David called me into his office at Book-IT – his glass-walled office on the upper floor, with who knows how many Book-IT staff trying to think of a reason to hurry past and get a quick look inside – and dumped me.

'I don't understand,' I said, and I genuinely could not compute what he was telling me.

'Oh, Loren. We've had a good time. But I wasn't intending this – me and you – to be something exclusive,' said David, 'I mean, you're great! But the thing is, there's this other girl, and I want to see where that relationship might go.'

There was another girl? But how could that even be? I was so shocked that I burst into tears.

'Oh, Jesus,' said David, rushing to close the door (not that it helped, because: glass-walled office). 'Oh, Loren, please. Stop this. Stop this now. Don't cry.'

To be clear, he wasn't upset. People were walking past and gawking in. He was embarrassed.

'Please stop, Loren,' David said, looking around for something to mop up my tears. 'Loren, please. This is crazy. The last thing in the world I wanted to do was to hurt you.'

Again, this made no sense. If he didn't want to hurt me, then why was he leaving me?

'But we've been happy,' I said, chest heaving. 'Why not find out where this is going? Leave her and stay with me. What has she got that I haven't? I thought we were in love.'

Oh yes, I went there. And it gets worse. You know all those rules about keeping your dignity after a breakup? About not calling and texting and sobbing? About keeping your head high? I broke all of them. *All* of them. I called David long after he'd made it clear that he didn't want me to call anymore. I texted him vague messages like, **Thursday 6pm best for me** to see if he might text me back, saying: **Sorry, what?** so I could then pretend that I'd sent the message to the wrong person (that didn't work, either). I turned up on his street corner, where I jogged up and down in one spot in my Lycra gym pants, hoping that he might come out and see me and say, 'Wow, Loren, you are gorgeous. Come on back to your rightful place – in my bed.'

None of it worked. David had dumped me, and he wasn't playing games. His calls and texts to me just stopped. Bang. So brutal. Like I hadn't existed. I remember Molly telling me: 'Look, it's probably for the best. Cutting you dead, it's harsh, but it's so much better than letting you hang on, wondering whether he might come back ...'

Which was all well and good, but I was hurting like hell. When I wasn't at work or jogging, I was moping.

'I don't understand,' I sobbed to Nadine. 'What did I do wrong?'

'This isn't about you,' she said. 'I told you, this man is a player. Now, enough. Week after week, you're in bed. You need to get up. You need to stop. You need to move on.' With that, she tried to drag the covers off me.

'I can't move on,' I said, snatching them back. 'I'm devastated. I've got a broken heart.'

'You have not got a broken heart. You have a broken head. You dated. You broke up. This happens, Loren. To thousands of girls in this city, every day. You know what you must do. Get back on the donkey.'

She meant the horse. But who wanted a horse? Not me. I wanted David, a situation made infinitely worse by the fact that I was still seeing him – literally, I was still seeing him every day, because we worked together at Book-IT – until one day, when he simply disappeared.

* * *

'What the hell happened?'

I was standing outside David's office, looking in. The entire staff was doing the same. His desk – a desk that I knew intimately from all the times he'd called me in to sit on it – had been wiped clean.

'Where is everything?'

All the things that normally covered his desk – the baseball signed by Derek Jeter, the two computer screens he needed to watch the stock market, the miniature rake resting in the sandbox – were gone.

David's posters – WINNERS GET UP ONE MORE TIME – were gone, too.

'Why doesn't anyone ask me what happened, because I happen to know.' It was whiny Marvin, the least likeable of the unpaid interns we had slaving at Book-IT.

'What do you know?' I said.

'The guy who worked in there,' said Marvin, 'the jerk with the dollar-sign cufflinks like he's Michael Douglas in *Wall Street* and hello, it's the new millennium?'

Yes, that was David.

'Well, he got a call to come in on the weekend, and then when he got here, lawyer types were waiting for him,' Marvin said. 'Guys in suits. Guys with ties. They had this big, closed-door meeting. Next thing, he walked out.'

'How do you know all this?'

'Because I got a call to come in, too. I was standing right here when he came out of there. The lawyers, they told me: "Go in, pack up all his stuff, and take it to him." Which I did. He lives on Mercer. You should see the apartment. It's got all this fancy furniture: that famous leather chair with the footstool, one of those arc lamps.'

Yes, I remembered.

'But what did he say?' I said anxiously. 'Was he upset, or ...?'

'He wasn't upset. He just said, put those things there, and those things there, and while I was doing that, he told me that it was no big deal, he was planning on leaving New York anyway.'

That hit me like a hammer. David was leaving New York? But why? To go where? And how was I going to get him back if that happened?

'He's going back to his home town.' Marvin shrugged. 'He said something about his mom being sick, and he felt sad to be going because he would have stayed a bit longer to keep the company out of trouble.'

'Out of trouble? What does that mean?'

'He didn't say, only that he thought they'd regret asking him to go because he was the one holding everything together. Like, how arrogant can you get?'

I looked back into David's empty office. His title at Book-IT had been Vice-President, Capital Raising, meaning he was in charge of finding investors, and since we were a start-up – i.e.

not making any money – he could well have been holding the place together.

'Maybe he's right,' I said, 'maybe we are in trouble.'

I rushed home from work to tell Nadine.

'So they must have caught him,' she said, because Nadine is smart like that.

'What do you mean?' I said, because I'm dumb like that.

'The amount of money he was throwing around – the apartment on Mercer, all those fancy clothes and paying for every round – it had to be coming from somewhere.'

'But he was really high up, and they were paying him a lot,' I said indignantly, and loyally.

'Sure they were,' said Nadine, grinding her cigarette butt against the fire escape. 'Believe me, Loren, nobody gets marched out of the building on a Sunday unless they've been stealing.'

* * *

David left Book-IT in the summer. I stayed on, as did most of the staff. Whatever calamity he predicted might come from his departure never eventuated. We went from strength to strength. I got promoted from a cubicle to an office, and I promoted myself from the smallest bedroom in our little apartment to a one-bedroom apartment on the Lower East Side.

There was no contact between me and David, and I do mean none. He had lost his Book-IT email when he left and I couldn't find a forwarding address; he'd had to hand back his cell, and I didn't have his new number. Nadine encouraged me to quit moping and enjoy New York, which I did, to a point, but when your heart gets broken, it gets broken, and there's not much you can do to fix it, except give it time.

And then *bang*.

Yes, you guessed it. I ran into David. Literally. I crashed into him, on the corner of Park and 45th.

David was first to speak. 'Hey, hey, hey, easy there, girl,' and then, as we collected ourselves, he said: 'Oh my God, it's Loren Franklin! What are the chances? How the hell are you, Loren? How long has it been?'

It had been four years.

'You look amazing,' he said. 'What the hell are you doing with yourself?'

Truth be told, right at that moment, I was struggling to get a word out. It was just such a shock to see him again, and he hadn't changed at all. He still had the dark hair, the blue eyes, the deep voice, and I don't know, I just couldn't seem to get a hold of myself.

'Me? I'm not doing anything,' I said, 'I'm just walking along.'

'Oh come on. You must be doing something. You're not still at Book-IT?'

As a matter of fact, yes, I was, but for some reason I said: 'No,' and then: 'I mean, yes! Yes, I'm still at Book-IT. Not at the same job.'

I was talking gibberish.

'So they promoted you?' he said. 'It was only ever a matter of time. You'll end up running that place.'

'Why did they fire you?' I spluttered, thinking: *Oh, gee, Loren, did you really just say that?!*

David threw back his head and laughed. 'Is that what they told people? They didn't fire me! I quit. I had to go home to Bienveneda. Mom had a bit of a health scare. But now I've started a business there. Capital Shrine. I do capital raising, investment, same as I used to do for Book-IT, but now I do it for me.'

'Oh right,' I said, and then – inexplicably – 'and you come to New York?'

Like he wasn't standing in the streets of Manhattan? Like capital raising doesn't happen in New York? I wanted to slap myself.

'I do,' said David, smiling. 'I come quite often. I've been thinking about getting a place here because you know, the hotels are a bit dingy and small.'

I didn't know. I'd never stayed in a New York City hotel. I heard from people that they were small, but would David be staying in a small room in a dodgy hotel? I didn't think so. To look at David – and I couldn't take my eyes off him – was to see a man doing well for himself. Maybe I couldn't have put a price tag on it then, but his elegant suit must have been expensive, and the cufflinks were still there.

'But hey, what about you?' he asked. 'Still in that little apartment of yours? The one you shared with Nadine? You know I saw her at something the other day ... not saw-saw, in person, but in a magazine. Magnificent.'

I felt a twinge of jealousy. I knew the shots he meant. Nadine had made the cover of *Fancy*. She wasn't wearing much: knickers and lipstick, and she had a cigarette dangling from her bottom lip. It was all very black-and-white and arty, and no, of course I wasn't still sharing with her. Nadine had taken off one weekend for what she said was a test shoot for a Hollywood pilot, after which we'd never seen her again, except in magazines. Nadine had made it.

'And what about Emma what's-her-name?' said David. 'Do you still see her?'

I didn't. Emma was also gone, off to Boston to do her MBA.

'So, you're all alone?' he said, in mock sympathy.

'Ha-ha! I'm not alone, no ...'

What was I talking about!? I was living alone in my newly leased, one-bedroom apartment, which I somehow found myself telling David came with a washer–dryer combo that wasn't in the basement but in the kitchen ...

'Woo hoo,' said David, smiling.

Was I standing there on that busy corner, surrounded by honking cars and dog-walkers, rabbiting on about my washer–dryer combo? Apparently yes. To myself, I said: *Just shut up, Loren, can you just shut up? Because you're coming across as such an idiot. No wonder this guy left you.*

But hey ... he wasn't leaving now. No. David was still standing where we had stopped, on the street corner, chatting and smiling. The pedestrian lights had changed not once, but twice. We were in people's way and he did not care. Let them push around us. David was busy, gazing at me.

'Hell,' he said, 'I've got to go. But hey, what a coincidence. And do you know, when I was flying in from LAX yesterday, I thought to myself, wouldn't it be cool if I ran into Loren Franklin? And here you are. So weird. And you look so great. But hey, listen, I have to get moving. But it was so good to see you.'

'Right. It was so good to see you, too.'

David smiled. 'And hey,' he said, leaning in to kiss my cheek, 'if you're ever over on the West Coast, promise me you'll look me up?'

'I promise.'

'Good stuff,' he said, and then he was gone, swallowed up by the sea of people that is Manhattan on a midweek day.

And me? I almost collapsed. Had there been a wall behind me, I would have slumped against it and slid down, down, down, right onto the ground. David Wynne-Estes had returned to the city for one day and he had walked straight into me.

Forget the fridge filled with cold and dead things, over which we'd once met. Was this an omen? Also, what was it that David had said: If you're ever on the West Coast, promise you'll look me up.

Like I was ever on the West Coast. I was never on the West Coast. The West Coast was where I'd grown up. The West Coast was in my past. My future was in New York City. No way was I going back to Bienveneda. I mean, that's just madness.

* * *

Who agreed with my decision to try to chase David down after that chance meeting? Well, I was no longer in touch with Nadine, but I could imagine her response, as she sucked back on a ciggie: 'Have you lost your mind? This man, he is a player. This man, he is never settling down.'

Maybe so, but I felt like I had to give it a shot.

Why?

Where is the woman who has never recalled a past encounter and wondered deep down in her heart, if he was the one, The One Who Got Away?

I'm not talking now about the first guy you ever dated. That would be crazy. Who looks back on the first guy they ever dated and thinks: Wow, I wish I was still with him? Nobody. Alright, almost nobody. No, the guy I'm talking about is somebody who came along after you'd already had a serious boyfriend or two. He was somebody you hung out with for a while and maybe you weren't even sure if you wanted him, or else you met him on holidays and had a bit of a hot fling with him, or else he was married, in which case we just won't go there.

It doesn't matter. All that matters is that you were with him, and now you're not but he still plays on your mind. Sitting in traffic, you find yourself wondering: Why did we break up?

What would my life be like if we'd stayed together?

Would I be happier?

Would I be more fulfilled? More satisfied, sexually? More content on every level?

David was that guy to me. He was my One Who Got Away.

I'd been absolutely head-over-heels in love with him, I got dumped and I never quite got over it. Don't say I didn't try, because by the time we ran into each other on that street corner in New York I had been without David in my life for far longer than I'd ever been with him. I had dated other guys. I had been in what might even be called other relationships.

I still thought about David up to twenty times a day.

What was he doing? Did he ever think about me? Did he ever regret his decision? Did he ever think of tracking me down?

On the face of it, the answer to those questions was: No. Because he never had tried to track me down. But then again, what had he said when we ran into each other?

Don't forget to look me up if you're ever in town.

I was never in town. Bienveneda wasn't the kind of place I ever felt like visiting. In part, that was because my mom had passed. Dad was still there, as was Molly, but, I don't know, the place no longer felt like home.

On the other hand, David was there. And I guess I just had to know, was there something between us, or not? I wanted – maybe I even needed – to find out and so, a week or so after that chance encounter, I reached out to Molly.

hey, I texted, **miss u**

Molly's reply came straight back.

hey! I miss u 2 sister!

It was exactly what I was hoping she would say.

maybe we should get together how about i come and see u?

Molly texted back: **YES – when?**

The most obvious time seemed to be Dad's birthday, which was then about three weeks away. It wasn't a big birthday – he had already turned fifty – but Molly said that if I was going to be in town, she would organise a party, which sounded like fun.

'Where do you think he'll want to go?' I said.

'Where do you think?' she replied, 'BENIHANA.'

I laughed. Is Benihana my favourite restaurant? No, but I had good memories of going there with Dad and even now, I can remember how glamorous I once thought those sweating Japanese chefs were, with their headbands, and their skill at setting fire to onion stacks.

'Perfect,' I said. 'It'll be like old times.'

I didn't tell Molly that I was hoping to also see David while I was in town. She wouldn't have been happy, not after how he'd dumped me.

Anyway, I flew into LAX on the Friday, and spent the Saturday with Molly. Her condo is on the Low Side, so there was no real risk of bumping into David, but I still found myself on high alert as we cruised around the shopping centre, searching for something for Dad.

The party was on Saturday night, and Sunday was a bit of a hangover day, but by Monday, I was more than ready to run into David.

To this day, he doesn't know it, but I had engineered the meeting from the start. From what I could tell from looking on Google – is that stalking, or is that due diligence? – David had opened an office in Bienveneda, between the new Cupcake Heaven and the old Citibank.

There was a Starbucks nearby.

Was luck going to be on my side? That was the question I was asking myself as I headed out on the Monday morning. On the face of it, yes. The day was gorgeous. I'd rented a Mustang to drive from LAX into Bienveneda – it's about three-and-a-half hours, one way – and with the sky so blue and the skinny palms waving in the breeze, it felt right to put the top down as I cruised into Main Street.

My goal was to find a parking space about 300 feet away from David's office, so I'd have to walk past his front door to get to the Starbucks. I had to go around the block twice before I found one, and I remember thinking: *Please don't let him see me doing laps.*

Anyway, I found one, parked, and took a few steps in the direction of Starbucks. I had no idea – none at all – as to where David's desk was in relation to the front windows, or whether he was even at work. Would he be able to see me as I walked by, and would he come straight out?

Apparently not, because nothing happened.

Damn it.

I continued on towards Starbucks, where I joined the line for coffee, thinking, this is no good. What if David hadn't come into the office? What if he was at the gym? Or worse, in New York? What if he couldn't see the street from where he sat?

I gave my order. The girl behind the counter spelled my name incorrectly (they always do). The barista took ages, which was fine. Time spent amidst the souvenir cups and the foil bags of coffee beans at Starbucks was time during which David might move towards his window.

'Caramel frappuccino for Loron?'

I took the cup off the counter, and popped a straw through the domed lid. Alright. Time to try again. I stepped out of Starbucks and began walking towards the rented Mustang, and I swear to God, I was about to click the locks on the car, when David called out.

'Loren? Loren Franklin?! Hey, stop, Loren, is that you?'

I had to do a double-take. David wasn't wearing a suit and sure, I'd seen him in workout gear, and I'd seen him in boxer shorts, but I'd never seen him dressed for business in California. David was wearing red Bermuda shorts, with a baby-blue polo and a bright-pink belt. He looked like Tommy Hilfiger. Not the designer. The ad.

He looked, to be frank, a bit dorky.

I was wearing white. All white. White jeans. White T-shirt over a push-up T-shirt bra, with cream ballet flats. The effect I was going for was easy, breezy California. My hair was up in one of those carefree, dancing ponytails that take forever to get right.

'It is you!' said David. 'Loren Franklin! What the hell are you doing here?'

I'm hoping to run into you! That was the honest answer, but I didn't say that.

I said: 'David! Oh my goodness, that's right, you came back here! I'd completely forgotten. You work here? In this street?'

David nodded. 'I do. This is my office. Capital Shrine. I've been back here, what ... ages now. But what about you? Visiting your folks or ...?'

'Yes,' I said, sipping my frappuccino, 'it's my father's birthday ... we had a big party on Saturday night ... I'm heading back tomorrow.'

'No way,' said David. He was using his boat shoe to stand half in and half out of his office. 'I mean, look, don't run off ... what are you doing now? Do you want to get something to eat?'

I hesitated. I even checked my watch, like I had somewhere else to be.

'Well, alright,' I said. 'Sure, why not?'

* * *

We went to the Jetty, the bar where the yachties go for cold beers after a good day's sail. It's faux-casual, in that you need a Ralph Lauren polo shirt and George Hamilton tan to really fit in.

'Hey, David, so great to see you!' said the girl on the door. 'It feels like it's been ages!'

David said, 'Great to see you, too, Candy,' and kissed her cheek.

Candy?

'You want outside?' she asked, sneaking a glance at me. 'I can seat you guys outside.'

'Oh, babe, that would be excellent,' said David.

'Of course!' she said.

David stepped back to allow me to go first. I followed Candy's nut-brown legs out to the tables on the deck. David followed right behind, guiding me into my chair by putting his hand on the back pocket of my white jeans.

Alright, I thought, *that's a good sign.*

Candy seated us as close to the edge of the deck as it was possible to get without the table falling into the bay. I knew the Jetty by reputation but had never actually been there before. It was so pretty. There were boats bobbing on the water directly in front of us.

'It's our best table,' Candy said.

'You're too good to me,' said David.

Candy smiled. 'I'll go get you guys some water. Tap water okay? And I'll bring you some menus.'

I waited for her to be out of earshot before I said: 'Current or former?'

'Candy?' said David, all innocent.

'Yes, Candy. Tell me you haven't.'

'Haven't what?'

I thought about what to say but only for a split second. Then, all cool, I said: 'Buried your face in her pussy, David.'

He was shocked. I was pretty shocked myself. That wasn't like me. As a rule, I don't go for dirty talk. David had tried to encourage me a few times in New York and I had been absolutely hopeless at it, but I'd learned quite a bit in the time we'd been apart, including the fact that alpha men like David tend to prefer a woman with more confidence – including sexual confidence – than I'd had in my early days in Manhattan.

'Maybe that's *your* fantasy,' David said, eyes wide. 'Want me to call her over here and ask if she's on the menu?'

'Sure,' I said, smiling. 'You do that. But if she is on the menu, I get to taste her first.'

'Fair enough!' said David, impressed. 'Here she comes now!'

Candy was skipping back across the floor in her bright-white sneakers. She had two water glasses in one hand, and a couple of over-sized menus under her arm.

I was quite sure that David had a raging erection under the table, and that he was using his linen napkin to try to cover it.

'Alright!' Candy said, smiling her radiant, Californian smile. 'Here's some water. Now, what else can I get you guys to drink?'

David said: 'You know what? This is something of a reunion for us. I think champagne is in order. What do you say, Loren?'

'Champagne sounds good,' I said, 'but you know, I don't have a lot of time. Maybe we should order?'

'Oh right,' said David. He was taken aback. 'Okay. Well, do you want to look at the menu, or should I just order for both of us?'

'Yes, order,' I said, 'I don't much mind.'

'Okay, well ...' David cast his eyes over the menu. 'Well, I guess we'll have the oysters, maybe some octopus ... is that blackened on the grill? Okay, we'll take that, maybe with the lime mayonnaise. And I don't know, fries?'

'Fries are great,' I said.

Candy nodded as she took it down. 'You guys have a big appetite today!' she said.

'Loren has an appetite,' David said, looking cheekily over his massive menu. 'Maybe we should ask her, what else do you fancy, Loren?'

'Oh, I'm fine for now,' I said, winking back, 'but maybe we'll get dessert.'

Candy wasn't in on the joke – she was the dessert – but she smiled, and gathered up the menus. 'Super! I'll get that underway for you!'

As soon as she was gone, David tried again. 'So ... what kind of dessert did you have in mind?'

I pretended like I didn't get it, and David took that as a cue to back off. The champagne came, and he raised a toast. 'To old friends!' We clinked and drank and shared some small talk. The food arrived, but who had an appetite? Not me. There's no denying that the atmosphere was electric: twenty minutes into lunch, I was wet through my G-string, and David surely knew it.

Neither of us wanted to leave.

'Hey, don't you have to get back?' he asked at one point.

'I'm having too much fun,' I said. 'Don't you have to get back?'

'I'm the boss,' David replied, all swagger. 'I don't have to do anything.'

We smiled at each other. David picked up a fry, dipped it in mayonnaise, and offered it to me. I burst out laughing. We kept on drinking. The sun started to sink and the other customers began to leave, and the point came when we had to go, too.

Candy brought the cheque. David paid, and we rose together.

'That was so much fun,' I said.

David appeared surprised. 'Don't tell me we're done? You promised me dessert.'

'Oh, look, I'd love to,' I said, 'but I've been out all afternoon already. I only ever told Molly I was popping out to Starbucks. I've got to get back.'

David seemed to be devastated. Alright, that might be pushing it, but he did look dismayed, and he was still trying to talk me around as he drove me back to my car. 'Are you sure? Because when am I going to see you again?'

I held my nerve. Given how much I'd had to drink, I probably shouldn't have gotten out of his car and into mine, but I did, and I made it back to Molly's safely, thank goodness.

'Where have you been?' she demanded, as I crashed through the front door.

I didn't want to go into the story with her so I fudged and weaved.

'You reek of alcohol,' she said accusingly. 'Don't tell me you drove?'

'Don't lecture,' I complained. 'I just bumped into an old friend and we had lunch.'

I could tell she wanted to scold me – Molly can be funny like that – but I wasn't having any of that nonsense. I curled up on the sofa beside her, so we could, like I'd promised, watch re-runs of *Friends*.

'No, we shouldn't watch this,' Molly cried, halfway through the first episode. 'It'll make you miss New York too much.'

'Do you know what?' I said dreamily, 'I haven't even thought about New York, not once, all day.'

* * *

Did you make it home okay?

I was sitting in my office at Book-IT when my cell phone buzzed with a message from David. He was in his office in Bienveneda, but his mind wasn't on the job. I don't want to sound smug, but it seemed like he was thinking about me.

I'd been thinking about him, too.

Hey, are you there?

I hadn't replied to David's first text. That was another thing I'd learned in the time we'd been apart: guys don't seem to mind when you play a little cool.

I'm here, I responded.

Call me, he texted, **I want to hear your voice.**

This was working out better than I'd hoped, and yet I felt so anxious. Spending time with David in Bienveneda had confirmed for me what I'd always suspected – I was crazy about him – and I really didn't want to blow it.

I texted back: **lunch was great … next time you're in nyc we should def catch up** … and then I waited, and ping!

CANT WAIT. NEED YOU NOW.

I suppose there's no real point in going over how fast things moved from there. David made plans to get on what may even have been the next flight to JFK and within weeks we were again an item, meaning I had to tell Molly, because how else was I going to explain why I was suddenly in town all the time?

'But don't worry,' I said, 'this time I have one foot on the brake.'

Molly was concerned. 'You have exactly no feet on the brakes,' she said, 'I can tell from your voice. You're in love with this guy.'

'No, no, no,' I said, but who was I kidding? I wasn't just in love. I was planning on moving.

Six weeks after that lunch at the Jetty, I had my résumé up on LinkedIn, with the preferences set to California.

'It just makes sense,' I told Molly, 'all this commuting is driving us both crazy. And you should see my Verizon bill. The phone sex alone is costing me a hundred dollars a month.' (Ah, yes, the phone sex! Who remembers phone sex? *Suck me, lick me, touch me, fuck me, suck me, lick me, touch me, fuck me …*)

'Also, with the business I'm in – online – there are a lot more opportunities on the West Coast,' I continued. 'I mean, a lot more.'

'The way you're talking, it's like this is a done deal,' said Molly.

'It's not,' I said, but in truth, I'd already had two offers. One of them was to work at a place called Facebook. In fact, I remember saying to Molly: 'I don't know, it seems a bit risky …'

Argh!

The second offer was from the *LA Times*, which was where I went.

'It's more solid than Facebook,' I said, 'and it's in LA. I can live in Santa Monica! That'd be nice. I'd be by the beach, out of the cold.'

'Closer to David,' said Molly.

'Closer to David,' I agreed, without even thinking.

'You're a fool,' said Molly. 'How do you know he's not going to break your heart. I mean, again?'

'No, no, not this time,' I said. 'This time, I'm in charge.'

* * *

'David?'

'Hmm?'

'That guy – the one from Bienveneda Golf? He's just sent you another email.'

It was a holiday weekend in California, and I was seated at the kitchen bench at David's place on Bienveneda's High Side. We'd been dating for something like six months, and I guess I'd become a regular there, so much so that the housekeeper knew how I took my coffee.

David was on the patio, doing his bicep curls. His laptop was on the bench in front of me, bleeping like mad.

'Ignore him,' David grunted.

'I can't ignore him. He's been sending emails for an hour and it's driving me crazy. Why don't you just get back to him? It's not like he wants you for a bad reason.' I held up the screen so David could see the messages coming in. 'Can't you see all these dollar signs? He wants to give you money.'

'I don't want his money,' said David, curling the hand weight up towards his chest.

'But why? Isn't that what you do? Take people's money? Invest it? Turn it into more money?'

'Technically yes,' said David, grunting again, 'but I don't do it for everyone, and I don't do it on demand.'

He placed the weight gently back into its rack, and reached for a gym towel.

'I don't get that,' I said, closing the laptop. 'What's wrong with this guy's money?'

'Not a thing,' said David, stepping into the kitchen to reach for my juice, 'except that right now, I'm not taking it.'

'Well, it's driving him crazy,' I said, swiftly moving the glass away from his grasp.

'And that's the point,' said David.

How was that the point? I genuinely wanted to know. David knew exactly what I did at work – I managed the Lifestyle pages for the *LA Times* – but I had only the vaguest idea what it was that he did for a living.

'Look, investing is nine-parts a confidence game,' David said, opening the laptop so he could begin deleting emails. 'I get requests like this all the time. People want me to take their money and make a fortune for them. For one thing, it's not that easy. For another, I don't take money from just anyone. Believe me when I tell you that ignoring a guy like this makes good business sense.'

'I just don't get how,' I said, stretching out my legs so I could wrap them around David's naked torso.

'Well then, watch and learn,' he said.

I watched as David tapped away at the keyboard:

Dear Pete, thanx for your emails, but as outlined in our earlier conversation, Capital Shrine is not currently seeking new investors. I wish I could be more help, but my best advice is for you to find an alternative investment vehicle at this time.

'There you go,' David said, pressing 'send'. 'Now watch what happens.'

Within seconds, a flummoxed email came back: Cut to the chase, David. What's the minimum spend?

David grinned. He replied: No minimum spend. Just no openings at this time. I'm sorry, Pete. I'll let you know if circumstances change.

Send.

'Okay,' he said, shutting the laptop, 'now, let's go do something fun, and then we'll see what he's saying when we come back.'

Something fun? I knew what that meant. I let David pick me up from the bar stool and carry me back to the bedroom. Emerging two hours later – wet from the shower this time, with a towel on my head – we returned to the laptop and sure enough, there were a dozen more messages from desperate Pete.

Can't we talk about this?

When do you anticipate an opening?

Is there some sort of message here I'm not getting?

'Are you going to answer him?' I asked.

'Nope.'

I shrugged. That didn't sound like great business sense to me, but how was I to know? I'd never run a business. Besides which, we had things to do. Our morning had been taken up with David's workout, followed by sex; our afternoon was to be consumed by David's desire to buy an expensive mountain bike (maybe followed by more sex) and he'd taken a table at a fundraising gala for the Booster Club for Bienveneda Grammar, his old school, to be held at the Nineteenth Hole that evening.

The gala was black tie, and I was excited about it. I'd never been to the Nineteenth Hole. It's members and their guests only, and that includes the ballroom. I'd ordered a silky red dress – it was floor-length, with one shoulder – to be delivered to David's, and I had new shoes – Jimmy Choo – plus David had splashed out on a pretty pendant, with the sun, the moon and a tiny gold star.

We arrived at the venue shortly after seven pm. Waiters stood by the door, holding silver trays of champagne. I was standing near the bar, waiting for David to return from the washroom, and admiring the decorations – the organisers had gone over the top with the nautical theme; there were giant plastic lobsters hanging from the ceiling – when a red-faced Pete came barrelling towards me.

'Where's your man?' he said.

My first impression was that Pete's tuxedo was too small. My second was that he was drunk.

'My man?' I said.

'David Wynne-Estes!' he said.

David – resplendent in black tie – joined us.

'I've been trying to raise you for like a month.'

'I'm sorry, Pete,' said David, 'I thought I emailed you this morning. What seems to be the problem?'

'The problem is that I can't get you to take my money,' Pete boomed, slapping David so hard on the back that David's whole body jolted forward and his champagne splashed, 'and that's making me feel bad.'

I reached for a napkin to mop David's hand. He took the napkin from me. 'It's fine, Loren.' Turning to Pete, he said: 'I'm sorry, my friend. I've laid it out straight for you; it's nothing personal, but I'm not taking new investors at this time.'

'What I don't get is why not,' said Pete. 'My money not good enough?'

'Please,' said David. 'Your money is fine. And I do appreciate you thinking of me. But again, we are simply not taking new business at this time.'

Pete's eyes narrowed further. I found myself clutching the little star part of the pendant David had given me. Pete was a big man, and he was furious.

'Well, I can't understand that,' he said, shaking his big head, 'because I happen to know from my wife that you took money from her hairdresser. But everyone knows that story, right?'

Some of the people standing close – ladies in their finery, and men in their bow ties – looked embarrassed.

'He took five thousand dollars from my wife's hairdresser and she's paid off her mortgage,' Pete boomed, 'but he won't take money from me.'

The woman standing closest to me – an older lady with a fox stole, including the paws, draped over her shoulders – gulped at her champagne. Were things about to get ugly?

'Okay, Pete,' said David, putting his hand onto the small of my back and gently moving me away from the bar. 'I've had enough, and I'm pretty sure you've had enough.'

We pressed on into the elegant crowd, but there was hardly a moment during the night when I couldn't see Pete's red face glowering at us.

Driving home, I quizzed David: 'Don't you care how angry he is? I got the feeling he was bad-mouthing you to everyone, all night long. And what is this about his wife's hairdresser? Did you really pay off her mortgage.'

David laughed. 'Of course I didn't,' he said. '*She* paid off her mortgage. And good for her. She works hard.'

'And he doesn't?'

'Fat Pete? He probably works hard, too.'

'But you're not helping him. Although I can't say I blame you after how he behaved tonight.'

David glanced in my direction. The roads were dark and wet, and he'd had a bit to drink.

'That doesn't mean anything,' he said. 'I'll take his money soon enough. Let me see if I can explain this ...'

And so he did: Capital Shrine was a private investment company. David was the president and the CEO, and therefore it was up to him to decide whose money to take.

'And I decided some time ago that I wouldn't take just anyone's money,' he said, as he guided the car through the streets of Bienveneda's High Side towards his home. 'Capital Shrine is the kind of place that people have to be invited to join. The idea is that we are exclusive. That's the image I want.'

'But why send an invitation to the hairdresser?' I said.

'I kind of did that as a favour for a friend,' said David, 'but it turned out to be one of the best moves I've ever made. That girl didn't have a lot of money, obviously. She has a small salon, but she has some good, regular clients who really like her – old-style High Side ladies who won't have their hair done anywhere else – and one of them asked me to help her. So I took her little nest egg, invested it, and we had a windfall. And she paid off her mortgage. And that's been good for me, because now she tells everyone, and everyone wants in.'

'But they can't get in,' I said.

We were paused in the dark, waiting for the garage door to roll up.

'Right,' said David, 'and that's deliberate. Because the more I keep the door closed, the more people want to bash it down. Take this guy – Pete – he's hearing about how everyone else is making money. He's greedy – nothing wrong with that – because he wants to make easy money, too. He's trying to get in and can't, so he's frustrated. He's telling everyone how frustrated he is, and that gets a person wondering if maybe they can get in. Guess what? Some can. But some can't. And as far as anyone can tell, there's no rhyme or reason, and that drives people crazy. But that's okay. Because in a few months' time, I'll have one of my girls call Pete and say: "David has an opening at Capital Shrine. We're taking limited investments" or whatever, and he'll be so excited, he'll tip everything in. I'll make sure he does well. And then he'll go around, grinning and telling everyone: "I'm in, and it's great." And that will make even more people want to get in.'

'That's genius,' I said.

'Yes,' said David, gliding his car expertly between the Porsche and the Prius, 'I know.'

* * *

There comes a moment in every relationship when you realise that things are getting serious. It's called Meeting The Parents. David's parents are Belle and Garrett Wynne-Estes. As far as I could tell, he hadn't taken a whole lot of girls to see them over the years.

I'd been dating David for about eighteen months when he said: 'Mom has invited you to dinner, and I suppose we better go.'

It was a big step because I knew David didn't have a close relationship with his parents. Their names had come up in conversation, and he'd pointed out his parents' house on those weekends when I was in town, but David made it plain that although he'd moved back to Bienveneda when his mom got sick – cancer, I think – they weren't the kind of family that got together for Sunday lunch.

That said, I spent half the day getting ready.

'Will it be formal? Is it more casual? What do you think I should wear?' I said.

'Whatever will be easiest for me to remove when we get home,' said David.

'You are no help at all.'

I'm not, as a rule, a wearer of linen dresses, but given what I knew of the High Side, a linen dress seemed appropriate. I went with a blue dress. I'm blonde, and blue suits me, as does red, but red seemed wrong.

Belle and Garrett's home is on the River Road. It has a high stone fence and double gates with the letters W and E, for Wynne-Estes, woven into the ironwork. We pulled up in David's Porsche. The gates opened slowly. David's jaw clenched the instant his wheels hit the long gravel drive.

'Are you alright?' I said.

'I'm fine,' he said, taking my hand.

Belle was first to greet us, swinging both doors open at once like they do in the South. 'Welcome,' she said. 'You must be Laura.'

'It's *Loren*,' said David.

'It's fine,' I said, embarrassed. 'It's not important. Thank you for inviting me.'

'Oh, we've been so looking forward to meeting you,' said Belle. She is one of those women whose tiny bones poke through their thin cardigans. 'We hardly ever see David these days and now we know why.'

David stepped into the hall, saying: 'Where's Dad?'

'Out back,' said Belle, clutching at her pearls.

'You have a lovely home,' I said, trying not to stare at the portraits on the wall.

'You like the house, do you?' Garrett came striding towards us. He wore a navy blazer and he was swinging a tennis racquet (or is that my memory playing tricks on me?).

'I do,' I said. 'I'm Loren.'

'I'm Garrett. This is an important house. A. Quincy Jones. Do you know him?'

My mind started racing. *A. Quincy Jones. Director? Film star?*

'Architect,' said Garrett, 'built the Palm Springs Tennis Club.'

'Oh really?' I said, looking around. 'Well, it's lovely.'

'Come and sit down, Laura,' said Belle, motioning me towards the sitting room.

'It's Loren,' said David.

'Loren, sorry, Loren. Come and sit down.'

The sitting room had a high ceiling with exposed beams, a white brick fireplace and low, elegant furniture.

'You sit here,' said Belle, patting a sofa cushion, 'and David, where will you sit?'

'I'm okay here,' said David. He was standing with one elbow on the mantelpiece.

'Perhaps a drink?' offered Belle.

'I'll organise wine,' said Garrett, excusing himself.

The coffee table was immense. It had a glass top, and books and trinkets underneath. Belle fished around to find some coasters. They were in a box with royal corgis on the lid.

Garrett returned. He had a bottle of wine – uncorked – in one hand, and the stems of four glasses laced through the fingers of his other hand. He placed three glasses on the coasters, before proceeding to fill his own glass, on the sideboard, to the brim.

'Right, then,' he said, turning back. 'Who else is having wine?'

'Wine would be lovely,' I said, pushing my glass forward.

Garrett stumbled over, and splashed some white into my glass.

'Anyone else?' he asked.

'I'll have some,' said David.

Garrett peered into the bottle, shrugged and poured what remained into the third glass.

'Alright,' he said, 'perhaps a toast?'

Poor old Belle's glass was still completely dry.

'Welcome, Loren.'

'Mom doesn't have any wine,' said David.

'Oh, I'm fine,' said Belle, red blotches climbing up her neck. 'I was just going back to the kitchen, to check on the dinner.'

Garrett stuck his nose into his glass, sipped, and sipped again. 'Nice, nice,' he said, holding it up to the light.

'Now, Loren,' he said, moving to take the seat that Belle had vacated, beside me on the sofa. 'I wonder if you might let me show you something.' He put his glass down on the coffee table and began feeling underneath to extract one of the books stored there.

'Oh, Dad, not now,' sighed David.

It was one of those awkward moments when you're trying to be warm and polite without really knowing what you're in for.

'David says you're from Bienveneda,' Garrett said.

'I am.'

'And your surname's ... Franklin?'

'That's right.'

'Our name, as you probably know, is Wynne-Estes,' said Garrett, rubbing the side of his moustache. 'Some people find it hard to pronounce. It's not that hard. Wynne-Estes. Sound it out ... Win ... Es ... Tes ...'

I smiled. 'Win-Es-Tes.'

'Good, good,' said Garrett, turning his attention back to the book he'd extracted from under the coffee table.

'Do we really have to do this, Dad?' said David, but his father ignored him.

'Budge up a little, Loren,' Garrett said, 'I want to show you something.'

I budged up.

Garrett had the book open. 'Now, see this here?' he said, tapping my forearm to ensure he had my full attention. 'This here is my family tree. Every branch of our family back to 1650 is in this book. Would you like to see?'

What could I say? 'I'd love to.'

David said: 'I think I'll go and see if Mom needs a hand in the kitchen.'

I thought: *Hey, don't leave me.* But he'd gone.

'Now see this, Loren,' said Garrett, finger extended towards a photograph of a man with a white handlebar moustache not unlike Garrett's own. 'This character here is my second cousin. Edward Garrett Wynne-Estes. Now, he ...'

And so it went on, for six long weeks. Alright, not for six weeks, but you get the picture. David's father is a drunk and a bore whose family tired of him years ago.

'How could you leave me there?' I admonished David afterwards.

'You're what my sister and I call fresh meat,' he said. 'Somebody new, too polite to ignore him.'

To his credit, David did rescue me. At some point, Belle came to say the meal was ready to be served, and while Garrett seemed content to ignore her, David then came into the sitting room, saying: 'That's enough now. Mom wants to serve.'

'We can finish later,' said Garrett, reluctantly closing the book.

Like most of the big homes on the High Side, Belle and Garrett's place has a formal dining room. There is a table with eight chairs; David, Belle and I took three in the middle, and Garrett sat at the head.

Belle had set the table with placemats, napkins in napkin rings, a salt dish, even a soup tureen. I got the feeling these things were the 'good' things, taken out only for guests. The glasses came in sets of three: red, white and champagne, but there was no champagne and hardly any wine, except in Garrett's glass.

'Tell me, son,' he said, at one point, 'how is the gambling business?'

David was sawing away at the steak on his plate.

'It's fine,' he said, which surprised me. David is opposed to the idea that his business – buying, selling, trading, and investing – is essentially gambling on the stock market.

'You know, Loren, I had a very successful concrete company,' said Garrett. 'Quite a few of the buildings you see over here sit on Garrett Concrete foundations.'

'Is that right?' I said politely.

'We were expecting David to take over that business,' said Garrett, with his eyes on his plate. 'You know we sent him to business school in New York with that in mind, but no. David had his own ideas, some of which went pear-shaped.'

David's grip on his knife and fork tightened but he did not speak.

'Now he's started this new business,' Garrett said, gulping more wine, 'which is gambling on the stock market from fancy offices on Main Street. So let's see how that goes, shall we?'

I picked up my glass and sipped and smiled. David said nothing.

Belle twisted her pearls, saying: 'Is there anything left in that bottle there, Garrett? Maybe Loren would like some more.'

'I'm fine, really,' I said.

'She's fine,' said Garrett, touching the napkin to his moustache.

Coasting home in David's Porsche that evening, I said: 'So ... I get the feeling that your dad doesn't approve of Capital Shrine?'

David had his hands firmly on the leather steering wheel. Never had a car been pointed so determinedly towards home.

'He approves enough to ask me to make a little more of his pathetic nest egg,' said David, 'but I guess he's going to have to wait, too.'

* * *

'You are making what again?'

Molly was perched on one side of the bench in David's kitchen. I was on the other side, studying a menu. Molly's voice was muffled because she had a bag of ice against her lips to try to bring down the swelling from her most recent fillers (none of which, I should add, were flattering, but each to their own!).

'Engagement Chicken,' I said.

'And where did you read about this?'

'I told you: *Glamor* magazine.'

'And whose idea was it?'

We had been through this.

'You know the radio shock jock, Howard Stern. It came from his wife,' I said, placing a plucked, pink chicken on the chopping board. 'She was dating him for ages and he hadn't proposed. Then her mom – or somebody – told her about this recipe. Engagement Chicken. It's absolutely guaranteed to make a man propose. And I mean, it must have worked, because they got married.'

'You think he married her for her chicken?' said Molly.

'I have no idea,' I said, 'but at this point, anything is worth a try.'

The recipe calls for a whole chicken with a lemon up its butt.

'And how do you make it?'

'As far as I can see,' I said, peering at the laptop, 'all I have to do is screw the lemon in there.' I plucked a lemon from the fruit bowl, scraped it over the cheese grater a few times to loosen up the rind, and began screwing it into the chicken's cavity.

'Very glamorous,' said Molly, eyebrows raised. 'And can I just say that I can't believe you're taking relationship advice from Howard Stern.'

'I'm not taking advice from Howard Stern,' I corrected her, wiping my hands on my apron. 'I'm taking relationship advice from his wife.'

'You've gone nuts.'

'I'm not nuts,' I said, placing the chicken on its tray into the oven. 'I just really want to know where this relationship is going.'

David and I had been dating for close to two years. I was back and forward between Santa Monica and Bienveneda every other weekend. I had my own beeper to his garage. He'd met Molly. He'd met my dad. I'd taken his side against his parents.

Why hadn't he proposed?

Friends had ribbed us about it. Clients were always asking and I had no idea what to say. I couldn't work it out. Did he think I was too young? Maybe. I wasn't yet thirty, but David was coasting towards forty, and it wasn't as if he was going to marry somebody his own age.

I was in despair about it, which probably explains why I was doing something so stupid as making Engagement Chicken, and you know what, maybe it worked, because next thing I knew, everyone in town was reading the same headline: THE WEDDING OF THE CENTURY.

That's how the local newspaper, the *Bienveneda Bugle*, broke the news.

A little birdie tells us that Bienveneda's most eligible bachelor, David Wynne-Estes, has popped the question and if what we're hearing is correct, this is going to be the Wedding of the Century.

Was it the chicken? Alright, probably not. More likely it was me being patient, and David being ready. The point is, he did pop the question – and he did do it right, meaning down on bended knee at the end of the Bienveneda pier, with a diamond the size of an iceblock – and I accepted.

I accepted knowing that David wasn't perfect. Who is?

I accepted knowing that I didn't quite fit into his world. David's sister, Janet, seemed to understand this. 'Who will you have?' she said, shortly after we told her.

'I'm sorry?'

'The wedding planner? Who will you have?'

I didn't know that I needed a wedding planner.

'I think I can do it myself,' I said, 'and Molly is going to help, and ...'

'Don't be silly,' said Janet dismissively. 'This is not the kind of thing you can do on your own. And you can't just let anyone do it. Let me think about it.'

A day or so later, she came to the door at David's and pressed a card – a completely square business card, with gold trim – into my hand. 'Here.'

'J.J. Kim? You know him?'

'I know him, and I've told him about the wedding,' Janet said evenly, 'and my advice to you is to use him and nobody else.'

I waited a day or so before putting the call in. J.J. Kim was California-famous for his over-the-top appearances on the breakfast shows. He had purple hair, held vertical with product, and a super-smooth forehead, like Janet's. The gold on his business card was a nod to the chunky gold rings he wore on all ten fingers.

'So you're the lucky lady marrying David Wynne-Estes?' he cried when I called. 'Now, don't you worry, I know just what you need.'

He knew what I needed? How about what I *wanted*?

We had our first meeting at J.J.'s offices in Hollywood. His chair was a giant plastic hand. Molly had insisted on coming along, she said for moral support, although I suspect to ogle J.J.'s plastic surgery. ('It's too much,' she told me afterwards, 'just too, too much. He's got, like, tennis balls in his cheeks. Too much!' and it was all I could do not to say, 'Molly? You have tennis balls in your cheeks, too!')

I opened by saying: 'You know, my mom's no longer with us, so when we're thinking about the bridal table, it'll be David's parents, and then my dad with Molly's mom, who is Val …'

'Wait, wait, wait,' cried J.J., throwing himself back against the giant fingers behind his head. 'What do you mean, bridal table! Bridal table? You want a bridal table? There will be no bridal table!'

'No bridal table?'

'No, no, no, no,' J.J. said, wagging a finger from side to side in an exaggerated motion, 'we will NOT be having a bridal table. Oh no. I have in mind something very special for you.'

Molly said: 'Something special like what?'

J.J. looked triumphant. 'Thrones! I have in mind the exact same thrones that Posh and Becks had at their wedding. The exact same! Because that is how I see this wedding. You are – okay, David is – Bienveneda royalty. So you need thrones.'

J.J. was by now squealing.

Molly was doing her best to keep a straight face. It was a struggle.

'But how will that work?' I said. 'Where will everybody else sit?'

'In the garden,' said J.J., clicking his fingers theatrically around his own head. 'You'll have your golden thrones under a canopy in a lavish garden, with fairy lights and waiters dressed like motor mechanics, and we'll have driftwood benches and sophisticated milk crates for tables ... can't you just see it?'

Sophisticated milk crates? I could not see it. 'Where would people put their plates?'

'On their laps,' said J.J. Kim, exasperated. 'This isn't going to be a chicken-and-beef wedding you know, Loren. This isn't going to be people sitting at a round table with a white cloth, a glass of Merlot and a bread roll. This is going to be something special. Delicate dishes. Tasting spoons!'

'Tasting spoons?' said Molly. 'Our dad is six-foot-seven and shaped like a queen-bed mattress. You're going to have to give him more than a tasting spoon, especially since he's going to be paying.'

'He's what?' If my expression was anything like J.J. Kim's, we must have looked like two open-mouthed dolls at a sideshow carnival.

'Your father is paying?' said J.J., aghast.

'Oh no,' I said. 'Oh, Molly, surely not.'

* * *

A few days later I was having dinner at Dad and Val's. It's a house I know well, because throughout my childhood I spent occasional weekends there, sleeping on a trundle on the floor near Molly's bed, as part of the custody arrangement my parents worked out.

Dad was seated where he pretty much always sits, in the recliner near the flat screen TV I'd bought for him for the most recent Father's Day, to replace the big box they'd had for years.

We'd all finished eating (actually, my father and Val had finished eating; I was on J.J.'s famed wedding diet) and I had stayed in the kitchen long enough to pretend to dry the dishes, but Val's not silly.

'Go talk to him,' she whispered.

I nodded, and went to find Dad. He was well into his nightly routine – feet up, crime novel open – but he took his feet down from the ottoman when he saw me coming.

'Wedding of the Century,' he said. 'Impressive.'

'That was a stupid thing for the *Bugle* to write,' I said, fiddling nervously with my engagement diamond.

'When does a newspaper not write something stupid?' Dad said. 'But the main thing is, I don't want you worried, Loren. Whatever you're planning, I've got it covered.'

Oh, my goodness, he so did not have it covered.

I took a deep breath. 'Well, here's the thing, Dad, you don't have to pay.'

By this stage, Val had come out of the kitchen, carrying two cups of tea on saucers, with plain biscuits.

'What are you talking about?' said Dad, taking the cup. 'We've planned for this day, haven't we, Val?'

Val did her best to smile but she looked terrified. 'Indeed we have.'

I thought, *Oh, God bless you two, but really?*

'Please listen, Dad,' I said, as he took his first sip of tea. 'There are a lot of people on David's side ... people that I've never even met, people who are clients, who apparently have to come to this wedding, and we obviously don't expect you to pay for people that I – let alone you – don't even know.'

Dad picked up one of his biscuits and had a nibble. 'Why are they coming if you don't know them?'

'Because,' I said, 'it's good for business. David has these clients. He calls them the Big Fish. Big catches. He makes big money from them. They have to come because, you know, if they get invited, it makes them feel special. It's a way of showing them they have a personal relationship with David, that he's not just interested in them for their money.'

'But isn't that the truth? He is only interested in them for their money, surely,' said Dad, nibbling some more. 'Why does he have to pretend to be their friend?'

I thought, *You old bastard. You're not stupid. You know exactly what I'm trying to say.*

'David's not actually pretending,' I said. 'I suppose what I mean is, he wants to show his appreciation to certain big clients by having them at the wedding.'

'Well, I don't know,' said Dad. 'What do you make of this, my love?'

'Well,' said Val carefully, 'if David sees the wedding that way – as a way to entertain clients – and, I mean, if he wants to put in, maybe we should let him.'

Dad's eyebrows shot up. 'Have you gone mad?' he said. 'Of course David's not paying. I'm paying. Loren here is my daughter. I'm the father of the bride. My job is to cover the cost of the wedding. And I mean, how much can a wedding even cost?'

Was he kidding, or did he really have no idea? A wedding can cost nothing more than seventy-five dollars for a licence at City Hall or a wedding can cost ... well, the sky's the limit, and J.J. Kim was aiming for the sky.

'I guess that depends ...' I said.

'It doesn't matter,' said Dad, picking up his novel, 'because we have it covered. Don't you worry. It'll be fine.'

I looked over at Val. The conversation was over.

'Well, if you insist,' I said, rising to smooth my skirt, 'and thank you, Dad. It's generous of you.'

Dad sipped, satisfied to have won the argument. I stayed a while longer, then Val walked me out to the car.

'What are we going to do?' she whispered.

'Don't worry, I'll just send him a few bills,' I whispered back.

'Oh, thank you,' she said. 'I mean, there's just no way ...'

'Stop,' I said, putting a finger to my lips. 'Of course there's not.'

* * *

'The quote for the cake has arrived,' I said, opening the email on my laptop.

'Let me guess,' said David, 'is it nine hundred dollars?'

We were curled up on the L-shaped sofa in David's house, with David in the 'big corner' and me with my legs down the chaise.

'How do you even know that?' I said, because the cake was in fact $900.

'Your wedding planner copied me in,' said David. 'I think even he's worried.'

'How can I send this to Dad?' I said. 'Can't you just hear him? He'll be saying: "Nine hundred dollars? What kind of cake do you get for nine hundred dollars? Is it a gold-plated cake?"'

'For nine hundred dollars, it should be a gold-plated cake,' said David. 'And just out of interest, what kind of cake do you get for this exorbitant amount?'

'I got the croquembouche.'

'The what?'

'The croquembouche. It's a tall cake in the shape of a triangle, made of balls stuffed with custard and dribbled with treacle.'

'Well, whatever you want,' said David.

'It's more like what J.J. Kim wants,' I said, cuddling closer, 'which today was flamingos ...'

'Flamingos?'

'Pink flamingos,' I confirmed, 'because that's retro, not kitsch, or maybe it's retro kitsch. I can't remember. Plus, we have three suites at the Bonsall.'

'Three suites!' said David, moving his hand into the space under my yoga singlet. 'Do we get to try them all?'

'They aren't for us.' I slapped his hand away. 'They're for me – well, for me and my bridesmaids – to get ready.'

'You need three rooms to get ready?'

'Apparently,' I said, and actually, we did need to hire rooms because where else would we get ready? Not at David's. He'd already claimed his house for himself and the groomsmen.

Not at Molly's, because she had a one-bedroom, one-bathroom apartment, and there were four of us; and certainly not at Dad's, because that's really Molly's childhood home, and this was my wedding.

'I'll organise connecting rooms,' J.J. said, 'with views out to the ocean and interlocking doors, but still some sharing of bathrooms, because, you know, fun!'

* * *

The plan was for Dad to pick me up from the Bonsall precisely thirty minutes before the ceremony. Being ex-military, he was of course on time.

'Daniel Franklin, reporting for duty,' he said, when he rang me from the foyer.

'All right, Dad. Coming.'

Molly turned to me. She had her hair in a French knot, and her lips were wet with gloss. 'It's time.'

I didn't need to be told. I was probably the only bride in the history of the world who was ready on time. Molly picked up the bouquet. The problem of how to carry our phones was solved by cousin Lisa (she's on Dad's side) who had a hard-shell clutch.

'Let's go, let's go,' cried J.J., making shooing motions.

We crowded into the corridor, and began making our way towards the exits. The Bonsall has an old elevator, but it also has a wide, spiral staircase and J.J.'s idea was that I should take the stairs.

'I want you coming down like this,' he said, with nose in the air, and fingers trailing on an imaginary balustrade behind him, 'and then you stop halfway and you don't move again until every eye in the foyer is on you.'

The only face I wanted to see in the foyer was Dad's. Given his size, he was hard to miss. He was pacing the marble when he glanced up and saw me.

'So, come on,' I said, after a pause, 'how do I look?'

How much Dad could see of me under all the layers of veil I couldn't say for certain, but he said the right thing.

'Like an angel.'

For a moment, it looked like my big old ex-military dad was going to cry, but no, because of course Molly was also there, competing for his attention.

'Hey, hey, hey, but what about me?' she asked, coming down from behind where I'd paused on the stairs. 'How do I look?'

Dad laughed. 'Lovely,' he said, 'but how about *me*?' J.J. had ordered Dad into a tuxedo. Dad shoved his arms down so his hands were flat by his sides, and he began to waddle. 'I'm a penguin!'

'A king penguin, maybe!' said Molly, twisting her body so he could see her dress.

'Shall we go?'

That last came from Janet. Skylarking in the foyer made her uncomfortable, although it was difficult to tell from her expression, since Janet had more Botox in her forehead than even J.J. Kim.

'Yes,' I said. 'Let's go.'

I extended my hand down the stairs. Dad reached up and away we went, with my kitten heels clicking across the marble floor. From the corner of my eye, I could see some of the other guests staring. Dad was used to that. He's a big man, and children, in particular, love to gawp at him.

The staring in the foyer wasn't at him, though. I don't want to sound like I'm bragging, because I'm not, but J.J. Kim had done a good job.

I looked pretty. With pearls in my ears, and with the sparkly tiara, and the big rock twinkling on my finger, and all the veils, I might even have been described as beautiful.

Our group approached the brass-bound glass doors. Bellhops bounced forward. J.J. Kim's plan had been for me to glide out of the foyer and straight into the waiting limousine, but that didn't happen because the driver had stepped away for a smoke.

'Hey, hey!' cried J.J., arms flapping.

The driver took a final puff of his cigarette and flicked it into a flowerbed. 'No hurry,' he said, 'we're early.'

'Early, early!' cried J.J. 'We're not early! We are right on schedule.'

'Settle down,' said the driver.

J.J. was flapping his arms like a lunatic. I laughed. What's a wedding without a mighty scrap between the pink-suited wedding planner and the laid-back limo driver?

I made my way into the car. Molly was supposed to lift my skirts in but she was too busy flirting with a bellhop. It was fine. Everything was fine because I was marrying David.

The church we had chosen for the ceremony meant nothing to my family, or indeed to David's. J.J. chose it because it was pretty and would look 'a-MAZING' in the photographs. It stood atop a hill with views of the ocean. I could see guests on the manicured lawns.

'We can't be late,' said J.J., fretting.

We weren't late. We were bang on time. J.J. flicked his arm like a conductor, and the bridal waltz began to play. I put my hand into the crook of my father's elbow and stepped into the church.

'You okay?' asked Dad, patting my hand.

'Never better,' I said.

I could see David through my veil. He was standing at the end of the aisle, near the preacher, with his hands lightly clasped in front of him.

'Well, hello,' I whispered, as I reached his side.

'Well, hello to you,' he whispered back.

'Who would have thought it – I finally got you all to myself,' I said, smiling.

David laughed, and why wouldn't he? Did this wedding mean that he was going to change his spots?

I mean, please.

* * *

The reception was at Parsons. I'd been so nervous about the thrones, but to J.J.'s credit, they looked lovely, and kind of medieval, standing there in the Parsons' forest, surrounded by wonky toadstool tables.

I saw Dad looking around. By the time we were done with photographs, it was close to six pm, and the sky had turned pink. A team of waiters was sending out floating lanterns across the lake, and a brass band had started to play.

'I paid for all this?' said Dad. 'Pretty good value!'

'You did so well,' I agreed. Then, when he wandered off to refill his glass, I yanked Val aside and whispered in her ear. 'Tell him to go easy on the booze,' I said.

'Sure,' she said.

He didn't go easy, and Val didn't either. The booze was free, and one glass in Dad's hand would go down in a single gulp. Gulp! Gulp! I watched, amused and fascinated. By speech time, he'd be plastered.

'Make sure he gets some food down,' I whispered to Molly but honestly, the food wasn't going to touch the sides. First course was a scallop floating in bubbles at the end of a soup spoon.

'What's this?' asked Dad, sniffing at it.

Val screwed up her nose. She wasn't sure, either. 'Seafood?'

'I don't see much food,' said Dad, who just loves that kind of joke.

'Be quiet and eat it,' said Val, so Dad slurped the scallop down, while commandeering a waiter to bring him a bread basket, from which he snatched two, then three bread rolls, all the while drinking beer, and then wine and more wine.

Just as I'd predicted, he was soon bent out of shape with Garrett matching him, glass for glass, except that Garrett didn't have to give a speech.

'Alright, ladies and gentlemen!' the MC cried. 'Let's hear from the father of the bride!'

The crowd – Big Fish included – roared their appreciation.

Dad got to his feet. He was as red as a tomato, his bow tie was wonky, the front tails of his shirt were out, and one silky button, right in front of his shirt, had burst over his belly.

'Alright, alright,' he said, shifting from one enormous foot to the other. 'Is this thing on?'

He tapped, and the microphone screamed. The MC rushed forward, adjusted things – shirt button included – patted Dad's broad back, and stepped back, grinning.

'Well, now,' said Dad, wiping his brow with the back of his hand. 'First of all, thank you everyone for coming. As most of you will know, I've got two daughters. I've got Loren here, who is the bride' – at this point, the crowd whistled and cheered – 'and I've got Molly, who is younger. And they're both pretty good-looking, right?'

The crowd whistled.

My face flushed. In truth, I felt a bit miffed. Molly had lived with Dad for a long time, longer than me. She definitely calls him Dad, but I am his only biological child. I found myself thinking,

Hang on, you are my father, and this is my day, but there was no time to get sore, or to stay sore. Dad was on a roll.

'That's right, they're both pretty good-looking,' he said. 'Loren's the eldest, and she's definitely been the ambitious one, going off to college and getting a job in New York City, and to be frank with you, I wasn't expecting to be marrying her off in her hometown, but what do you know? Here we are.'

Somebody shouted: 'Hear, hear!'

Dad stuck a finger into his collar and gave it a pull, trying to let in air.

'What's more, we're here to see her marry a fellow born and bred in Bienveneda,' he continued, prompting more cheering.

'Not from the Low Side, mind you!' said Dad, grinning over the microphone. 'Although that's where my lot is from. In case you can't tell by the number of sleeve tattoos we've got. No, no, no, I'm kidding. But no, Loren's decided to go with somebody from the High Side. And people say never the twain shall meet!'

The crowd was really laughing now, and Dad, loving an audience, ramped things up.

'So yes, here she is, marrying David Wynne-Estes,' he said.

The crowd cheered and clapped some more. Dad took a moment to mop more sweat from his brow with one of the linen table napkins.

'Well, I have to tell you, I was a bit wary when Loren told me who she'd chosen,' he continued, 'and that's because my side has always thought people on this side were a bit up themselves!'

The crowd roared again, although not David's parents, who looked at each other with eyebrows slightly raised.

'And this guy here, this David Wynne-Estes, we're told that he's done particularly well for himself setting up his own business, getting hens to lay golden eggs or whatever it is he does.'

The Big Fish, especially some of the younger ones who had flown in from New York, loved that. One of them hollered: 'Hell, yeah!'

'And I'll be honest,' Dad said, 'since the two of them got engaged, I've had a few people say to me, well, your Loren, she's done pretty well for herself, hasn't she?'

The crowd went to clap, but Dad held up his hand, shook his head and said: 'No. No, no, no, I've had a few people say that to me, but let me tell you, I've got no idea what they're talking about. Because from where I'm standing, looking at my daughter there, it's David that's the lucky one.'

The crowd went: 'Awww ...'

Dad nodded. 'That's right,' he said, gazing directly at me. I was trying not to cry, because it would be Panda Eyes if I cried.

'And I hope you know I mean that, Loren,' Dad continued, 'because I love you. Maybe I wasn't the best father that ever lived, but you are the best daughter a man could wish for, and I wouldn't change a bit of you.'

I put my hands together and blew a kiss in Dad's direction. Then I glanced at David to see his reaction. He was leaning way back in his throne, so much so that the two front legs were off the ground.

Dad pointed a pistol finger at him. 'And now to my new son-in-law. It's a pleasure to welcome you to the family, David ... and make sure you take care of my girl.'

The crowd was clapping and cheering and looking to David for a response but David wasn't getting up. He wasn't settling the chair on which he was balanced. He wasn't reaching into his top pocket to take out a speech of his own. No, he was reaching down towards the ground, to where he'd left his half-drunk bottle of beer.

He picked up the bottle and tilted the neck in Dad's direction.

'Well, you don't have to worry about that,' he said. 'Loren's in good hands now that she's with me.'

* * *

About a month after the wedding, I was on my knees in the en suite, vomiting. 'I feel awful.'

'That's the second time this week you've said that.' David was tucked away in the walk-in wardrobe, dressing for work.

'I cannot be pregnant,' I said.

'Sure you can,' said David, coming out of the wardrobe. He was grinning and fastening a cufflink. 'We've been doing it often enough.'

'Please stop,' I said, mainly because David was right. We were only just back from our honeymoon, which had been a cruise down to Cabo, followed by a few weeks in a private villa owned by one of his clients, which was more like an estate, with an army of housekeepers and a militia patrolling the border.

'What does this guy do?' I'd asked David. 'Run a drug cartel?'

We had nearly run out of condoms on day three – surely a good sign on a honeymoon – and when we arrived in the villa I'd been loath to add them to the list of things I wanted the housekeeper to get from the market (mangos, bananas, Trojan Pleasure For Her). Plus, we'd had a lot of tequila, and so we probably weren't as diligent with the remaining condoms as we should have been.

* * *

'You're pregnant,' my doctor confirmed, snapping off her silicone gloves. 'No question. You are.'

'No way,' I said, struggling back into a sitting position, and then of course came the double whammy. It wasn't one baby; it was twins.

'This wasn't part of the plan,' I moaned to Molly, because the plan had been for me to come home from the honeymoon and find a new job in Bienveneda (I couldn't stay on at the *Times*; the commute was too great).

But David was ecstatic.

'Twins,' he said, staring at the two bleeping lights on the screen in the office of Bienveneda Ultrasound. 'I cannot believe that. That is just fantastic.'

Oh yes, fantastic, except if you have to carry them.

I'm not going to pretend that I loved being pregnant. Some women do, but I am not one of them. Likewise, I'm not going to pretend that David's pride in having conceived twins translated into him being amazing during my pregnancy because he wasn't amazing.

Some days, he was horrible.

Let me see if I can explain. Three months into the pregnancy, I was as big as a woman at full-term with a singleton, and I had pain in my lower back. I don't know if that was because of the way the babies were pressing on my spine, but I moaned: 'Can you please rub my back?'

David was propped in his usual corner of the L-shaped couch with his iPad at the ready.

'Sure,' he said, reaching forward with one hand to rub his knuckles over my spine.

'No, I mean, I need you to massage my back for me. I'm in agony.'

'I don't know what you want me to do,' David said grumpily. 'I'm not a massage therapist. If you're in pain, you should go to see somebody.'

'I don't want to go to see somebody,' I said, dismayed. 'I want a massage from my loving husband.'

David turned his attention back to his iPad. 'I don't feel comfortable,' he said. 'What if I hurt you? And how am I supposed to concentrate on what I have to do here, if I'm giving you massages every night?'

Does that sound cruel to you? And yet I could see his point. Mine was a twin pregnancy; David wasn't a specialist in pregnancy massage. He was a specialist at making money, and God knows we were going to need it. We had been inspecting new houses, and researching new and bigger cars. We were going to have two children at Grammar before we knew it, plus, down the track, there would be college fees.

Maybe it was me who was being selfish. It wasn't like we couldn't afford a massage therapist.

I decided not to push it and changed tack, instead.

'How did the girls in the office react when you told them about having twins?' I asked.

'They're thrilled for us,' said David, 'and Fat Pete was in today – you're nearly bigger than him now, you know – and he was saying, "Double trouble. Ha-ha! This is going to make you want to work even harder." Like I don't work hard enough for that fat bastard.'

Part of the pleasure of twins is the reaction of other people. Everywhere I went – the pharmacist, the tiny baby boutique on Main, the stroller specialist at Macy's – they were all saying the same thing:

'Twins! No way!'

'Twins! How lucky!'

'Twins! What a blessing!'

And they're right. Twins are a blessing, but I'm not going to gloss over the fact that David wasn't supportive. I'm guessing that everyone has seen photographs of guys who get really into their wife's pregnancy? Who post pictures of themselves on Instagram, holding their wife's belly, and saying things like: 'We're expecting a special delivery!'

That was so not David.

David was more, 'You're pregnant, and therefore fat and uncomfortable. I get it. I just don't know how I'm supposed to help.'

In fairness to him, I wasn't my best self, either.

Five months into the pregnancy, I was starting to resemble a whale. The weight and the pain in my lower back had driven me to insomnia, which made me grumpy. I had swollen feet, and I developed that strange condition where I couldn't stand the smell of anything too strong or too chemical.

I had joined a group on the internet, called June Babies, which may have been a mistake.

'I sent my poor husband out for ice-cream and peanut butter last night,' cried one mom-to-be. 'Poor thing is being driven crazy by my cravings.'

Nothing like that was happening in my house. I could only imagine David's response to such a request: Couldn't I get the housekeeper to go in the morning?

Speaking of which …

It was six am on a Sunday morning during my eighth month of the pregnancy. David had called from work the night before to say he was heading out for drinks with clients. I'd expected him home around ten pm, maybe midnight, but midnight came and went, and so did one am, and two am, and before long, it was dawn.

He hadn't come home, and I hadn't been able to sleep.

Where was he? Had somebody spiked his drink or had he had an accident? Should I call the local hospitals?

I was just about to call the police when I heard the garage door lift. David's car seemed to crawl, as opposed to roar, into its usual space. I eased myself off our bed – my weight, at that point, was around 160 pounds – and padded down the hall to the kitchen.

'Where have you been?'

Startled, David grabbed his chest. 'Jesus, Loren,' he slurred. 'You scared me half to death.'

'Where have you been?' I repeated. I was standing with my hands on my hips, my feet wide apart, and my bitch face on.

'I told you. I had to have drinks. Now I need water,' said David, rocking from one side of the kitchen to the other. 'Water.'

'Have you tried the tap?'

'Tap. Yes, tap. And Advil?' He opened the cupboard where I kept saucepans. 'Where the hell is a glass?'

'Have you tried the dishwasher?'

'Dishwasher,' said David, but how was he going to find it? We had only recently moved into our new house on Mountain View Road, having purchased from a friend of a friend of a friend for an off-market $3.5 million. David had known his old house – the bachelor pad with all the gadgets – very well, but this house was different. Our new appliances were hidden behind smooth panels. We had a dishwasher – we had three (one for pans, one for glasses, one for general crockery) – but David would need all the luck in the world to locate them, especially blind drunk.

'You're not being nice to me,' he pouted. 'Help me find the dishwasher. I need a glass of water. I have a bad headache, you know.'

'Go to hell,' I said.

David sighed a big, woe-is-me, isn't-my-wife-a-bitch sigh.

'Well don't help me, then,' he said, staggering off down the hall. I watched as he bumped from one wall into the other, and as he fell straight down onto the bed, where he lay like a starfish with his finely tooled shoes hanging over the edge. The smell that was coming off him, I can barely describe it. Beer. Cigarettes. Cigar smoke. Rancid stripper smells? Probably. Then he started to snore, leaving me free to search through the pockets of his suit jacket and, when that failed, through his wallet, and what did I find?

A receipt for $5176.50, including tip and tax.

Let me just repeat that. I found a receipt for five thousand, one hundred and seventy-six dollars! Bang, gone, spent on whisky and whores at some Low Side joint called the Pink Cat.

Five thousand dollars!

I was furious. I was also exhausted, and yet I felt like taking my huge carriage and dumping it on David's back. Squashing the breath out of him. See how he liked carrying all that weight when he was dead tired.

David slept for five hours. He woke to find me sitting in our kitchen, feet wide apart, and breasts resting on my stomach, and stomach resting on my lap. Not the prettiest picture, but then again, nor was he. In fact, what a sight he was. Messy hair. Dry mouth. Grit in the corners of his eyes.

'Christ,' he said, rubbing his thumb and four fingers against his forehead. 'I need that Advil.'

I got ready to unleash. 'Would you mind telling me ...'

'Oh, Loren, please don't start.' David was not pleading with me. He was holding a glass against the ice-maker, and his expression was of a man who didn't want an argument.

'Don't start? Would you mind telling me where you've been?'

'Christ, Loren,' he said, holding the ice in the glass against his forehead. 'Can you please, please give it a rest?'

'Excuse me?' I said. 'I'm your wife. I'm entitled to know where you've been all night.'

'I told you,' he said, with eyes still closed, 'I had clients in town. I had to entertain.'

'At Pink Cat?!'

I was throwing down my trump card but David did nothing more than wipe the back of his hand across his mouth.

'You're snooping now?'

'This isn't about me,' I said, amazed. 'This is about you. You spent five thousand dollars – five thousand dollars! – at a strip club.'

David didn't answer immediately. He paused to gulp down his water, then put his empty glass into the sink. 'It's not your business.'

I put my hands defiantly back on my hips. 'How is it not my business?'

'It's work.'

'How is it work?'

'It's work because I was with clients,' said David, in a tone that suggested that he was speaking to a simpleton. 'It's work because that's sometimes what I have to do: take clients to strip clubs. You have no idea, Loren. Clients come to town to see me about their investments. They come from LA. They come from New York. They're away from their wives. They're in a celebratory mood. They want to have a bit of fun.'

I could hardly believe what I was hearing.

'Strippers are fun? How does that work? Do their wives know about this fun? And it's five thousand dollars.'

That was probably my weakest card. I was stupid to play it.

'And what has that got to do with you?' said David. 'What does it matter to you, what it costs? It's their money: they invest with me. I take a cut of the profits, but it's actually their money. So it's going back to them. Besides which, is there anything you want that you don't have?'

'Excuse me?'

'I said, is there anything you want that you don't have? Another pedicure? A manicure? Something else for the nursery? Something else for the house? Because you do have the black Amex. It has no limit. As you seemed to have noticed.'

With that, he turned to leave the kitchen.

I managed: 'Hey, where do you think you're going?'

'To take a shower,' he said. 'I'm going to take a shower, and then I'm going to watch the ballgame. That okay with you, Loren? Or are you going to have a problem with that, too?'

* * *

Knowing what I knew then, why did I stay with David?

Two reasons.

I was eight months pregnant with twins.

I was also still in love.

Of course, I remember the twins' arrival as if it was yesterday: me lying on my back in the delivery suite, with a yellow-painted belly and mesh socks over my feet; David standing by my side in scrubs and a hairnet.

'You okay there, Mr Wynne-Estes?' a nurse had said. 'Wait, watch … he's going to fall.'

David didn't fall. He recovered himself in time for a nurse to catch him and so he was there, to see our girls arrive.

Hannah and Peyton.

Oh, how I love those girls.

My C-section had been booked for nine am. I'd have preferred something a little later but nine am suited David – his intention was to return to the office after the birth – and it suited our doctor, who was his client.

David drove me to the hospital at eight. I don't recall feeling nervous as they swabbed me with antiseptic. My exposure to babies before I had the girls was essentially nil. I had no younger siblings – alright, Molly, but I didn't know her as a baby – and no nieces or nephews, not even on David's side, since Janet has no children.

'You're going to need help,' said the midwife at Bienveneda Private. I wasn't so sure. Mom had raised me without help (and without Dad around, since he was in the military when I was born).

'Right,' said the midwife, when I explained, 'but that was … a different time. You'll need a baby whisperer. In fact, you'll probably need two.'

'One for each baby?' I said.

'One for each shift. Six pm until midnight, and then midnight until six am. You'll probably have an hour alone before the day nanny comes at seven, but you should be okay for that.'

I remember thinking, *Is she serious?* She was serious.

'The main problem you're going to have,' she said, 'is finding somebody good at such short notice. This is something you really should have organised by now.' (To be clear, this conversation took place during a pre-natal; the girls hadn't yet been born.)

Part of me wanted to shrug the whole thing off, but by week's end, I had hired a 'girl' – Maria – to come home from hospital with me, and by the end of our first week at home with my daughters, Maria had hired another 'girl' – Sophia – because, she said she couldn't be expected to 'do twins' on her own.

'So, how many staff will you have in total?' said Molly, when she heard.

'I guess … four? No, five. I'll have the two night nannies, the day nanny, David's old housekeeper and the gardener. And the boy who does the pool, so six if you count him, or seven if you count the lady who comes to clean.'

'Seven staff,' said Molly, shaking her head. She was cradling Hannah, or maybe Peyton.

'I know,' I said, 'it's ridiculous.' And it is, but then again, I quickly got used to having all that help. In the early days, it felt necessary because the girls weren't good sleepers. Then came the teething, which was difficult. Then Hannah started to walk while Peyton was still crawling, which prompted a round of appointments with an occupational therapist, because shouldn't they be doing things together and obviously it was just easier to have a nanny stay with Hannah while I tended to that, plus, who was going to keep the house clean, especially now that David's business had geared up, with an associated rise in the number of events – galas, fundraisers – he needed me to attend.

Before long, I found myself having a meltdown over the phone – one time, stupidly, to Molly – because 'Nanny A hasn't arrived, and Nanny B won't answer her texts, and there's a function tonight, and I just can't see how I'm going to get there. I mean, they just switch off their phones,' I wailed, 'when I need them to be answering me.'

'Maybe the poor girl's phone is dead?' suggested Molly.

'But it's not the point,' I said. 'It's not supposed to be dead. She's on call. I get so sick of this. You pay good money, but it's like everyone says, you still can't get good help.'

There was a pause on the line.

'What did you just say?' said Molly.

'Oh, I'm just so frustrated,' I said.

Molly was laughing, but it was a strange kind of laugh. 'No, did you just say what I think you said? Did you just say that it's so hard to get good help these days? I'm going to scream if you said that.'

'You don't know what it's like. David is out of the house most of the day. He goes to the gym three mornings a week. He plays golf. He plays tennis. He's got the sailing club. He has these dinners. I'm supposed to get to most of them. But I've got things on, too. He's hooked me up with all these committee people who are raising money for this, that and the other. I'm supposed to go to lunch with the wives of his clients. I'm supposed to help organise fundraising dinners for the hospital. I'm supposed to be part of the Booster Club at Grammar. You have no idea.'

'Lunches and dinners?' quipped Molly. 'I can't imagine how you cope.'

She was being sarcastic, but the truth is that I coped the same way everyone on the High Side coped: I had help, which Molly seemed to find hilarious because apparently you can't have help if you don't go to work.

'You're actually not fair on me,' I argued. 'It's alright for you. You have your business, and that's it. I have these events, small talk, meetings, it's endless.'

'If you hate it, don't get involved,' Molly said.

'I have to get involved,' I complained. 'David insists.'

Barely a week would go by without him arriving home from work with a new responsibility to dump on me. He'd stand there, all nonchalant, maybe undoing a cufflink, maybe undoing one of his white business shirts, when he'd suddenly say: 'Oh, look, don't let me forget, Jett Ryan's wife has this idea for denim-patterned diapers. I said you'd help.'

'Denim-patterned diapers?'

'Yes,' he'd say, 'because you're good at web design. And Jett's a big client. And he adores his wife. And she needs help. I'm not sure she knows how to turn a Mac on.'

I couldn't really refuse because, as David also liked to point out, it wasn't like I was doing anything else.

'You don't have to work,' he'd say, 'and besides, don't you like the wives?'

The wives referred to the women married to David's Big Fish. Women who were rail thin and blonde, who got around town in Land Rovers and bug-sized sunglasses. Most were Bienveneda-born and Bienveneda-bred. High Side that is!

Did I like them? I didn't know. I wasn't sure. It was difficult to get to know them properly. These were people who had been through Grammar together (I went to the local high school; I don't need to tell you what side it's on) or else their children were at Grammar together.

'If we're going to get ahead in this town, we need these people on side,' David would say.

'I get it,' I'd tell him, and I did.

* * *

Is anyone still having sex?!

I didn't post those words to June Babies, but boy did I read the thread.

Not here! came the first chirpy reply.

Not here either! came the second.

So, I wasn't alone but it was disconcerting. Sex with David had been good from day dot, but it stopped dead during my pregnancy. That wasn't my doing. I was the one who reached out and got rebuffed.

'I don't like the idea,' said David, peeling my hands off his torso, 'there are babies inside you.'

'Oh come on,' I said, 'they're safely tucked away.'

David wouldn't have it. 'I'd rather wait it out. The idea of poking around in there ... it feels like I'm invading their space.'

I could have pushed the point, but who wants to have sex with somebody who feels uncomfortable? Not me, and anyway, it wasn't like I felt particularly attractive during pregnancy. Some women do. I get that, but I didn't. I felt swollen and tired and gross. Then came the months during which I was breastfeeding which wasn't attractive to David, and again, fair enough, because my breasts were like blue-vein balloons, with cracked nipples on top.

The girls weaned at four months, after which my boobs became like long socks. David was keen to resume relations but I felt self-conscious. One particular night, he rolled towards me, wrapped an arm around my waist and began feeling around. Back in the old days, he'd have found something he liked, but this was after the babies had left me with an apron of flesh around my middle.

'Well, well, what's this, then?' he said, giving me a squeeze.

I slapped his hand away. David had grabbed hold of my post-baby roll. I hated my post-baby roll. I recoiled from his touch, but David wasn't having that.

'Come on, babe,' he said. 'You're still hot to me.'

Is there even a worse thing for a husband to say?

Thankfully, one of the babies cried. I got up. I didn't have to get up. We had a night nanny to do that, but I wanted to get up. David rolled onto his back. I was gone for maybe twenty minutes and when I came back, it was clear to me that David had masturbated.

Oh really? I thought. *That's our sex life now? Me feeling crap and you wanking?*

I would have had it out with him, but he was already asleep.

I started exercising. Yoga, Pilates and spin classes, but I didn't kid myself. I lost weight but my skin was so stretched after the twin pregnancy that after a certain point, it doesn't snap back. The only solution was plastic surgery. That's the business that Molly's in – cheap Mommy Makeovers – but I didn't really feel like going to Molly – who is two years younger, with no kids – and showing her my baby roll and my saggy boobs. I went to Beverly Hills instead. They did a good job. I look better than I did, but I will never look as good as I did before I had the twins.

Not that it matters. Occasionally I will agree to sex, but I want it to be over quickly. It's been more than five years since I felt raging desire. Part of that is the roles we've taken up. He's Breadwinner. I'm Wife. Worse, I'm Mother.

When did I sign up for that?

I'm also never off the clock. Our family hardly ever takes a vacation together, because David is always working. The girls and I have been to Disneyland, Orlando, Bermuda and New York; David did not come. He has been to New York without us, many times. That is the dynamic.

One time I talked David into an old-fashioned American-style holiday. We drove down to Palm Springs, with the girls watching the screens in the backs of the car seats. We didn't take any of the nannies, and I thought that would be fun, like the Griswolds. Who was I kidding? Having driven all day, we arrived at the little resort shortly after four pm. David asked the hotel clerk for the wi-fi password. That was his priority. It was 107 degrees and there were no empty beds by the pool. David made a fuss and an attendant came and cleared some damp towels off beds that had been 'bagsed' or 'saved' by guests who weren't at the pool.

I changed the girls into swimmers and put blow-up rings around their waists. I applied the sunscreen, ordered fries and drinks, and splashed around with them. David sat and swiped. Two hours in, I wouldn't have minded a bit of a swim. A swim-swim, across the pool, not a splash around in the shallow end, without one of the girls hanging off me, pulling me under, saying, 'Mom, Mom, watch me, watch me,' or 'Mom, Mom, be a dolphin! Let me ride on your back.'

I turned to David, lounging with his iPad on the bed beside me, and said: 'Is it alright if I go for a bit of a swim?'

David popped out one of his ear buds. 'Sorry?'

'I said, do you mind if I go for a bit of a swim?'

'Why would I mind?'

'Because, you know, could you watch the girls so I can have a swim ... by myself.'

He said, 'I don't get it ... why don't you just go?'

I tried to explain. 'Well, I can't ... I mean, if I go, they'll just jump on me.'

Peyton was in fact already pulling on my leg, saying, 'Yes, Mom, come for a swim!'

I think David knew perfectly well what the problem was, yet he kept saying: 'Just go if you want to go.'

I got up from the sun-lounger, and told Peyton, 'Mom's just going for a swim.'

'YAY!' she cried. 'Mom's coming in!'

I tried to peel her hands off me. 'No, no, Mom's going to have a swim on her own ...' but that made no sense to either of my daughters.

'No, I'll swim with you, Mom!' cried Hannah.

'No, no, you girls stay here with Daddy ...'

But of course they didn't want to, and my swim descended into chaos, with the girls hanging off me as I tried to make my way through the water.

What I'd wanted – what I had been asking for – was for David to put his iPad down and take control. To say: 'Come on, girls, let's go get ice-cream.' Or: 'Let's go see what's in the gift shop.' To get the girls excited about something other than being in the pool with Mom. To take them – bouncing on the balls of their feet – away from the pool so I could slide quietly into the zone that people live in when they aren't responsible for small children.

But no. I had to get splashed in the face, climbed on, and pushed down, until I came up spluttering and thinking: *So this is my life now. I'm a nuisance to my husband and a pool toy to my kids.*

That was, what, two years ago? Maybe closer to three. Did things at any point improve? I can't say that they did. Things stayed about the same.

Oh, who am I kidding? Things got worse. So much worse.

* * *

The tap on the shoulder. Who doesn't love the good old tap on the shoulder to bring down their whole world? It happened to me.

I was standing in the Kiss-and-Go lane outside Bienveneda Grammar. I had lifted Hannah down from the back seat of the Range Rover, and I was in the process of lifting Peyton down when I felt it.

Tap, tap, tap.

'Mrs Wynne-Estes?'

I turned around. 'Yes?'

It was a mom I didn't recognise. She handed me an envelope.

'I'm sorry to do this,' she said, face all prim, 'but you deserve to know.'

I'd been smiling when I turned, probably because I was thinking, *This is a mom I haven't met before. Maybe she has a party invitation for the girls, or a note about Booster Club; maybe this is about the problems Grammar parents are having with cars moving too slowly through the Kiss-and-Go. Smile and take the note, and worry about it later.*

But there was something about the way she strode away that made me think, *No, this is different.*

I reached into the car for Peyton's *Frozen* backpack, and slipped it over her shoulders, checking to see that the water bottle was in the side pocket. I kissed the top of her blonde head, and I called out: 'Hold hands!' as the girls skipped towards a teacher who was signalling to them to come inside.

I climbed back into the driver's seat and turned on the ignition. I wasn't going to open the envelope then and there. Why? Because I was in Kiss-and-Go, where everyone's impatient. And because I knew what the letter would say.

I put the SUV into drive and coasted home. Part of me thinks I must have been on autopilot, because what streets I took, I can't tell you. I beeped the garage open, and parked beside one of David's cars. I sat in the quiet of the garage for a moment, collecting my thoughts. I rode the elevator up one floor, and sat down at the kitchen table, conscious of one of the housekeepers. She was running the Dyson over the carpet; the gardener was making a scratching noise with his rake outside the window; the pool boy was scooping leaves from the surface of the water.

I opened the envelope. The note wasn't handwritten. It was printed off somebody's computer, in good old Times Roman, the idea being it would be untraceable.

Dear Mrs Wynne-Estes,

    You don't know me, but I am one of a number of moms who can no longer stand by and listen to the gossip without letting you in on Bienveneda's worst-kept secret …

Which was that David was having an affair with a woman at work. I didn't have to be told her name. I could guess. It would be Lyric Morales. We had met, twice. Once when I had dropped by David's office and there she was, all big lips and curves. Luscious and willing. That's how David would see her. As opposed to out of shape and sagging, which is how he sees me. Buxom and pert, instead of the Hanging Gardens of Babylon.

It wasn't just how she looked; it was the way she looked at me. I should have known something then. Maybe I did, and maybe I couldn't face it.

The second time was at a party to celebrate the big five-O birthday of one of David's Big Fish clients. Who didn't see Lyric that evening? Her silk dress was slipping off her shoulders, and she had cut-outs over her hips.

'Is she even wearing underwear?' I asked.

David looked flustered. 'Who?'

'Miss Half-Naked over there,' I said. 'Honestly, David. You want a certain kind of standard at the office, surely. She looks so cheap.'

I definitely knew then, didn't I?

I think I probably did.

And so, what to do? That's the question I asked myself upon opening the envelope. What's a wife supposed to do when confirmation of her husband's affair is placed in her hands?

Did I say: 'Oh. Alright. So this is how my marriage ends. David leaves to take up with a twenty-something with lips like a fish; I sign up for Match with a profile that says: Single Mom of Two.'

Or did I say: 'No. I'm going to stay and fight.'

Was there anything to fight for? Maybe David didn't want to be married to me anymore. Perhaps he was in love with Lyric, and utterly done with me.

I started to cry, and cried more when the realisation dawned on me that everyone at Bienveneda Grammar had known for who-knows-how-long what I was now discovering. That was humiliating. One of the things I had loved about being Loren Wynne-Estes was the fact that David had picked me from a group that included girls with much better pedigree.

I could hear them saying: 'Poor thing never really did fit in.'

Also: 'Have you heard? David's wife? Well, she's soon to be his ex-wife. Yes, I know! It was probably inevitable.'

A voice interrupted my thoughts.

'Madam? Please?'

It was Marie-Claire, our new housekeeper. She had come into the kitchen and I hadn't noticed. She wanted me to lift my feet so she could vacuum underneath. My reaction wasn't rational.

'Get out!' I screamed. 'Just get out!'

Poor Marie-Claire. She dropped the Dyson and bolted for the door. You would think the housekeepers on Bienveneda's High Side would be used to crazy white ladies, but perhaps not.

I'm going to have to tip her big this Christmas.

The important question was, what was I to do?

Was I supposed to call David? Was I supposed to wait for the day to pass, and go to pick up the girls as normal? I could hardly bring them home and have things out with their father while they cowered in their bedroom.

So I called him at the office. It's something I rarely do. What would I call him for? To chat? We had long given up on that. To say: 'Can you pick up milk?' I could pick up the milk. The housekeeper could, or the nanny.

He didn't answer my first call. Normally, that would be a clear signal: 'I'm busy, Loren. Whatever is the problem, I'll have to call you back.' I'd be reluctant to try again. Not this time. David not answering his phone intensified my rage. My imagination was in overdrive. If he's not picking up, why not? Busy fucking *her*, probably!

I called again, and again.

Finally, he answered. 'Loren? What the hell? What's wrong?'

'Why don't you tell me?'

The line went quiet.

I knew. And he knew I knew.

'Loren?'

'David.'

I could hear him thinking: *Oh shit*.

'What's the matter?' he said cautiously. No question, he was hoping that he was mistaken. He wasn't, and I knew that he knew it.

'I think you know what it is,' I said.

Pause.

'Okay, Loren,' he said. 'Do you want to talk?'

Confirmation. I exploded. I threw the phone. The battery came off and rattled against the floor tiles. The feeling I had in that moment is one I wouldn't wish on anyone. It was like cymbals going off in an all-white room.

I picked up the phone. Put it back together. My hands were trembling. David had been calling. Texting. Trying to reconnect. If I didn't respond soon, he'd come home. But I didn't want him in the house. I called him back. Put on my calmest voice.

'Listen, I'm on the way,' he said.

'No,' I said. 'You don't come here. There is no here for you here. No home.' I was speaking gobbledegook.

David's voice came back broken up. Had I damaged my phone? Maybe. Or else he was dropping in and out on his way up Mountain View Road. 'If you ... explain ... not what ... think ...'

'Don't tell me, "It's not what you think,"' I said. 'I'm not an idiot.'

'Let me come home. Let me explain.'

No. I could not have the conversation that I had to have, in our home. Not in the place where my precious daughters kept their pretty things. It would filthy up the place. I'd never get it clean.

Somehow, I agreed to meet David at the In-N-Out Burger. Yes, the In-N-Out Burger. Oh, the irony! There is no point going over what I said to him when he got into the passenger seat of my car. I can barely even remember. Inside my head was all white fog. Except that David said yes, he'd been having an affair. He was desperately sorry. He didn't even like Lyric, let alone love her.

I screamed at him: 'Then why are you fucking her?'

I'm embarrassed to write what he said: David said that he has a sex addiction.

I laughed in his face. To see David sitting there in his expensive suit in the seat beside me, saying: 'No, I think it's serious. It's a proper mental disorder. I've been googling and it is a real thing.'

OMG, as the girls might say. What a crock. It made me want to choke him. But you can't do that, can you? I demanded details. He wasn't forthcoming, saying he couldn't remember how or why it started. No, of course he didn't love her. He loved me. But things had changed between us. We hardly ever had sex. I never seemed interested. He didn't want to push me, but he was starved for sex. And Lyric was willing. He had been weak. He had been stupid.

'You're right,' I said, 'you have been very stupid. And it's going to cost you.'

David nodded. 'But wait,' he said, suddenly looking desperate. 'There's something else.'

There was something else? Something else like what?

'We're broke. I'm sorry, Loren. I've been trying so hard to keep this from you, and I wish there was another way to say it. There isn't. We are in real financial trouble.'

Hearing those words – we are in real financial trouble – did something strange to my head. David kept speaking but all I could hear was a drumming noise. I kept thinking, *This cannot be true.*

I managed: 'How can we be broke?'

'Right,' he said, 'well, it's complicated.'

It was actually quite simple. David had been stealing from Peter to pay Paul. He'd been taking money from new investors and giving it to older investors to make it appear they had made a huge profit, in the hope that they would brag loudly enough to encourage men like Fat Pete to turn up and beg to be allowed in.

'It started out kind of innocent,' he said, running his hands through his hair, 'and I figured, as long as I'm still making money, I can keep a handle on it. But remember a couple of years back, the stock market had been up, and then it suddenly went down?'

I remembered. There had been a financial crisis. Stock prices had fallen. I knew that. But they'd come back.

'Right,' said David, 'but the problem is, some of the Big Fish wanted their money out. I managed to put some of them off, but others were insistent so I took funds from other investors ...'

My heart sank. 'And now they want out and you have nothing left?'

'Right,' said David. He was as close to tears as I'd ever seen him.

I sat quietly for a moment, as the news sank in. 'Well, this is not my problem,' I said, suddenly shaking my head. 'You may be broke, but we're not. I'm not. Because we have the house. And half of it is mine. Because you surely don't think I'm going to stay with you after this revelation, do you?'

And that's when David dropped his next bombshell.

'We don't have a house,' he said. 'I've borrowed against the house. I had no choice.'

'What are you talking about? How could you even do that without talking to me?'

'I had no choice. We were going under. I had nothing to sell. The cars are leased. My retirement fund is empty. I'm paying my staff – nannies included – out of loans. I've been doing it for you, Loren. Because I knew you'd be horrified. I've been trying to turn things around. And I can. I just need time. I need time. What I can't afford to happen – what we can't afford to happen – is for anyone to get a whiff of what's going on. Because if word gets out, and people start asking for their money back ... well, that would destroy us.'

I wish I could describe what was going on in my guts while David told me all this. The feeling wasn't a pain, exactly. It was more like churning. Like I might vomit, which I then did, right into the centre console.

'Oh, God, I am so sorry, Loren.' He popped the glove box and started groping around for napkins or baby wipes. 'I know it's a shock. I've betrayed my vows. I'm ashamed of myself. I deserve whatever I have coming. But you don't deserve any of this.'

I snatched the wipes from his hands and put one to my lips.

'What are you saying?' I managed eventually. 'If I walk, I walk with nothing?'

'But you don't have to walk,' said David, taking my hands in his. 'You can stay! Please! I'm begging you to stay. Because together, we can fix this. Think about it, Loren: if you go, I'll have to sell the house. And we'll have nothing to show for it. There won't be enough for a new house for you. There certainly won't be enough for two new houses. And how will that look? You renting on the Low Side with the girls? Me renting somewhere else? The girls being taken out of Grammar. That will definitely cause a run on the business. That would be a catastrophe.'

He had started to cry, and really, as far as I was concerned, that was the end of the conversation. I had never seen David cry. Never, not once. And so I decided – right then and there – that whatever happened, I would not divorce him. And yes, I realise that some people will think that I'm crazy, and maybe I am. Maybe I should have said, 'You think I care about money? This is not about money. You are a liar and a cheat who has run us into debt and put our girls' future in real jeopardy. I have been a kind and loving wife, who has been patient, *trusting* and true to you. And now I'm out of here.'

But how could I do that? Where would I even go? To Dad's? To Molly's? To a Low Side rental? How would I pay the rent? I have not worked since before the girls were born. Yes, I have a college degree. It's something, but it's not worth much on its own. What kind of job would it get me, after so many years out?

So I decided to stay. And it isn't only because of the money. It's also because – however awful he's been to me, however badly I've been betrayed – I love being Mrs Wynne-Estes and I love David. Which is ridiculous, obviously, but I do.

I love him.

I always have.

I love him, and I want to fix our marriage. I want to work through this with David, and I want to get past it. Which is why I think this Mexican vacation idea is a good one. Our therapist suggested it. I guess I'm pretty lucky in that Molly can organise it for me. I went over there yesterday, the first time I'd been in that cute little apartment for a while. We had a chat. She was all: 'The main thing is, where do you want to go? There's a Four Seasons at Punta Mita – sunset sailing, whale watching – or there's a golf resort at Bahia de Banderas ...'

'No golf!' I said, raising a hand.

We decided – she decided – on the villas at Cabo San Lucas on the tip of the Baja Peninsula. Two nights with a personal butler and dinner at the Michelin-starred restaurant, and an old-style Juliet balcony with views over the sea arch; and then five nights on a 100-berth sailing ship called the *Silver Lining*.

The cruise ship was my idea. I love cruising. You don't have to pack and re-pack. We'll have five nights to concentrate on each other and connect. But like I told Molly: 'Be careful what you book. I don't want the same ship as the first honeymoon. It was alright but this has to be fantastic. I don't want one of those monstrous, 1000-berth, floating cities. David would hate that. Something intimate. Something sweet.'

The brochure for the *Silver Lining* looked great. It's a small ship – two hundred passengers and eighty crew – but it's luxurious. I mean, four decks and three pools, plus one of those pools where you swim in the sea. It has waiters in black tie, standing ready to whip the cloche off your plate, and chefs in tall paper hats.

'I don't want yard-glass party people,' I said.

'There'll be none of those,' said Molly.

So anyway it's all booked and it's not just a vacation. We're calling it a second honeymoon. The girls will stay with Janet. Molly wasn't happy about that. I tried to wave it away saying they would just be happier staying at home which they will but also, I'm not sending them to live in an apartment on the Low Side. I'm just not. So, we'll fly down to Cabo and get on the ship and we'll head out to sea. We'll talk. We'll cry. We'll make love. We'll reconnect. Because what choice do we have? At the end of the day, I love him, and – as everyone who has ever been married already knows – when you love somebody, divorce is not an option.

Murder, yes, but not divorce!

Molly Franklin

'Forbidden fruit – there's a reason
why it tastes so sweet!'

Tweet by Lyric Morales

He broke her heart.

David broke my sister's heart.

He had been cheating. If that wasn't bad enough, he was broke and threatening to pull his little girls out of their lovely High Side school.

Had David walked into the house at that moment, I would have smacked him just for that.

I put the journal into my handbag and made my exit from the house, battling past the media pack without answering any of their crazy questions.

I was doing my best to keep my composure. It wasn't easy because I was fighting an image that kept appearing in my head. It was of Loren alive in the cold water, crying as the ship sailed away, leaving her alone in the dark.

I got into my car with the idea of heading over to David's parents' house to see if the twins were there. The problem was that I knew that at least one of the media cars from Loren's house was tailing me and I didn't want to lead the media to the twins.

I was still trying to figure out what to do, when my phone rang. I took the call, hands-free. It was Dad, saying that he'd told Mom, and she agreed with him: we had to go to Mexico.

I stopped my car and put my forehead on the steering wheel.

I hadn't really wanted to go to Mexico. I wanted to stay and confront David. But I couldn't let my father go to Mexico to search for Loren on his own.

'Okay, fine. Like I said, Dad, I'll get some things from my apartment and meet you back at home.'

I stayed the night in the narrow bed in my old room. It was impossible to sleep, mainly because of the images in my head but also because Dad couldn't stop trying to reach David. I've lost count of the number of ways we tried to track him down. I phoned. I texted. I went through Facebook and left messages there. I called the hotel where he'd stayed with Loren before they boarded the *Silver Lining*. We tried Janet, and we tried his parents, but nobody picked up.

Finally, we gave up, and went ahead and booked our tickets down to Mexico. Then we called Gail Perlot and left a message to let her know we were coming.

Gail called back. 'Oh, Molly, it's really not a good idea ... David is due to head home himself in the next twenty-four hours. I'm just not sure that you coming here will achieve anything.'

Dad told her to stop. He wasn't going to be turned away.

The plan was for Mom to drive us to LAX first thing in the morning.

Being Mom, she tried to pack a meal for us to eat on the plane.

'You won't like what they serve,' she said, using one hand to wipe tears off her cheeks and the other to cut Dad's sandwich into triangles. 'It might be spicy and that will unsettle you.'

I tried to dissuade her. 'Mom, no way is security going to let us through with a Thermos of chicken soup and a ham sandwich.'

But it wasn't about the soup and the sandwich. Mom just wanted to do something.

It took a little under three hours to get to the airport. We started in pre-dawn darkness and arrived in morning light. Mom let us out by the kerb. Dad leaned over to kiss her like it was for the last time. A security guard came and threatened us with a ticket. I felt like saying, 'Have some compassion ... he's just lost his daughter,' but what would have been the point?

'Be careful,' said Mom.

'Of course we will.'

I'd told Dad to bring on-board luggage only, but Mom had packed way too much for him, so we ended up having to check his suitcase in. That slowed us down, and then we got stopped at the X-ray machines.

'What's this?' the guard asked, signalling towards a dark shape in Dad's over the shoulder bag.

I tried to explain. 'Dad gets bad indigestion so Mom made that soup for him ...'

'Yeah, that's not going on the plane. He eats that now or it goes in the trash,' the guard said.

'Just throw it, Dad,' I said.

'I can't throw it. Your mom made this.' He stepped out of the line, unscrewed the lid, and began slurping down soup.

'Dad, we're going to miss the plane.'

That got him moving. He poured the rest of the soup out, and on we went, at least until we got stopped again.

'Why so many stamps for Mexico?' said the guy from customs, flicking through my passport.

'My business is there,' I replied.

'You have business in Mexico?'

I was about to explain, when Dad said: 'My daughter's missing.'

The border-patrol officer looked up. 'Your daughter's missing?'

'Off a cruise ship. It's been on the news.'

'In Mexico?'

'Yes, off the coast of Mexico.'

The border-patrol officer shook his head sadly and stamped Dad's passport and mine. 'Good luck,' he said, pushing the documents back.

Our plane was due to leave from the farthest possible gate. Dad did his best, but he's a big man and it was slow going even on the travelators. Eventually we arrived at the departure lounge. Dad squeezed himself into a moulded plastic chair. I used the few minutes we had before boarding, to check the news on my iPad.

Loren's disappearance was the top story on the *Bienveneda Bugle*'s front page. They had used one of the photographs from her Facebook page. It wasn't one that I remembered seeing. Loren was wearing the pendant she had described in her journal, with a little moon, a star and the sun. Her blue eyes were flecked with gold, and although her hair was tied back, one soft tendril had come loose. She wasn't even a little bit made up yet she looked so pretty. That was always Loren's luck. Maybe there were times when she felt down, but she was born gorgeous.

The story about her disappearance had been written by a reporter called Aaron Radcliffe. I recognised the name. He had been leaving messages on my phone, asking me to comment. How he made the link between Loren and me, and how he'd got my number, I don't know. In any case, he'd mucked the story up, because the headline said: HONEYMOON TRAGEDY – BRIDE MISSING OFF CRUISE SHIP.

Loren hadn't been on her honeymoon. She'd been on her second honeymoon, trying to save her marriage, although why she'd wanted to do that was beyond me.

Couldn't she see that David was toxic?

Anyone could see it.

* * *

'Come straight out and my driver should be there.'

Dad and I had landed in the airport at Cabo San Lucas. Gail had promised to send a car to meet us, but I couldn't immediately see anyone holding a sign with our name on it.

'It's okay,' I said, 'we still have to get our bags. Then we'll go out and find the driver.'

Dad's suitcase was easy to locate. Mom had strapped one of her purple belts around it.

We got through customs quite quickly, mainly because the line had dwindled down to nothing while we'd waited for Dad's bag. Gail's driver was easy to spot. He was holding a sign that said: 'Mr Wynne-Estes.'

'Hello,' I said to the driver, 'I'm Molly.'

Dad stuck out his hand. 'I'm Danny Franklin.'

The driver seemed confused. 'Family Wynne-Estes?'

'That's my son-in-law,' said Dad. 'I'm Danny Franklin. That's David.'

I stepped in. My Spanish isn't great, but I do know a few words. I said: 'No, that is us. I'm sorry. My dad's tired. Wynne-Estes. Yes. Thank you.'

The driver said: 'Your lady is missing from the ship?'

'Yes, that's right. My sister. Missing. We're here to see Gail Perlot.'

The name worked. 'Yes, Gail, we go, we go to Gail,' the driver said.

We stepped out of the airport into the heat. Drops of perspiration popped instantly onto Dad's forehead. The driver said: 'Come, come, come ...' His car was typical of embassy cars – it was an SUV with tinted windows and air-conditioning – but the ride was not smooth. The traffic out towards Gail's office was bumper-to-bumper, with mostly old cars that liked to honk and brake, on terrible roads.

'Bad traffic,' the driver kept saying. 'Bad traffic.'

'No kidding,' said Dad. He was holding onto the passenger strap.

Gail's office was in a building adjacent to the largest of the lavish hotels on the beach at Cabo, all of which are positioned to take advantage of views of the sea arch. Security inside the building was tight. We passed through a metal detector and had our digital fingerprints taken, before being allowed in.

Gail stood to greet us. She was an officious woman with a wide butt that made the vents at the back of her jacket flare. The centrepiece of her desk was a small, steel model of the flag-raising at Iwo Jima.

'I am so, so sorry to have to meet you under these circumstances,' she said, extending a hand with an old-fashioned engagement-and-wedding-ring combination. 'I can't imagine how this feels.'

'I'll tell you how it feels,' said Dad, wiping sweat from his brow, 'it feels like we're being given the run-around. It seems like nobody wants to tell us what's going on. Twenty-four hours we've been trying to reach David. No luck, but don't worry because I've got plenty of questions for him now.'

Gail's expression switched from empathy to something like anxiety. 'I'm sorry to have to tell you this, but David has left Mexico.'

'He's left?' Dad was wide-eyed. 'What do you mean he's left? Didn't you tell him we were coming?'

'I did tell him, but I know he flew out this morning. I was thinking that you might even run into him at the airport.'

So David knew that Dad and I were making a dash to Mexico yet he'd still upped and left?

'I'm so sorry,' Gail said. 'He got the nine am flight out. It's not a direct flight, but it's the first flight into the US. He'd have to go via San Francisco, and I don't know, can he drive from there? Down to Bienveneda?'

'Well, he can,' I said, 'but why would he? Didn't he leave his car at LAX? And why leave when he knew we were coming? You told him we were coming; I texted him. I've texted him a dozen times in the last twenty-four hours. I gave him our flight number. I said we'd see him. This sounds like he's avoiding us.'

Gail put her hands down on the desk. 'Well, I guess I don't know for certain, because I spoke to David only briefly this morning. He said the police here in Cabo had no further questions for him at this point, and he told me he wanted to get home to the girls, because the girls need to be told. Provided they don't know already. He was dreading the idea of them finding out from the television, although I gather his sister is keeping them away from the news.'

Dad looked astounded. 'But what is he going to tell them? That's a tricky conversation to have with five-year-olds, isn't it: "I killed your mother." I mean, what else is he going to say?'

'Dad, please,' I said, appealing for calm. 'We can't waste any more time on David. Can you tell us how the search is going, Gail? Who is out there? What can we do?'

'I know how agonising this must be,' she sighed, 'because any minute now, you're going to read online that the search has been called off. And I want you to know that's not quite right. There are still plenty of vessels out there. There's another cruise ship, and several yachts, plus the coast-guard cutter. They're under instructions to keep a lookout. But I do think, at this point, that we need to accept the likelihood that Loren will not be found.'

'Hey, hey, hey,' said Dad, rising from his chair, 'I think it's a bit early for that conclusion, don't you?'

'I am so sorry,' said Gail, for what seemed like the thousandth time. 'I wish there was something else I could say. I wish I could help. I really do. But I think we have to accept that Loren ...'

'Don't even say it. This is impossible to accept,' Dad said. 'Could you just accept this? Could you just walk away, if this was your daughter? You say you've talked to David, but you've let him walk out of here without talking to us. You say the Mexican police have no further questions for him, but how can that be?'

Gail chewed on her bottom lip. Her brow was furrowed. She seemed to be weighing up whether to let us in on something that she knew, that perhaps we didn't.

'What do you believe happened?' I asked. 'Do you think my sister jumped? I mean, did she leave a note?'

Gail shook her head, like no, that wasn't it. She paused a while longer, then said: 'As I tried to explain on the telephone, we – meaning the staff here, the embassy staff – wouldn't be in any position to hold David. Do you understand what I'm saying? We couldn't hold him even if we wanted to. This is Mexico. And the ship from which Loren disappeared, the *Silver Lining*, is Dutch. And those waters out the window there' – she pointed – 'that's the Pacific Ocean. It's not US waters. It may not even be Mexican waters. It could well be international waters that Loren went missing in. So it's a complicated situation, and my understanding is that the police in your home state – in

California, and even in Bienveneda – do know about this case, and they will be making a statement.'

'They will? But when?' I demanded. 'And what will they be saying?'

From her pained expression, it was clear that Gail knew more than she was saying. Dad could feel it, too. He kept trying to press Gail, asking: 'Did they search Loren's cabin? Have you talked to other passengers? Maybe we could see the surveillance tapes. Maybe we would notice something that the investigators don't even realise is important.'

Gail nodded. 'Well, when you say "we" ... there is the question of jurisdiction.'

Dad exploded. 'So, what, David answers to nobody?'

Now it was my turn to try to calm the situation. I put my hand on Dad's big knee. 'Please, Dad, please.'

Then, to Gail, I said: 'Okay, I get the feeling from what you're saying that there are things you're not telling us, and while I don't understand why you simply can't fill us in, no doubt there are reasons, and I'm prepared to accept that for now. But what *can* you tell us? When was the last time anyone saw Loren on the ship? Surely you can tell us that?'

'Yes. I think I can tell you that,' she said, visibly relieved, 'if you could just wait for a moment ...'

She picked up the phone on her desk and spoke into it. 'Carlos? Can you bring the USB? Yes, that one. Yes, please. Also, some coffee? Three cups. Thank you.'

She hung up and turned back to me. 'I can tell you this: on their last night on the ship, your sister and David attended the Captain's Dinner in the main dining hall. The Captain's Dinner is a special event – a gala evening, formal attire – and by all accounts, it's the highlight of the cruise.'

I had seen photographs of the Captain's Dinner on the *Silver Lining* website. It was black tie for men, and to-the-floor for women, with tiaras if you had them.

'According to the statement David has given to the *Federales* here – that's the Federal police – it was a lovely evening,' said Gail, moving her spectacles to better study the notes on her desk. 'There was dancing by candlelight. There was a string quartet. The evening ended around midnight, but David and Loren went back to their cabin early. They hadn't danced. Loren had eaten almost none of her meal. By David's account, he opened a bottle of French champagne from the minibar for Loren – at Loren's request – not because they felt like celebrating but because she was upset and wanted more to drink. They had one of the better cabins – a suite, or a stateroom – and they sat out on the balcony and talked about problems they were having in their marriage. At some point, David coaxed Loren into bed and I guess he must have fallen asleep ... and when he woke, Loren was gone.'

'So he pushed her off the balcony,' said Dad indignantly. 'Can't you see that?'

'No,' said Gail, shaking her head, 'no, definitely not, because we do have another sighting of Loren. It's hours after the dinner, but she is not on her balcony. She is in the corridor outside her stateroom ... and David is not with her.'

As Dad and I were processing this, Gail's assistant, Carlos, came into the room and served coffee.

'Here, let me show you something,' she said, before picking up her laptop and moving out from behind her side of the desk.

She put the laptop down so it was facing Dad and inserted a USB. He remained seated. I stood up and looked over Dad's shoulder. The image on the screen was grainy, but I only had to look for a half-second to recognise Loren. She was walking away from the camera, getting smaller and smaller as she made her way towards the end of the long corridor outside her room. She was wearing jeans, and she had the four fingers of each hand tucked into her back pockets, palms out.

'That's Loren,' said Dad.

'That is exactly how she walks,' I said.

Gail touched the arrow keys to keep the tape rolling. 'You'll see that she turns left at the end of the corridor here and, unfortunately, that's where the tape ends.'

'What do you mean?' I said. 'Where does the footage go from there?'

'The next camera is around the next corner, but Loren is not on it,' said Gail. 'They have looked at the film a million times but there's no sign. So all we can say for certain is, Loren went down this corridor, which comes out on the deck, and that's where we lose her.'

Dad started hitting the keys to bring the image of Loren back again. 'But what, she just disappears?' he said.

'Yes,' said Gail, 'but there's a black spot right there. The cameras don't cover every inch of the ship. They couldn't possibly.'

'So she went out onto the deck and …'

'And from there we don't know,' said Gail.

'But what's the time stamp on that?' said Dad. 'It must have a time stamp.'

'You're right. It does. The first sighting of Loren is here, at 3.46 am,' said Gail, replaying the footage, while pointing at the square-shaped numbers in the top right corner, 'and the last sighting of her, at the end of the same corridor, is at 3.47 am. So it has taken her less than a minute to walk that hall.'

'But she can't just disappear,' I said, 'she must go somewhere.'

'She must,' agreed Gail, 'but at this stage, that's the last sighting we have. The ship's management are going over all the footage from all the other cameras on the ship, from 3.46 am. So far, nothing.'

'What, nowhere?' said Dad.

'Nowhere. But we do see David.'

'I bet we do!' cried Dad.

'David stayed in the cabin until 4.50 am,' said Gail.

'How do we know that?' I demanded.

'The ship uses the same key-card system they have at hotels,' said Gail, 'like swipe keys. So we can see David and Loren go into their cabin well before midnight ...'

At this point, she went back a few frames on her laptop to footage that showed David in a tuxedo, guiding Loren, in a stunning halter-neck, through their cabin door.

'And here Loren comes out,' she said, showing the Loren-in-the-corridor footage again. 'And then there is no movement on that door until David comes out, shortly before five am.'

I put my face as close to the laptop as I could. The images were grainy but there's no question it was David.

'He says he's coming out to look for Loren,' said Gail, 'and he goes the same way. He disappears at the end of the hallway. So technically, he has followed Loren but he's a good hour behind her, and we very quickly see him again. Here he is on the lower pool deck, something like two minutes later. Here we see him rushing into the dining hall. He speaks to crew members there. "Has anyone seen Loren?" You can see him gesturing. The crew are shaking their heads, no, and now we see David again, agitated, asking the crew to raise the alarm.'

'Well, isn't that convenient,' said Dad, indignant. 'He's seen her on that first deck, pushed her off and then he goes and makes like he doesn't know what happened.'

I stepped in. 'There is no footage at all from that deck? But have the police – the *Federales* – interviewed any other passengers? Maybe somebody heard something? Or saw something? An argument? Because what is David saying: that she's fallen, or that it must be suicide, or what? Because that's ridiculous. Loren has young girls. Twins. Never, never, never would she leave them. Never. And if it's suicide, where's the note?'

'Well,' said Gail, sighing, 'there were something like three hundred people on the ship, including crew. This was to be their last night. People had gone from the Captain's Dinner to the disco. The casino was full. We've got a lot of people who have had a lot to drink, wandering around, heading to bed, even after Loren was out of her cabin. So far nobody saw her. And no, there was no note.'

I weighed up in my mind whether to tell Gail what I knew. It would mean breaking bad news in a shocking way to Dad. But it had to be done …

'Something you won't know, and David won't have told you: he had been having an affair, and Loren found out about it. Doesn't that tell you everything you need to know?' I said.

Dad looked thunderstruck. 'David's been having an affair!?'

'I'm sorry, Dad. I was going to tell you. It's all in her journal. But surely it's relevant?'

'He'd been having an affair with who?' said Dad.

Gail looked uncomfortable. 'Ah, yes, David did tell me that. He told the police that. I think it explains a lot about what happened, don't you?'

'That sounds to me like a motive to throw my daughter off the ship,' shouted Dad.

'Except that David did not leave the cabin with Loren. And we do not lose sight of him on the footage.'

'But you haven't found a note, have you?' I asked. 'A suicide note? Surely Loren would leave a note.'

'No, we haven't found a note. Although I did a quick internet search before you came. This year alone, six people have gone missing from cruise ships and in only two cases did people leave a note. And it's not just cruise ships. Very often in these situations, people don't leave notes.'

'No. Stop,' I said. 'Did you not hear what I was saying? David was having an affair. Loren has two children. Her girls are everything to her. Not in a million years would she leave them. I cannot believe that you are simply accepting what David is saying. His story reeks to high heaven.'

Gail closed her laptop. Her expression suggested that she did not necessarily disagree with me, and that she was resigned to the idea that nothing she could say would satisfy me. She carried the computer around to her side of the desk.

'I'm so sorry,' she said. 'I know how hard this must be to accept.'

'Yes, but it's not only the affair that's a problem,' I said. 'Did David tell you that his business was going under? Did David tell you that this trip was all about trying to prevent Loren from divorcing him?'

'What's all this?' said Dad.

'I'm sorry, Dad,' I said, exasperated. 'I was going to fill you in. I went to Loren's house yesterday. I found a journal she had written over the last few weeks. He was having an affair but there's more: David's business was in trouble. This trip was all about one last chance to try to patch things up. Loren was trying so hard. Really trying. You can tell from what she wrote, her heart was broken but she didn't want to give in. She didn't want to hurt her girls. But probably over the course of the five days on the ship, the reality must have dawned on her. Her husband was a liar and a cheat. She could take the girls and get out. And maybe that's what she finally told him she was going to do.'

Dad looked stunned. Maybe he wasn't all that surprised by the cheating – that would surprise nobody – but the idea that David's business was in trouble was astounding.

'Are you kidding me?' he said. 'David gets around town like a Rockefeller.'

'Please,' said Gail, putting up her hands for quiet. 'Some of what you're saying, David did in fact tell us. And I am not necessarily without sympathy for your position, but right at this moment ... This matter is not under our jurisdiction and this is out of our hands.'

* * *

When Dad and I left Gail's office he was in a white-hot rage. Gail insisted on putting us back into the embassy car, saying: 'I don't want you walking. You're upset. Let my driver take you to your hotel.'

'But we're not going straight to our hotel,' said Dad angrily. 'We're going to see the ship. I'm going to look that ship over. I want to speak to the captain. I want to speak to the crew. I'm not having this. My daughter jumped? There is just no way.'

'And I'll support you for as long as you're here,' Gail said gently, 'because that's my job, to support you and every other American citizen who needs my assistance. If you feel the need to visit the ship, my driver will take you. I can introduce you to the staff of the *Silver Lining*. They have an office down by the port. I am absolutely happy to do that for you.'

'We can manage on our own,' said Dad.

His tone was gruff. I could hardly fault him for that. On some level, he understood Gail's predicament. She was in no position to investigate. It was probably more than her remit to even sit down and talk to David in any detail, let alone Dad and me. Still, Dad wanted to know: had anyone checked David's phone? What about Loren's? Was there such a thing as a forensic team in Mexico and, if so, had they been into the cabin? Were there any signs of a disturbance? What about other passengers? What insights could they provide?

'He's obviously done it,' said Dad.

I didn't disagree with him.

'And it's so obvious that there's something they're not telling us.'

I didn't disagree with that, either. I mean, how could I?

Liz Moss

'Exclusive tonight on *Up Close with Liz Moss*: Liz sits down with David Wynne-Estes. Don't miss it.'

Tweet posted by Fox9

Hands up who has read *To Kill a Mockingbird*? Who remembers Atticus saying never ask a question when you don't already know the answer? Every barrister I know has that memorised, but reporters treat those words as gospel, too.

Don't go into an interview without knowing most of the story. Go in ready to catch him off guard, and not the other way around.

Long before I met him, I had an idea what David Wynne-Estes was going to say in our televised interview. He wanted to sit there under the hot lights and deny blame for anything and everything that went wrong in his marriage.

He wasn't to blame even for the adultery, because of course, men never are.

My interview with David took place in David's home town, Bienveneda. I'm a New Yorker and I hadn't previously been out that way. Bienveneda is pure California, with blue sky and Dr Seuss palm trees. And the High Side is big homes behind stone walls, guys in convertibles, and hot moms in white jeans, carrying small dogs.

It is not my cup of tea.

For the record, my network, Fox9, didn't pay for the interview. Given the size of the story at the time, we probably would have paid, but – despite being in what he was telling everyone was a poor position, financially – it seemed that David was not after money.

He was in damage control.

To give you a sense of the timeline, David had returned from Mexico and was living with his angelic blonde twins in the big house on Mountain View Road. Loren's family – her stepsister, Molly Franklin, and her father, Danny Franklin – had also returned from Mexico to their homes on the Low Side of Bienveneda, and the tension between the two camps was palpable.

'I've always admired you,' he said to me, by way of greeting. Was I meant to be flattered? Maybe, but I've heard it a lot. I've been doing *Up Close with Liz Moss* TV interviews for, what, twenty-seven years? Good Lord. It's a long time, and I've probably seen it all. Celebrities, sports stars, people triumphing over adversity, and plenty of people like David: flash rats caught up in horrendous crimes – think O.J. Simpson – trying to defend themselves in the court of public opinion.

Terms were hammered out not with David directly but with two consultants from Sally & Sons (often spelled Sally $ Sons, with a dollar sign, because they charge like wounded bulls). Sally & Sons are crisis-management specialists. For a fee, they will help anyone manage their reputation online and in the traditional media. Their advice for David, who can't have been as broke as he was claiming, was to get on the front foot. He had been trying a different tactic – say nothing to nobody – but then Molly had released extracts from Loren's journal to the public, via the *RealNews* website, and bang. The story exploded, and why wouldn't it? Releasing those extracts was such a good idea. Hardly anyone watches live TV anymore, so these big interviews are risky, but the journal extracts sent a million people – probably more – to the *RealNews* website, which is great for revenue. The demand was so intense, their server crashed. As their rivals, we couldn't have been more thrilled. That it crashed, I mean. For a while there – twenty-four hours – everyone wanted the journal extracts but nobody could read them. How *RealNews* managed to underestimate demand quite so catastrophically, I can't say. Demand was always going to be huge. This was a wife's private diary, detailing her husband's affair. People are obsessed with that stuff.

I'm not ashamed to admit that I was one of the people trying to get on the site. I had been following the story in the news, and I'd seen countless photographs of Loren on her wedding day, or out on the tennis court, bouncing around in new white shoes and a ponytail, or making Play-Doh models with her cute kids in the amazing kitchen of their dazzling house. To my mind, Loren came across really well in her journal. She was driven and spirited. She believed in her marriage. Her bad luck was to fall hopelessly in love with somebody like David Wynne-Estes.

By contrast, David seemed an absolute monster. He had refused to be interviewed by *RealNews*, and they punished him by including lots of clips of him running to his car with a hoodie over his head.

Plenty of people seemed to agree with me. The public – on Facebook and via the TV chat shows – were calling for David's scalp. He had to do something.

We – meaning the team at Fox9 – immediately got in touch, offering to tell his side of the story.

The deal we negotiated was for an hour-long interview, but we wanted something for our website, too, so we would also get David to write his version of what had gone wrong in his marriage, to post immediately after the interview went to air.

Fox9 doesn't have a studio in Bienveneda, so we had to make do with some rooms at the Bonsall, where David and Loren spent their wedding night. The Bonsall is your classic Californian hotel: flamingo-pink walls and cabanas by the pool. We asked the management to remove all the furniture except for a couple of overstuffed armchairs in front of a fireplace.

I sat in my armchair with a clipboard on my lap. I had my face tilted towards the light, and a makeup girl with a tool belt stuffed with blush brushes and cans of hairspray was giving me a last-minute touch-up when David walked into the room.

I watched as he stepped carefully over the cables strewn across the floor and settled into his armchair.

The sound girl immediately stepped between us, to pin a miniature mic to his lapel, and by the time she was finished adjusting his levels, she was smitten.

No, I can't explain how, but David has that effect on people. He's undeniably handsome, but there is also something of a little-boy-lost thing going on that women, in particular, find irresistible.

My job is not to get suckered by anyone's charisma. If I didn't get suckered by Bill Clinton, I wasn't going to get suckered by David Wynne-Estes (although, having interviewed them both, I'd say David might even give the old dog a run for his money).

So there I was, sitting opposite David, going over the questions I intended to ask. Remember, it wasn't for me to decide whether or not he was guilty, or even of what. That was for viewers to decide.

For all his natural confidence, David seemed nervous, although I suppose that's normal when you're on TV for maybe the first time. He had turned up groomed like a stallion and in a suit so beautiful that even our network chief was seen peering into the TV monitor to get a closer look. To my critical eye, the suit was slightly too big for David, but don't be fooled. That may well have been deliberate. Sally & Sons is not above putting a dodgy client into an extra-large suit to make him appear smaller and more vulnerable, like a little boy in a big-sized chair.

Plenty has been said about David's eyes. Are they really that blue, or does he wear coloured contact lenses? Having looked into them over an extended period, I would say that David's eyes really are blue, but the effect is amplified by the tan and the crinkles at the corners of his eyes.

My best guess is that David's tactic in our interview would be to throw himself upon the mercy of our mostly female audience. Yes, he'd been a bad husband and a lousy partner. Yes, he was a cad, but he was not a killer.

Would the audience buy it? I was dying to find out.

I called out to our director. 'Are we good?' I said.

'Ten seconds,' she replied.

I looked up at David and smiled. 'You good?'

He leaned forward and said: 'Be brutal with me.'

I'm confident it didn't show, but that set me back slightly in my chair. Be brutal? Who says that?

'I mean it. Ask me anything,' David said. 'I have nothing to hide.'

I looked over at the cameraman. He gave me the thumbs up to reassure me that we were recording. I kept my expression neutral and began.

'Alright,' I said, 'then I guess we'll start with your affair.'

* * *

'Your wife kept a journal.'

'No, she did not.'

Remember what I said about not asking a question if you don't already know the answer? Perfect example right there. Not that we couldn't edit it out, but getting a flat denial like that to something can throw you. His wife didn't keep a journal? The whole world had read extracts from Loren's journal on the *RealNews* website.

'I'm sorry, you're saying your wife didn't keep a journal?' I said.

'That's right,' said David, 'my wife – Loren – did not keep a journal.'

How great would it have been to have had a copy of Loren's journal on the side table next to me? I could have picked it up and waved it, saying: 'Then what's this?' That would have been good TV but bad luck because extracts from Loren's journal had been published online and I didn't have a printout.

'Well, then,' I said, 'what have we all been reading?'

David moved slightly forward in his seat, the way Tom Cruise does when he's being interviewed. Like he wants to get closer to you. Like he wants you to understand. My producer had specifically asked David not to do that because it mucks with the camera angles, but it's a classic Sally & Sons tactic. It makes the talent appear honest and transparent. They're moving in your direction. They're giving themselves to you. In terms of body language, it's the polar opposite of sitting with your arms crossed.

'Loren's journal isn't a journal in the sense of her writing her thoughts down at the end of every day,' said David. 'What people have been reading, Loren wrote all in one burst over about three weeks.'

'I see, and in your mind, that's not a journal?'

'Of course it's not,' said David earnestly. 'What people have been reading are basically notes – notes and thoughts – that Loren took down after I confessed to my affair.'

Again, classic Sally & Sons. David was throwing himself upon the mercy of the viewing audience by confessing the affair to them, with no prompting. No sallying. No dodging. But how truthful was he being?

After all, he hadn't confessed to his affair to Loren. He'd been caught out by a mom at Bienveneda Grammar, who had dobbed him in. Still, I let him continue.

'Loren wrote those notes late at night during the most difficult time of her life. She was hurt and confused, and trying to make sense of things. Which makes the betrayal of Loren by her family that much worse.'

That threw me. What on earth was David on about?

'Loren and I were at a turning point in our marriage. She was trying to decide whether she could stay with me. It would be a tough decision and she was trying to sort things out in her own mind. We had a marriage counsellor – Bette Busonne, who invented the Busonne Method – who was urging Loren to put her thoughts down on paper. And I remember Loren laughing – bitterly laughing – through her tears at that suggestion. This was when we were sitting in Bette's office, fairly soon after Loren found out about the affair. Loren was curled into her chair and Bette said: "Why are you laughing?" and Loren replied: "Because it's not going to take very long to write down how I feel. I feel like crap."'

'I'm not surprised,' I said evenly.

'Right,' said David, 'and Bette's advice was: "If you start writing things down, you might find that it helps you sort out your feelings and that will help you decide whether you want to stay with David." And that hit me like a hammer because my fear was that Loren would come down on the side of leaving me. So when Bette suggested that Loren go right back to the start of our relationship – right back to when we first met in New York City – and try to pinpoint when and why we fell in love and when things might have started to go off track, I was all for it. Because I thought, yes, that will help Loren see that my affair wasn't the problem. My affair was a symptom of problems we already had in our marriage. That things were rotten before I strayed.'

Oh, I see. Of course! We were already at the point where the affair wasn't his fault.

'Bette said: "Write everything down, don't try to censor your thoughts. By the time you get to the end, you will have an answer as to whether you want to stay with your husband." That's what Loren was doing, she was writing down her deepest, innermost thoughts for the purpose of figuring out whether she wanted to stay with me. That's not a journal. That is a sacred text and those words – those thoughts – they belonged to Loren exclusively. They were not for me to read, and I cannot imagine how Loren would feel knowing that her deepest, most private feelings have now been shared with the world and not by me, but by people who claim to love her.'

Did I mention that Sally & Sons charge a pretty penny? Now you can see why. That little speech, right at the start of our interview, was a masterpiece.

Playing it back in the privacy of the editing room a few days later, my producer said to me: 'That gentle sound you hear? That's the women of America, moving in to comfort this guy.'

I wasn't so sure. The women of America don't approve of adultery.

I decided to hit David with a few questions about his tacky betrayal. 'Well, for the sake of this interview, let's refer to Loren's private thoughts as her journal. You've read the extracts. We all have. So tell us, how did it feel, having to read just how badly you've hurt your wife?'

David didn't flinch. 'I didn't need to read Loren's notes to know how much I'd hurt her. Loren was my wife. I knew her intimately. I only had to look at her to see how much pain she was in.'

Masterful. I pressed on: 'And how did that make you feel?'

'I wanted to do whatever I had to do to make things right,' said David. 'I was responsible for Loren's hurt, and I was taking responsibility for that as we tried to repair our marriage.'

'Yes, we'll get to that,' I said, 'but how did you feel, reading Loren's journal?'

'Well, it was surreal, because I was there for many of the events she described, so I guess it was like looking at my life through a different set of eyes. The first time we met, the first time we broke up ...'

I raised my hand slightly off my lap, a signal I use when I want the talent to stop for a moment, usually so we can adjust the lighting or the sound, although mainly so I can interrupt.

'Yes, let's talk about that,' I said, 'let's talk about the first time you met. You are thirty-two and Loren is twenty-three, and the two of you have just begun working at Book-IT ...'

'No,' said David. 'I was already there. I had been there more than a year. Loren had just arrived. She was one of the new graduates.'

I smiled, and we started again. 'Okay, the two of you have just met. Loren has just arrived in New York City. She's landed a good job but she's not earning much money. You're a big shot. You've got the penthouse ...'

'It wasn't a penthouse.'

'Okay, it's not a penthouse, but to cut to the chase, you're a big deal, and Loren falls head-over-heels in love with you …'

'Which I knew nothing about.'

'I'm sorry?'

'That's the problem with this journal,' said David, leaning forward with his hands together and his fingers pointed in my direction. 'It's only one side of the story. And there are two sides to every story. Loren says that she fell madly in love and I dropped her and hurt her, but that's only one side of the story.'

'Alright,' I said, smiling. 'Okay. So what's your side of that story?'

At this point in the interview, we intended to show some photographs of Loren as she was at age twenty-three from David's collection, including one in which she was crouched beside a small snowman in Central Park. It wasn't a great shot – the pixels on those old digital cameras weren't great back in those days, and the snowman was pretty lame, with bent sticks for arms and a piece of fir tree on its head – but that was the point.

Loren, when she met David, was still young enough to be making snowmen in Central Park, and she was so pretty. In the shot, she wears a woollen beanie, jeans and snow boots, and she's got iPod buds in her ears. You can see the cords in her long, straw-coloured hair. She's got a radiant smile and soft-pink lips.

'Loren was gorgeous,' David said, 'but I don't mean just physically. She was also unlike anyone I'd previously met in New York.'

'How so?'

'She was shy. Shy like a deer, I used to think, like she was scared that the world wanted to hurt her, or something. I couldn't understand why. To me, she was beautiful and talented and it seemed obvious that she had the world at her feet. It wasn't until she told me about her parents' divorce – how her father ran out on her to live with another woman who had a daughter about the same age – that I began to understand. Maybe your viewers already know this, but Loren's family – her father, and her stepsister, Molly – have put themselves forward as the people who have Loren's best interests at heart. In truth, Loren was betrayed by her father at a vulnerable age. He left his marriage to live with Molly's mother, and Loren's confusion about that – why was he living with another little girl and not me? – was something she carried right through to adulthood. She was extremely wary of getting involved with anyone, very wary of being hurt, and the manifestation of that was, she tended to play her cards close to her chest. So I had no idea that Loren had fallen for me until we broke up and she started to cry. She says in her journal that I was embarrassed by her tears, but in fact I was shocked. She'd never let on as to how she felt, or not to me, anyway. The idea that I was "The One" – you could have knocked me over with a feather.'

I had been sitting slightly forward in my armchair, but now I sat back, with my hands folded over the clipboard on my lap.

'Well, then,' I said, 'how did you feel when she told you? Because she makes it very plain in her journal that she was distressed.'

'Well, it's complicated,' said David, to which I could just imagine our audience rolling their eyes. 'On one hand, I was surprised. On the other hand, I was moving on.'

'From Loren?'

'No, from Book-IT, and from New York City. Loren suggests in her journal that something untoward happened at Book-IT, that I was marched from the building or something, and that may have been the impression left by others, but the truth is – and I did tell Loren this – the partners did not want me to leave. And you can check that with them.'

I made a note on my notepad, as if to remind myself to do just that. 'Go on,' I said.

'The guys who founded that company – two guys I met in college – had led me to believe that I was part of the ownership structure. Then I discovered that they were on track to make a fortune, but I was not part of it, because I didn't have a stake in the company. I was an employee. I asked them to rectify that, and they declined. So I decided to move on. And they weren't happy. And I realise that some people are going to think I'm heartless when I say that Loren was a casualty of my decision to cut my losses in New York City, but I had no idea about the depths of Loren's feelings for me. Loren was gorgeous. We were having a great time, but if I'm being honest, I probably wasn't ready to settle down at that point, and I mean, Loren was young, so it didn't occur to me that she was thinking of settling down, either. And yes, there were some ... scenes afterwards, but I wasn't too concerned. I thought, Loren will find somebody else in the blink of an eye and she'll probably never think about me again.'

* * *

'I have zero interest in concrete.'

We had taken a break from filming. One of David's minders had disappeared down the corridor in search of the ice machine. Another was in a corner with her hand over her cell phone. David and I were standing in front of the refreshment table (white tablecloth, percolated coffee, a selection of teabags in a timber case). I had opted to stay in the interview room during our break, which was unusual for me. My practice is normally to leave the room, lest I get caught up in small talk. On this occasion, I'd instructed one of the cameramen to keep his tapes rolling – covertly – so as we might catch a little of David off-guard. If that sounds somewhat sneaky, remember that he'd come with minders. I was determined to get under the layers of polish.

'I'm sorry, you said ... concrete?'

'I figured that you were about to ask me why I went back to Bienveneda,' David said, dipping his tea bag over and over, 'and I'm going to tell you that I had no interest in running my father's concrete company.'

'Oh, I see,' I said, nodding.

We already knew all about David's decision not to work for his father. We have teams of researchers at Fox9 whose job is to dig into people's backgrounds. David wasn't trying to fill me in. He was trying to bond with me and, again, there is no denying that there is definitely something charming about him. I renewed my pact with myself to keep my guard up.

'Actually, David, when everyone gets back, I think we'll start by talking about how Loren followed you to Bienveneda,' I said, taking my teabag out of the cup and placing it on a saucer, 'because people will want to know: why did she follow you? And when did you fall in love with your wife, David? That's a good question for this next session, too. In fact, why don't you try to come up with an answer for that.'

I turned with my cup too quickly, because I sloshed some tea over my saucer, although thankfully not on the cream jacket. An assistant zoomed forward to take the cup from me and check my clothes, but it was fine, and thank God. Sloshing your jacket in the middle of an interview is a disaster. You have to film the whole first session all over again, because otherwise, the viewer will wonder why you suddenly got changed.

We resumed our positions. The makeup girl stepped forward to apply a light dusting of powder to David's face.

'You've got a tough job trying to make me look handsome,' he said.

She grinned at him. 'You look just fine.'

'We're rolling,' said the cameraman, with his eye up tight to the viewfinder.

I had an opening statement ready: 'You weren't in love with your wife.' Our producer had written it for me, knowing it would be a good line for the promos. I thought it might also catch David off-guard, but it didn't.

'I was madly in love with her,' he said.

'But not when you first met?'

'Well, okay,' said David, 'what happened was this. I left Book-IT and came home to Bienveneda. My family is quite small. I have a sister, Janet, and then my parents, and we are close. My mother had some health concerns, and I agreed to come home to Bienveneda to help out and I suppose my father hoped that I would take over his business, but I had an idea for a business of my own.'

'Capital Shrine?'

'Right. There's no big secret to what I was doing. I was taking money and investing it, and sometimes you win and sometimes you lose. And for a long time, I was winning. I'm still very proud of what I was able to achieve, especially in those early days, creating wealth for people who don't seem to have the time of day for me now.'

The collapse of David's business – which was no more than a Ponzi scheme – was a well-known part of his story, chronicled in some detail by the *New York Times*, among others. I needed to steer the conversation back to Loren, so I asked David: 'At what point did Loren re-enter your life?'

'Well, it's interesting,' he said, 'because, as everyone knows from her journal, what basically happened was, I ran into Loren on Park Avenue in New York during a business trip, and I was a little nervous because, who knew: was she still cross with me? But Loren seemed to me to have moved on. She was doing well at work. She had a new apartment. She looked great and we had a pleasant exchange, after which I got on with the rest of my schedule for that day, whereas Loren seemed to have decided that the meeting was fate, which is something I knew absolutely nothing about until very recently. The way I understood things, I just happened to run into Loren again, this time in Bienveneda when she came to town for her father's birthday weekend. The fact she had engineered that meeting – planned it over many months – was a secret that Loren kept from me.'

'And that's when you had the now famous lunch at the Jetty?'

'Right,' said David, flushing. 'We decided to have lunch at the Jetty and it was a, ah, very pleasant afternoon. Loren was in excellent form. Very different from the shy girl she'd been when we first met. But the plotting and scheming behind that encounter … well, again, I had absolutely no idea about any of that. I had no idea about Loren's ongoing obsession with me. You would think, after we became engaged, got married, had two children, that it would be something that we joked about, something that became part of our story, but she never, ever mentioned it. Never. So of course it was disturbing to read all about it in Loren's journal.'

By David's account, it was during the lunch at the Jetty that he realised that he was still attracted to Loren.

'She had grown into a woman who was sexy and fun,' he said. 'I definitely tried to convince her to come home with me that day. She knocked my socks off. She turned me down, and I remember watching her drive off, with her ponytail swinging. There wasn't a guy in the street who didn't notice her.'

'And you were intrigued?'

'Right, but like most men, I believe it's a mistake to appear too keen. My feeling has always been that women don't want the men that want them. Women want the men they have to catch. So I waited a couple of days before I called her ... but yes, from there, the relationship very quickly became serious. And Loren was not wrong: I had decided that I wanted to get married, and Loren seemed to be the perfect candidate.'

I tilted my head. 'The perfect candidate?'

'Don't take it the wrong way,' said David, 'but yes, she seemed perfect, and to be honest, my big worry was that she might say no. Loren was still under thirty. I remember talking to her about children, and she said: "Oh God, not for years." Plus, if we got married she would have to move back home to her home town. She used to joke about how she'd "escaped" from Bienveneda. It had been hell for her, growing up here, feeling rejected by her own father. So to my mind, there was a real risk that she might turn down my proposal.'

'But she didn't,' I said.

'No, she didn't,' said David, eyes filling with tears, 'she said yes, and I was absolutely, one hundred per cent over the moon.'

* * *

THE WEDDING OF THE CENTURY!

I knew from Loren's journal that those words had appeared somewhere in the *Bienveneda Bugle* in the lead-up to Loren's big day, so we mocked them up in a newspaper-style headline to flash across the screen.

'And how does it feel when you see those words?' I asked. We were by now well into the second hour of the interview and I still had no great 'gotcha' moment, but that was fine. These things take time.

'I'd forgotten that headline,' said David when the camera came back to him, 'and it's obviously crazy when you think of the kind of weddings some people have. Kim and Kanye! But look, it was an incredibly fun night and huge for Bienveneda. People flew in from New York and drove in from LA, and Loren loved it. Being a princess. She laughed about the thrones, but she absolutely loved it. And after the wedding, we had the most amazing honeymoon. A cruise around Cabo that was just ...'

David paused, and began rubbing his brow, as if stressed.

'Well, the memories I have of that honeymoon, they're all ... I mean, Loren loved cruise ships. She loved the idea of them. The romance. Not having to pack and re-pack at every stop. She loved dining with the captain. The old-style glamour. And, you know, she was so happy on our honeymoon ... look, can we take a break?'

The last thing we'd normally want to do while David was getting emotional was cut, but it was too late.

'Sure, let's all take a break,' the cameraman said, then stepped back from his viewfinder.

'Could we perhaps get David a glass of water?' said the girl from Sally & Sons.

'Of course,' said the producer, and signalled to one of our assistants to bring a glass to David so he wouldn't have to untangle himself from the lapel mic.

'I'm sorry,' he said, sipping.

'It's fine,' I said patiently.

'Are we good?' asked the producer.

'All good,' said David, placing the water glass down by his feet.

The cameras rolled again.

'So, we were talking about your honeymoon. How soon after the honeymoon did Loren fall pregnant? It was very soon, wasn't it?'

'We hadn't planned on starting a family for several years,' he said, tugging a little on his collar, 'but God had other plans, obviously. And the girls were a gift. They are a gift. Although the pregnancy was difficult for Loren. And clearly, given what she's written, I should have been much more supportive, but there didn't seem to be all that much that I could do. I remember joking with some of my friends at the golf club: "My wife is pregnant and she can't stand me." They all sympathised. But they also warned me, "Get used to it. You're not her number one anymore and you never will be again."'

'But hang on a minute,' I said, tapping my pen against my clipboard, 'this isn't about you not being supportive. Loren found a receipt for a strip club in your wallet ...'

'No, no,' said David.

For a moment, I thought he was going to deny it, which would have been great because we had the receipts, but he didn't deny it.

'I did go to the strip club. I absolutely did, and it was absolutely wrong of me. But I'm not the first businessman to be dragged to one of those places by clients and I won't be the last. Like it or not, strip clubs are part of life in corporate America, and we, as a nation, definitely need to have a conversation about why that is.'

Oh please. Was David now trying to shift the blame for his own actions onto corporate America?

'As for what happened later,' said David, 'I can't be the first husband to have noticed that his wife's priorities had changed after the babies arrived. And if the average husband has problems with one baby, I had double trouble.' He grinned. 'Our girls were – are – gorgeous, but they put huge demands on Loren's time and energy. Not that she didn't have plenty of help. I made sure that she had all the help she needed. At one point, it seemed like we had more staff than family in the house. And yes, I have seen what Loren wrote: that I stopped seeing her as Wife and started seeing her only as Mother. But that isn't true. If anything, it was the opposite. Loren stopped being Loren and became Wife and Mother. The relationship we had before we got married – travelling, watching our favourite shows, having frequent sex – came to an abrupt end, as Loren's attention shifted to our girls. Which is appropriate and natural, of course.'

I smiled. 'Of course, but David, forgive me. I don't wish to sound like I doubt you, but what about what Loren has said about you being repulsed by the idea of having sex with her, before and after the babies arrived?'

He rubbed his forehead with four fingers of one hand. We had been talking for some time; the producer had done what she always does and turned the air-conditioning down just a touch; David – predictably – was beginning to sweat under the lights.

'That's not true,' he said. 'Loren put on weight with the pregnancy, but she was far more concerned about it than I was.

Loren was my wife. She had given me the greatest gift – two
beautiful children – and I still found her very attractive, but she
began to brush me off. The incident she mentions – when I put
my arm around her waist and cupped her belly – was a joke.
I was nibbling on her shoulder. I said something like: "What's
this, jelly-belly?"'

My eyebrows shot up. David said 'jelly-belly' to a woman
who had just given birth to his children?

'I see your expression,' he said, 'and I get it. Guys can be such
idiots. Obviously it's not funny. I should've been more sensitive,
but I thought she'd push back against me and laugh, and we'd
end up making love. She didn't. She froze. Yes, I should've known
better, but the idea that I was mocking her, or taunting her – that
is simply wrong. And look, even saying that, yes, we were having
problems in that department. Sexually. And yes, I felt locked out.
I was frustrated. Sexually frustrated. I know it sounds immature
but it's the way I felt. Locked out of my own life and locked out
of my own wife.'

For the first time in our interview, David's voice was rising. I
was interested to see where frustration might take him.

'And did you resent that?'

'No,' he said. 'No, because to resent that would be to resent
the girls. And I would never resent them for anything. Never.
But then, yes, I resented not having much sex in my relationship,
because over time, our sex life dwindled to almost nothing.
Maybe once or twice a month she might agree to sex, but I
could tell she didn't enjoy it. And I wanted sex. I wanted to have
sex with someone who wanted to have sex with me. Can you
imagine how it feels to have to admit that, here, today, publicly?
It's excruciating. But it's true. I wanted sex. I needed sex. I'm a
man! Maybe all men don't need sex but I do. And I don't think

that makes me a bad person. It makes me human. But Loren
was just not interested. She was paranoid about her weight, her
body shape, the girls waking up, everything. Here was a woman
who had once had a healthy libido, a woman who had loved
having sex – who loved having sex with me – who completely
changed on that front. Loren's libido after the girls arrived was
the elephant in our bedroom. Because it's hard for a man not to
take his wife's lack of desire personally, right? What was wrong
with me? I was an excellent provider. Loren had everything she
could possibly want or need, and yet ...'

David seemed genuinely distressed.

'So you were putting in, but you weren't getting out,' I said
gently.

'Right,' he said, looking relieved not to be judged, 'and I was
unprepared for that. I had always been attractive to women. I
know how that sounds, but it's true. I had never gone long
periods without sex, not since, I don't know, I was an adolescent.
Sex has always been an important part of my life and there I
was, shut out of intimacy in my own marriage.'

'And what did you do to try to rekindle the flame?' I asked
sympathetically.

'Everything,' said David. 'Everything. I bought Loren
presents. Flowers. Never chocolates. I could get in big trouble for
bringing home chocolates. I would try to coax her. I would move
closer to Loren on the sofa, and say things like: "Let me try to
turn you on." That's how I'd frame it, let me try to turn you on.
Not, "I want to have sex with you now and you must agree."
Not, "I demand my conjugal rights." Not, "Look, you can just
lie there, and you don't even have to pretend to enjoy it."

'I would coax and tempt and flirt and, I don't know, just
try. But she was not interested. And it was not a point I was

willing to push because, a year or so after the girls arrived, Loren began suffering from terrible migraines. She would take to the sofa in a dark room and not get up. The nannies would tend to the girls. She would refuse to attend important events with me. I tried to reason with her. Not only for my sake. For her sake. I'd say: "Loren, you should get up. You have to come out. You know it's important. I've purchased a table at this dinner. I've invited clients. We need to go." She would move a hot water bottle to her abdomen, or apply a cold press on her forehead and she would say: "Can you please leave me alone, David? I don't feel well." I'd be saying: "I can't go on my own. How does it look, me turning up alone to everything?" She would complain: "But all you ever talk about is business and golf. I hate business. I hate golf." I'd say: "You can talk to the wives." She would say: "The wives don't like me. The wives judge me." It was all in her head, of course, but that was still a problem, because when a businessman has a wife who doesn't get on with other people's wives, well, it was like driving a one-wheeled wagon.'

'I see,' I said, 'and did you seek counselling at any point?'

'Yes, of course,' said David. 'I urged Loren to come with me to see a therapist. She agreed at first but then decided that she couldn't tell the marriage counsellor that we weren't having sex much, because Loren was embarrassed about it. We were seen in the community as an attractive, successful couple. She was worried that our secret would get out. I said: "Loren, we can't go and see a counsellor and be less than honest. There'd be no point." And she understood that. So we didn't go anymore. And so things got worse. And I suppose in the end, I gave up trying with Loren, and I tried instead to solve my own problems by … by … by …'

'By inviting somebody else into your bed?'

David looked weary. 'Yes,' he said, 'by inviting somebody else into my bed.'

* * *

Be brutal. Ask me anything. I have nothing to hide. Those were some of David's words to me, and now it was time to find out exactly how true they were. I started with a direct question: 'Who is Lyric Morales?' I don't know what I expected – maybe for David to dodge and weave – but he answered.

'She was my mistress.'

I could just see the audience – Mr and Mrs Kafoops we call them; a generic couple, aged in their sixties – turning to each other in front of their TVs, saying: 'Has he got no shame?'

'And how did you meet her?'

'She worked in my office.'

'Meaning you were her boss?'

'Yes. I was her boss and we had an affair. But I did not initiate it.'

I raised an eyebrow. 'You didn't?'

'No,' said David, his tone steady. 'Not that it matters, because I should've known better. But that's the truth. I didn't seduce her. She seduced me.'

I thought, this is your first mistake. You're older, and wealthier, and more charming, and her boss. Yet it's her fault that you fell into bed?

'You're quite the cool customer, aren't you?' I said.

'What do you mean?' replied David. 'Did you expect me to lie? I'm not going to lie. It's embarrassing having to go over these things in public. It's disrespectful to my wife, and for that matter to Lyric Morales. But what choice do I have, other than to defend myself against what's being said?'

'Very well,' I said, 'then perhaps you should tell us how it happened?'

I knew perfectly well how the relationship between Lyric and David had started. David had by then given one of his three statements to the detectives at Bienveneda, but having him go over the details would be great TV.

'Well, I went into the office one day,' he said, looking uncomfortable, 'and I even remember the weather, because it was towards the end of the June Gloom. The morning fog we get in Bienveneda was lifting. It was blue skies, and I remember swinging along the coast road, thinking what a great day it was. My mood was buoyant. At that stage, I don't think I had too many money problems. Problems at home with Loren, certainly, but on balance, the day had started well. I was first to arrive at work. That wasn't unusual. We had a small staff – just three or perhaps four girls at that point – and our offices weren't large, but I always enjoyed going there.'

Ahead of the sit-down interview, I'd asked David to take us to his old offices on Main Street. He no longer has keys, but we asked him to put his hands up to the glass. I did the same. The offices of Capital Shrine were basically three rooms with extremely clean lines. There was a low, white sofa – leather, I presume – in the reception area, and an elegant coffee table made of one solid piece of blue glass.

'There's my dreams, shattered,' he'd said. It was the first time I saw him truly grief-stricken.

Now, back in our interview room, he was composed.

'I'm a person who likes routine,' David said. 'I would start each day responding to emails and dealing with whatever dramas

had risen overnight. I had three computer screens on my desk to
keep track of our investments. The girls – my staff – would come
in at around nine am to start their days. With the exception of
Lyric, they were all quiet girls. I never insisted on silence but I
did not want a wild and crazy office. I didn't like office birthday
parties, for example. The cake, the candles, the giggling. I liked
a quiet, smooth, dignified office, and my girls – the office girls –
understood that.'

Part of me wanted to say, 'Sounds like so much fun,' but I
kept that to myself.

'Generally speaking, the mail would come in at around
eleven am,' he continued. 'There wasn't much, because most mail
comes in by email these days, but there would always be at least
one or two big envelopes. The girl on reception – her name was
Sunny Bechara – would toss out what I didn't need to see – junk
mail, basically – and bring the rest to me. On this particular day,
I noticed a chunky package among the other parcels she put on
my desk. It was a padded envelope with my name, handwritten
across the front, in gold-coloured pen. The envelope smelled of
perfume. Of course, it had already been opened because that's
the way things were done: Sunny would open the mail, and staple
whatever important documents were inside to the envelope so I
didn't have to go fishing for whatever was within, but she hadn't
done that with this envelope.'

'Really,' I said. 'Why not?'

We were heading into painful territory and we both knew it.

'Right,' said David. 'Well, I mean, just as a reminder, I had
a glass-walled office. Everyone could see into my office, unless I
closed the blinds. But why would I close the blinds? So my hand
went inside the envelope and out came ...'

He paused.

'Yes?' I prompted. 'Go on.'

'Out came a pair of panties.'

'Not yours, I take it?'

David gave a short, sharp laugh. 'No, not mine,' he said, collecting himself, 'definitely not. And I was mortified. I could see Sunny and some of the other girls outside my office, trying a little too hard to appear busy, so, no question, they'd all seen the package, and no question, they had all been gossiping about it and were dying to see what I might do.'

'And what did you do?'

'I stuffed the panties back into the envelope,' he said, making a stuffing motion with his hands. 'I was embarrassed. But look ... I was also intrigued. I mean, who had sent them? Was it a joke, or was somebody interested in me? That was a thrilling idea. It shouldn't have been, but it was. It had been so long since anyone – Loren – had shown any interest in me, and I guess I was ...'

He was searching for the right word, so I suggested one. 'Flattered?'

'Yes, I was flattered. I didn't want to respond to the package straightaway because of the girls outside, but later that day, I sort of put the envelope under my jacket and went out to my car, and I took the panties out, and the note that came with them, and that's when I knew that the parcel was from Lyric.'

'I see,' I said, 'and how would you describe your relationship with Miss Morales up until that point? Was it friendly or ...?'

'Friendly,' said David. 'From memory, I'd only hired Lyric something like two months earlier. She came from Puerto Rico five or six years earlier, when she was maybe nineteen. Possibly twenty. I think nineteen. She had started out in LA, doing nanny work and household cleaning, the normal starter jobs. Then she did a secretarial course. How she ended up in Bienveneda I can't say for certain, but she was living in one of the new, rent-controlled apartments that had been built near Bienveneda's Lemon Grove – that's a large orchard behind the houses on Mountain View, where I live – and she came into the office, looking for work. And she was striking. Absolutely striking. Very tall – almost as tall as me – with dark hair, like a Sofia Vergara type. Look, that doesn't matter. The point is, Lyric had started working for me, we had a friendly relationship, and now it seemed that she wanted more, because she had included a note. It was a riddle, with a play on her name. Something about songs. Love songs. Lyric. It wasn't hugely sophisticated. The words, I forget, but clearly, the note was from her.'

'Alright,' I said. 'And what happened next?'

'Well, I went back to my office,' said David, 'because I was confused about what to do—'

'I'm sorry,' I interrupted, 'you were confused?'

'Yes, because of the way I felt. I mean, I was aroused. Can I even say that?' He glanced at the cameraman and his own support staff, as if seeking permission. 'I mean, it's humiliating, but that's the truth. I was aroused. Excited by the idea that somebody was interested in me. I knew what I had to do, which was fire Lyric. But she had made sure to send the parcel on a day she wasn't in so I would have to call her to fire her, which I kept putting off until I went back out to my car later that night when, yes, I did call her.'

'From the car?'

'Right. On the speaker phone, from the underground car park, I called her, and she spoke before I had the chance. She said: "Hello, boss." I was going to say something like, "Well, this is inappropriate," but instead I said: "Thank you for the gift," and it seemed like Lyric was feeling pretty confident about how I would react, because she said something like: "Oh, I'm sorry, I've completely forgotten. What did I send you again?" And I could see what she was doing. If I took the bait – if I answered her question – then I would essentially be entering into a relationship with her. And obviously, the decisions I made in the moments that followed were extremely bad ones. What I should have said was something like: "Lyric, I'm flattered, but I'm a married man." But I was starved for affection, and so I found myself saying ... ah ... do I have to say this?'

'I'm sorry,' I said, as if I didn't already know. 'Say what?'

'Well, everyone knows,' said David wearily. 'It's in the statement I gave to the police. I said, "Thank you for your panties." And then Lyric said ... she said: "And did you taste them?"'

He gave a small shrug.

I let him sit in hideously embarrassing silence for a minute before saying: 'Alright. Go on.'

'Well, the effect that a conversation like that ... I was blown away. Again, aroused. And next thing I knew I was arranging to go back to my office – I hadn't even pulled out of the car park – but I was arranging to go back inside because Lyric was on her way. She let herself in through the doors on Main Street. She pressed the button on the wall outside my office and the glass door slid open and she dropped her skirt at the door. And I'm not proud of what happened next ...'

'You mean the sex?'

'Yes. We had sex. And from that day on, I guess we were having an affair.'

'You guess?' I said.

'Yes,' said David. 'I mean, yes, from that day on, we were having an affair. And that word – affair – it's important because to me, it was always an affair. I never wanted more than that and maybe this is naïve, but Lyric didn't seem to want more than that, at least, not at first. Some of your viewers may find this difficult to understand, but Lyric was the kind of woman who seemed to enjoy the trappings of an affair. I'm not a psychologist, but the secrecy – the thrill of maybe getting caught – seemed to appeal to Lyric. I did not want to get caught. I had so much to lose. I was in love with my wife. With Loren and our girls. My loyalty … and that's clearly the wrong word in this context, but my loyalty was absolutely to them. I loved my family. But I also needed sex. And Lyric understood that. Or she seemed to understand that. My relationship with her was fun. I treated her well. But at the end of the day, it was an affair, and she understood that I, one hundred per cent, would not be leaving my wife for her.'

* * *

'You had a secret email account, didn't you?'

'Excuse me?'

'You had a secret email account. One that you used exclusively to communicate with Miss Morales.'

David seemed surprised that I would bring that up. He shouldn't have been. Viewers love secret email accounts. We had gained access to David's from a source within the Bienveneda Sheriff's Office, and we had paid her back with a couple of front-row tickets to a Katy Perry concert.

David shot a look at his minder.

She nodded, as if to say, 'It's okay. Let's see where this goes. If things get hairy, I can always step in.'

David looked back at me. 'Yes, I had a secret email account.'

'And do you remember your address?'

'My address?'

'Your email address.'

David shifted in his seat. He didn't want to answer but that was fine. I could answer for him.

'I have some of the messages here and they have your address on them,' I said, producing a piece of A4 paper from under the cover of my clipboard. 'And if I've got this right, you're Big Dave? Bigdave@capital.com? And Lyric would be ...?'

'Forbiddenfruit@capital.com,' he said, nodding grimly. 'I mean, stupid. They're stupid names. A stupid, private joke between us. Big Dave and Forbidden Fruit, that's how we signed off to each other.'

'And this Forbidden Fruit, I suppose we can guess what that means?'

'I suppose it's obvious,' said David, 'because, look, the banter between Lyric and me had a strong, sexual flavour to it. That's the nature of those relationships. They're charged.'

'So I see,' I said, leafing primly through the pages of printouts. 'And I guess at this point, we should perhaps explain how charged this particular relationship became?'

David sighed. 'Well, this is humiliating but yes, I can explain what happened. I get that it's important. I want to be open about it. Several months into the affair, Lyric and I developed what I considered a game, whereby I would call her into my office for what she called "the inspection". The idea was to ensure that she was wearing panties because of course, she had initiated the affair by sending her panties to me. The inspection could happen at any time. I might call Lyric into my office first thing on a Monday morning or at two pm on a

Wednesday afternoon. She would get no warning. If she wasn't wearing panties, I'd be allowed to, to, to ... to discipline her.'

'Meaning?'

'Normally, playful spanking,' said David, abashed. 'So, that was the game. The inspections would take place on my desk. Lyric would come into my office, she would sit opposite me – usually on the desk, facing me – and I would look up her skirt, and Lyric would get pleasure either from the spanking or from the inspection itself. Either way, she seemed to enjoy it ...'

'If we could just pause there,' I said, slightly raising my hand, 'I think you mentioned earlier that you had a glass-walled office?'

'Yes,' said David, shifting uncomfortably, 'and that, too, was part of the thrill for Lyric. The possibility of getting caught, or of somebody walking by and looking in.'

'That seems like an awfully dangerous game, David, if you didn't want your wife to find out.'

'Right. It was a dangerous game.' He leaned down to pick up the water glass by his chair. 'Because yes, the office walls were glass. And over time, Lyric grew bolder. She would come into my office for the inspection and rather than things happening quite quickly, she would stay sitting on my desk with her back to reception and insist that I pleasure her. On one occasion, I said: "Do you think we should draw the blinds?" She said: "Forget the blinds." Again, I'm not a psychologist, but Lyric was an exhibitionist. She knew that any of the girls walking past would see her sitting on my desk and that they would know from her position what was going on. I would be a fool to imagine that she didn't enjoy that segment of the game. Clearly, it was part of the thrill.

'Lyric soon became ... I guess the word is emboldened. And I probably threw a little too much caution to the wind, as well.

We became more reckless. The chances of us getting caught increased. I hadn't wanted anyone to find out about us, but over time, I guess people did start to find out about us. The girls in the office knew, and they must have talked, or else Lyric must have said something, because six months into the affair, a blind item appeared in the *Bienveneda Bugle*, saying: "Which Wolf of Wall Street type enjoys private music lessons?" Music. Lyric. It could only have been about me. So people knew, but Loren still had no idea. I waited for her to say something after that blind item came out but she didn't and I guess I grew cocky. Nobody was going to say anything. Nobody was going to tell Loren, and Loren was never going to find out. I could have the best of both worlds.'

'Meaning,' I said thoughtfully, 'you could have your cake and eat it, too?'

'Oh, I don't know about that,' said David, 'because you always have to pay the piper, don't you? But yes, in terms of keeping it quiet, I became reckless. Or stupid. That's probably the word. I began taking Lyric to work functions, which sounds extremely reckless, but Lyric was a colleague. It's not uncommon for a boss to take a colleague to a work function, and Loren didn't want to go anyway. She had her migraines and said everything was boring. Lyric loved a glass of champagne. She was extremely attractive and some of the outfits she had, you could see people's jaws drop. So I had this ideal situation, where I wasn't begging Loren to go out with me, and I wasn't pestering Loren for sex. And look, I don't expect any sympathy ...'

I cocked my head as if to say: 'Well, thank goodness for that.'

'And fair enough, but it was exhausting trying to keep all those balls in the air: having Lyric at work and Loren at home, managing the business through difficult times, being a husband and family man at home with the girls. There were days when I felt I was being pulled in every direction. And there were some hairy moments. Loren writes in her journal about an event she attended where she met Lyric. That was one of the most frantic nights of my life. I was trying to keep the two of them apart. Lyric was doing her absolute best to insinuate herself into every conversation that I was having with Loren by my side, and honestly, I could have throttled her ... well, not literally,' he said hurriedly. 'No, no, no, I mean, I wasn't angry. Because by this stage, things were getting completely out of hand with Lyric because ... and I'm sure you already know this ...'

David paused.

'Oh, we know,' I said. 'You mean, by this stage, Miss Morales had almost complete control of your life, didn't she?'

He looked weary, but having come this far, there was no backing out. 'I guess that's right.'

'Because she was no longer having sex only with you, was she? She was also having sex with your clients? And you knew about that, and encouraged her, didn't you?'

'No, I don't think that's fair. I didn't ask her to do it, and I'm not sure you could even say I encouraged her, but yes, she was having sex with my clients and, yes, it was with my consent.'

* * *

How was it exactly that David knew that Lyric was having sex with his clients? He knew because he was there. He knew because he was the hidden, silent, slightly delirious witness to her dangerous games.

'How many of your clients did Lyric have sex with?' I asked, knuckling down for what I knew would be one of the toughest parts of the interview.

'I'm not entirely sure,' said David, who seemed far less rattled than you might expect. 'But a key fact is, this wasn't something I asked her to do. I'm not sure I can explain it, other than to tell the blunt truth. I was working late one night. Lyric had stayed behind to keep me company, which was something she often did. One of the Big Fish called the office ...'

'Big Fish being big investors?'

'Big clients, yes. And I had been avoiding this particular Big Fish because he had been demanding a meeting with me, which could only mean he wanted his funds out of Capital Shrine, which was unfortunate because I had no funds to give him.'

'And why was that?' I asked.

'Well, I guess it no longer matters,' said David. 'But back in those days, I was terribly worried about going broke. The problem with investors is, they put their money in when times are good, but then, when times go bad, instead of riding it out, they come looking for their money, which has usually been lost. It's not a big problem. If you can afford to ride it out, most investments will come good again. But because so much of my success at Capital Shrine depended on the idea that I was somehow immune to the bad times, I didn't like to tell people that their money had been lost. So I had fallen into a bad habit, where I would borrow a bit of money from this client to pay that client, and so on.'

'And that works only to a point?'

'Right. It works only until you run out of money and, for some reason, a rumour had taken hold in Bienveneda that my business was going under. This was before it was actually going under. People hear rumours and they get nervous, and this Big Fish was one of the nervous ones. He'd invested a lot – probably more than he could afford – and now he wanted his money back with interest.'

'Now, I'm not an economist,' I said, 'but it seems to me the correct thing to do in a situation like that is to say: "I don't have your money. Your investment has taken a loss, and my suggestion to you would be for you to stay in until your position recovers."'

'But there's a risk in doing that, because statements like that can cause a run on your business,' said David. 'So when people came looking for their money, I tried to give it to them. But too many people had come at once, and I was angry about it. Because a lot of those people – people who, by the way, had described me as a buddy; people who would pat me on the back at the Nineteenth Hole – didn't really need to withdraw their funds. I knew these men personally. I had been to their homes. One of them was in the process of buying an apartment in New York. They did not need the funds that were tied up in Capital Shrine, yet they came demanding it and ...'

'And that annoyed you?'

'Yes, it annoyed me because it was so unnecessary. So I had been avoiding this Big Fish but now he was calling again. I had my head in my hands and Lyric said: "What's going on?" I didn't want to tell her, mainly because I had been too terrified to confide in anyone about the problems I was having at work. But Lyric wouldn't let up. She said: "Have we got money problems?" And I don't know, it was such a relief to finally tell somebody. I explained everything. Lyric listened. Loren would have been hysterical, but Lyric seemed completely calm. Finally she said: "What can I do to help?" I said: "I don't know, we just need to keep putting him off until I can think of something" and Lyric was great, she said: "You'll think of something. All you need is some sexual healing," and then she tried to arouse me but it wasn't going to work. Stress was impacting my libido. I couldn't even fake it, and I guess that's when she understood how bad things were. Because our relationship was normally so charged. So she pulled back from me and said something like: "Hey, this is serious! This is just not like you at all."

'I said: "I'm so sorry. I feel like I'm failing everyone. You, my wife, the business, everyone." And that got her riled up. She did up the buttons on the front of her shirt, and said: "Tell me what I can do." My instinct was to say, "Well, you can't do anything," because I had enormous problems and I couldn't see what Lyric could do to help, but she – and I can't stress this enough – she quite spontaneously came up with the solution. She said: "Well, why don't I meet him?"

'At first I didn't understand what she meant. I said: "Why don't you meet him? And say what?" Then Lyric winked, and sat back in the office chair and crossed and re-crossed her legs, and this was one of those occasions where she was not wearing underwear in the office. She said: "Perhaps he could inspect me?" And I was blown away. I said: "Would you do that?" She said: "Of course," as though the idea was … I don't know, like she was delighted. She said: "It might even be fun." I didn't know what to say. I didn't want to encourage Lyric, but I felt like my hands were tied. So I watched while she called the Big Fish back.'

'Go on,' I said.

David sighed. 'Well. Our telephones were the headset type, with the small microphone on a stick that goes over your mouth. I watched Lyric holding the microphone to her mouth. She was breathing into it, saying: "I have just received word from Mr Wynne-Estes. He won't be returning to the office this evening, but he understands that you would like to withdraw your investment from Capital Shrine and he asked me to begin the process with you. I understand that you're in a hurry, so if you're available to come to the office now, I'd be happy to go over the paperwork with you." She was winking at me as she said this. I felt distressed by what Lyric was planning, but she seemed to be enjoying herself and the Big Fish was obviously going to pull his money out and destroy us as soon as he could, because he told Lyric that he would come in straightaway.'

'Alright,' I said, 'go on.'

David turned slightly in his chair. He was searching for his water glass, which was again down on the carpet near his immaculate shoes.

'So, the Big Fish arrived within fifteen minutes of that phone call,' he said, sipping. 'Lyric used that time to reapply lipstick, spray herself with perfume. I went into my office and pressed the button for the blinds. We had those motorised blinds that would automatically stop when they got an inch from the floor. I mentioned earlier that I had three screens on my desk; one of them could be tuned to show clients entering or leaving our underground car park. I watched the Big Fish drive towards our gate. He had a brand-new, top-of-the-line European sedan. I resented that he had arrived in that car. That car seemed like proof that he didn't need to withdraw his money and maybe when I saw that car, I thought, to hell with it. Let Lyric do as she pleases.

'So Lyric buzzed the Big Fish inside. I was still in my office, but besides being able to see into the garage, I could also see what was happening in Lyric's office – she had asked me to give her an office, and I'd agreed – because she had set up a tiny camera on her desk so that I could watch her from my office. She liked to do things like pleasure herself with a tiny gold vibrator she kept in her drawer, and she had it set up so I could watch her on my Mac while I was at my desk. It was another silly game. A titillating

game we played, to arouse each other when we were supposed to
be working. Stupid, but it meant I could see what was going on
at her desk.'

'And to be clear, the camera at Lyric's desk wasn't just
transmitting those images, it was recording them?'

'Yes,' said David, 'and obviously, recording what went on
was the wrong thing to do. But Lyric was years younger than me.
She grew up in this age of social media, with everyone sharing
nude selfies and Facebook posts and whatever else. She didn't see
privacy the same way as I did. She was more "buyer beware". If
a person had sex outside their own home, they might get filmed
and that film might get shown on Facebook or Instagram. I think
all young people know the risks, whereas people my age, or your
age, Elizabeth? We just haven't gotten used to everyone having a
camera, a recording device, a social media account.'

He brought up my age. I'm not sure I have forgiven him for
that.

'Anyway, Lyric recorded this Big Fish as she had him make
his awkward way back to her office. He was very overweight,
with a stomach hanging down over the front of his suit pants
and a double chin. Lyric asked him to come to her desk. His
opening words were, "Where is he? Hiding in the office?"

'My heart missed a beat. What if he opened the door to my
office? But it was hard to open my door. It was a sliding door
with one of those green buttons. Even when you told people
to press the button to the left on the wall, it could take forever
for them to get it. And Lyric was a smooth operator. She had
the Big Fish follow her back to her office, where she said she
had his investment information, and the way she was walking,
anyone would have followed her, and that's when she began her
seduction.

'The little camera would have been blinking, but I'm not sure the Big Fish would have understood that it was on. Plus, this was after hours, the office was dark, and the camera was well hidden. Lyric handed him some paperwork, saying: "I've pulled your file. Please read over the information so we can be sure this is the investment we're talking about." She picked up a half-empty glass of red wine – we had been drinking together after hours – and began to refill it. "Can I get you one?" she asked him.

'He must have been in a foul mood. He said, "Not for me. I want to get through this and get out of here. Where do I sign?" Lyric stopped pouring and sort of leaned over where he was sitting, and Lyric had … well, she was well-endowed, and her shirt buttons were popping. Plus she always smelled like a perfume counter, so he would have gotten a good look and a good sniff of her, and the way she was sitting on the edge of the desk, he would have been able to see what I'd already seen, that she was naked beneath her skirt. The Big Fish swallowed hard. Lyric was using a fingernail to point to a sentence on the papers he was holding, saying: "I think you sign here," or some such. Her breasts were tumbling out and it was too much for him. Within three minutes of arriving, he was on his knees. I mean, literally. He got onto his knees – pretty clumsily, it wasn't easy for him, big guy that he was. It was quite a scene. And they … well, you know what they did, everyone does, I guess. And ultimately he left, even more red-faced than when he'd arrived.'

'But crucially,' I said in a tone that suggested distaste, 'he hadn't taken the paperwork?'

'Precisely,' said David, seeming to forget for a moment that this was not a cause for celebration. 'He had not signed the paperwork, and I was so relieved, I pressed the button to open my office door and went straight in to find Lyric throwing back the last of her wine. Her skirt was still up around her waist. My fear was that she'd feel disgusted with herself, but I couldn't have been more wrong. She looked pleased. I asked her: "Did you enjoy that?" and she made it absolutely clear that she had. She'd loved it. Her power. His submission. The way he'd been thrashing at her, like it had been forever since he'd seen such a beautiful woman, let alone been allowed to touch one. Her mood was extremely elevated. Like a natural high. A super high. And obviously, I should have been more conscious of the winking camera at this point but ... look, I forgot it was there and then, later, when I remembered, Lyric just laughed and said: "Oh my goodness, we filmed you, too? Don't worry, we can erase that."'

I held up my hand to get David to pause for a moment. 'Wait, you didn't insist that she erase that?'

'No, I didn't. Because that would have appeared ... I don't know, as if I didn't trust her,' he said. 'And I had a whole bigger reason to have to trust her because she was now an ally in my sinking business. She was helping me stave off the collapse. And I found myself feeling grateful to her, dependent on her ...'

'Which perhaps explains why she soon became your vice-president?' I said dryly.

'Right. It was that night, that I made her vice-president. I mean, it was stupid, but I said: "I think you've just graduated to a level beyond executive assistant!" Like a joke. But with Lyric, nothing was a joke. She said: "Yes, I certainly have and I'd like a new title, please." I said: "Given how you've just saved the day, maybe I should make you president." Obviously that was a joke. She said: "No, you're the president. I can be vice-president," and like an idiot, I agreed. Because I thought they're only words. What I had forgotten was, they were recorded words.'

* * *

Who was the woman that approached Loren Wynne-Estes outside the gates of her children's school? My team at Fox9 had put researchers on it and we were never able to find out. Was it another mom from Bienveneda Grammar?

'No, I don't believe it was,' said David. 'Believe me, I've been over this in my mind, and I have to wonder whether Lyric didn't have something to do with it. Which is kind of crazy because I'd made it very clear to Lyric that, if Loren found out, it would mean an immediate end to the affair.'

'Which is what happened?'

'Which is what happened. I was as good as my word on that point. The very second that Loren found out, I ended the affair with Lyric. And Loren's account of how it all unravelled is basically right. She called me during work hours, and I instantly knew why. We met up and she said: "Is it true?" I said yes and Loren started to cry. I was flooded with pain but also relief. Clearly, I had wanted the secret off my chest. Living a double life was destroying me. Loren said: "Who is it?" I said: "Lyric, from the office." Loren said: "I knew it," and put her forehead on the steering wheel and then banged her head on it, which scared me. I said: "I'm so sorry." Loren wanted to know how long the affair had been going on, and she said: "Do you love her?" I was amazed at that. Obviously I didn't love Lyric. I loved Loren. I said: "No, of course not, I love you, and I love the girls." Loren said: "Then why?"

'I told her the truth, or at least a close version of it. I said: "I don't know. I've been under pressure at work. We've been having problems," meaning the sex. And Loren knew that's what I was getting at. She started to cry again. Then she said: "I'm sorry."

I said: "Don't be crazy. What on earth do you have to be sorry about?" She said: "I'm to blame," and I said: "No, you are not," and we went back and forth, with Loren saying: "I've starved you out." I said: "You're being ridiculous," but Loren couldn't be convinced. She was crying and I was trying to comfort her. She kept saying: "How am I ever going to trust you again?" Which was ironic, because at this point, she only knew about the affair.

'So it was then that I decided to tell her about the financial problems we were having. Some people have interpreted what I said to Loren in the car that day as some kind of threat, but it wasn't a threat. It was the reality. We were broke, and if Loren walked out and forced the sale of the house, I'd have nothing to give her. If she stayed, there was at least a chance that I could trade us out of the mess we were in, provided, of course, that nobody else tried to get their funds out.'

'And what happened next?'

'Well, everyone knows. Loren agreed to stay. She lifted her head off the steering wheel and said: "It's her or me." Which was an absolute no-brainer. It was always going to be Loren. She said: "You go into your office, and you tell her she has to leave," and I agreed. Then she leaned over me, forced open the door on my side of her car, and I had barely managed to get both feet on the ground when she roared out of the car park.'

'And from there, you went back to the office?'

'Right, and I called Lyric into my office, and I told her that Loren knew about the affair and – as I had warned her, countless times – the affair was therefore over. And her rage ... well, it was incandescent.'

Making scratching motions with his hands, David continued: 'She leapt across my desk and began clawing at my neck and face. I grabbed both of her hands with mine. I told her to calm down, but her eyes were wild. She went storming out of my office, onto the street, breaking a heel on her way out the door. And I instructed the girl on reception to clear her desk.'

'Just like that? That seems … rather brutal?'

'Maybe it was,' said David, 'but yes, just like that. I picked up a cardboard box and told Sunny to put Lyric's things in there and send the box to Lyric. And of course, Sunny knew about the affair, so I guess that yes, that's when what I suppose you would describe as the dangerous consequences of the affair began to dawn on me.'

* * *

SEX! LIES! VIDEOTAPE!

'I take it you've read this?' I asked, holding up the newspaper.

'I have. It's an old copy of our local paper,' said David.

'For the sake of our audience, I hope you won't mind if I read out some of what it says here?'

'Do your worst,' he said.

I won't quote it exactly, the text is online for anyone who wants to read it, but the story basically said that David had encouraged Lyric and others on staff to engage in orgies with clients, and that he'd taped the sessions.

The suggestion was, of course, blackmail.

David objected. 'Wait, wait, wait … that's what the story says, but look, those claims are just ludicrous. I was not running a brothel from Capital Shrine.'

'But this report, it's based on police sources.'

'That's what it says,' said David sarcastically, 'but it's false. Because yes, it's true that Lyric didn't stop with just that one Big Fish. Yes, things did get out of control, and some of the people she lured into our office were in positions of power. Yes, there was a politician, and yes, a prominent businessman, but these were not orgies and there was no brothel.'

'Well, if this article is wrong,' I said, folding my hands into my lap, 'perhaps you can tell us what did happen.'

'I'm happy to do that, because I have nothing to hide. The first of the Big Fish wanted to see Lyric again. She told me he had called her the next day, with some nonsense about having forgotten to sign the forms. With no encouragement from me, she played up to him. She said: "Yes, I noticed that. And I'm glad that you forgot. Why don't you come over and we can go over the whole thing again." And she said things like, "No, not now. After hours. And perhaps some wine for you this time?"

'And of course he did come to the office, and I stayed in my office, again with the blinds down, while Lyric worked her magic. And once that pattern was set, she just kept at it. We had so many recordings of Lyric with this Big Fish, it was ridiculous. Also, incriminating. Lyric would buzz this guy in, and he would go lumbering into her office, where she would be sitting without her skirt on. Heels, yes, but no skirt and she would hold out a glass of wine to him, and he would take it and there was absolutely no ambiguity about what was going on.'

'But Lyric wasn't seeing only that one Big Fish. She was seeing other clients?'

'That's right,' said David. 'He wasn't a one-off and he wasn't the only one. Lyric played her game with a couple of other clients. And, look, at the time, it seemed like a dream come true because none of these clients were inclined to withdraw their money. But there was no brothel. No group-sex sessions ...'

'But you did have another lover on staff.'

'Not a lover. No. Look, I'm perfectly happy to be completely honest with you and your viewers. On one occasion, Lyric called Sunny into my office. This was during an inspection. I had no idea what she was up to. I leapt back from what I had been doing to Lyric. Sunny came in, and I suppose she had no idea either, but it wouldn't have taken long to figure it out. Lyric swivelled towards her, on my desk – and she was wearing no underwear. Lyric said something like, "Leave if you want, but if you're staying, close the blinds." Well, that was a signal to the rest of the staff if I ever saw one.

'And Sunny hesitated. She had been with me longer than Lyric. She was less experienced at probably everything in life. Her job was a simple one: answering phones, filing documents. She looked at me, sitting in my office chair, and I didn't know what to signal to her – my mind was just blown by these events – but then she turned and went back towards the door and I didn't know what she was going to do: leave, or quit, or whatever. But she pressed the button for the blinds and the blinds came down, and she came back to my desk, at which point, I lifted her onto the desk, and Lyric opened Sunny's thighs, and displayed her underwear to me, saying: "Well, it seems that she's been a good girl, Mr Wynne-Estes. She's properly attired. You'll be rewarded for that in a moment, Sunny, but remember, these inspections will be taking place regularly, and should you ever forget your panties, you can expect to be disciplined."

'Sunny said: "What does that mean?" and I demonstrated some of the discipline with a few slaps of my hand on Lyric's behind. It was all a bit of a game. And Sunny didn't seem to be at all concerned about it. I said: "You have passed the inspection, Ms Bechara, but let's see how things look tomorrow," and that was the end of it. The absolute end of it. There was no tomorrow.'

'And do you know why not?'

'I don't. All I know is that Lyric somehow managed to co-opt Sunny into joining her at her apartment – not at work, at her apartment – when the Big Fish came to visit, and that was something I knew nothing about. Absolutely nothing. I know it happened. The police told me it happened. But I knew nothing about it.'

'But you knew that Lyric was seeing your clients at her apartment?'

'I knew that eventually,' said David, stressing the point. 'It was a while before I knew that. I assumed that Lyric was mostly seeing my clients in her office, and that she was recording them in her office. And, to be honest, I didn't understand why she was recording them. I told Lyric, we don't need to record them. We weren't planning to blackmail them, or I certainly wasn't. The idea was to keep them as clients, with their money still in Capital Shrine investments, so that I might buy some time.'

'But wait just a moment,' I said. 'If we can just go back to this Big Dave email account … if I have the timing right here, it was around this time, or shortly afterwards, that you started telling Lyric that you loved her.'

An assistant from Sally & Sons took a quick step forward.

David said: 'I—'

'And that you no longer loved Loren,' I said.

'I—'

'And that you wanted to leave your wife, but you were concerned about the financial wreckage.'

'But not—'

'And that you could not wait to start, and I quote, "a new life" with Lyric.'

'Look,' said David. His tone was angry. 'If I could just be allowed to answer. Yes, it's true I said those things. Some time after Lyric began seeing these Big Fish, she also began pressing me for a time frame to get out of my marriage. I didn't want to lose Loren and the girls, but ...'

'But?'

'But like a fool, I began telling Lyric what she wanted to hear: that I would get out of my marriage as soon as I could. She asked me to set a date and I did. I said, okay, end of this year, but I had no intention of sticking by that date. It was a date I plucked from the air.'

'But hold on,' I said, 'this email I have here clearly says: "Yes, I am in love with you. Yes, I want to be with you."'

'Not true,' said David.

'It's not true that's what it says?' I waved the printout at him. 'Or not true that you didn't love Loren?'

'It's not true that I didn't love Loren.'

'But that's what it says, David.' I held the paper higher. 'That's what it says right here.'

'I know that's what it says. But that was written when I was trying to keep Lyric onside. When I would've said anything to keep her involved in my business. Because she was saving my business. I said those things to Lyric, but I loved Loren. I didn't want to leave my wife, and I desperately didn't want her to leave me ...'

'And yet,' I said, 'when Loren forced out the truth about your affair, you still didn't tell her the whole truth.'

'How so?' said David, sounding confused.

'The sex tapes. You didn't tell Loren about the sex tapes. You told her about your affair. You told her about your financial problems. But you told her absolutely nothing about the fact that you had captured a number of powerful men having sex with your assistant on tape, did you?'

'No, that's true,' said David. For the first time in our
interview, he sounded grim. 'You're right. She had no idea.'

* * *

Of all the curious characters in David Wynne-Estes's life, surely
the most curious is his daffy marriage counsellor. As far as I
can tell, Bette Busonne has no actual qualifications to work as a
therapist, yet she commands around $350 an hour to guide her
clients through what she calls the Busonne Method.

What's the Busonne Method? To my mind, it's one of the
craziest therapies I've ever encountered and I would have killed
to get Bette on air talking about it, but on that score, we were
out of luck.

As part of our negotiations with David, my team had asked
his team whether he objected to us heading out to see Bette.

David had groaned at the very mention of her name. 'She's a
quack.'

'Then let us expose her,' I argued.

'Oh, be my guest,' he said, 'but I think you'll find she's
gone to ground,' and so it proved. My staff telephoned Bette's
office, and her home. We sent emails and letters by registered
post. Finally, we turned up on her porch with a camera crew
in tow.

I rapped on the door, using the old-style knocker. David had
already told us that Bette's consulting rooms were behind the
lace curtains to the left of the front door as you face the house. I
saw those curtains move. I didn't see Bette – she is seventy-three
years old, without a facelift, so I'm sure I would have recognised
her – but her dogs started to yap.

I put my face close to the window, saying: 'Ms Busonne? It's Liz Moss. I'm with Fox9. We'd like to talk to you about Loren Wynne-Estes.'

She shouted back: 'Go away or I'll call the police.'

I said: 'I'd like to talk to you about the Busonne Method.'

She shouted back again: 'What goes on between myself and my clients is confidential.'

I pressed a piece of paper to the glass. 'I have a letter here from David, releasing you from your obligations in that regard.'

'I don't care what you've got,' she said. 'Go away.'

We stayed until a patrol car arrived and the police asked us to leave, but if Bette thought that was the end of it, she was wrong. We staked her out for a few days, and eventually got footage of her shopping at Whole Foods. We also had David's account of their sessions – a written statement – which we intended to place on our website for everyone to read. The statement said:

As part of the process of restoring my marriage after my affair, I agreed to attend couples counselling. I don't know where my wife first met Bette Busonne, but she told me that Bette had developed an unconventional approach designed to help couples heal.

My wife held Bette in high regard and before the first session warned me that she expected me to follow all of Bette's instructions to the letter.

Bette's approach is known as the Busonne Method. Her mantra is: The Whole Truth. Lies are toxic and will poison the path forward. Honesty As Policy.

Loren was permitted to ask me questions and I was required to answer completely and honestly.

Loren's first question was whether I had ever told Lyric that I loved her. I had, so I said: 'Yes, I did,' and that hurt Loren deeply.

I tried to explain, saying, 'But I didn't mean it, and I wasn't serious,' but Bette jumped in, saying: 'And what else did you tell her? Did you tell her that you didn't love your wife?'

I said: 'Yes, I did say that. But I didn't mean that, either. This was a very complex situation.'

I was prepared to explain, but Loren was already a weeping mess. I couldn't see the point of making her suffer any further, but Bette's approach is to be as hard as nails. I was happy to confess to the affair. I had already apologised and my instinct was not to go over things that could only hurt my wife.

Bette snarled: 'You don't think she's already hurting?'

Yes, Loren was already hurting, because I had cheated on her. And now she wanted to see this counsellor in whom she apparently had great faith.

So I said: 'Lyric wanted me to get out of my marriage. She was a volatile person. She could explode with very little warning, which is why I had to tell her what she wanted to hear.'

Bette said: 'Loren, how do you feel, hearing that your husband told his mistress that he didn't love you?'

Well, I'll never forget how Loren looked at that moment. She was curled into her chair with her feet tucked under her bottom, almost like a small child. Her face was streaked with mascara and her nose had started to run.

I said: 'Can we please stop? Look at my wife. She's in agony.'

'Well, I'm sure she is, but who's to blame for that?' said Bette, and then she sent us home with what amounted to an order to talk about the affair for a further twenty minutes after the girls had gone to bed, and not just that night but every single Thursday night for the next eight weeks.

I was aghast. As I understood it, as soon as the girls were reliably asleep, I would have to take a seat in our sitting room while Loren would sit opposite and assail me with questions about the affair.

'She can ask anything she wants,' Bette said, 'and you, David, will answer. Anything she wants to know. Specifically. About the affair. But only at that precise time of day and only for twenty minutes. After that, Loren, you must let up. You are not permitted to harangue David for hours on end. You get twenty minutes and then you stop. I expect you BOTH to stick to these rules.'

I tried to object. 'I don't see what good can come of this. It's like rubbing salt into a raw wound.'

Loren swung around and cried at me, 'I knew you would do this,' meaning that I would try to get out of therapy, so I agreed to go ahead.

Loren had already told Bette that questions about my affair swirled around in her head all day. Where did we meet? What did we do? Did we talk about Loren? What had I told Lyric about my sex life with my wife? How many people in Bienveneda knew about the affair?

Bette's theory was that Loren would keep obsessing until she had answers to these questions. I didn't necessarily accept that, but if the Busonne Method was going to save my marriage, I was determined to give it a go. And at first, it wasn't too bad. Talking about the affair in a tentative, almost curious way did seem to give Loren some relief. She would cry and sometimes she would attack me, but the twenty-minute limit on question time meant that I was soon off the hook.

By the third week, Loren had exhausted most of the more basic questions and had begun demanding intimate details of what had gone on. Would I kiss Lyric before sex and if so, what kind of kiss? Would I kiss Lyric on the neck? Would I kiss Lyric on the breasts? Did we have oral sex? If so, was I performing oral sex on Lyric or the other way around? My role was to answer these questions and that was extremely difficult because, whatever I said, Loren would sob or fly into a rage. Week after week this went on and I began to doubt the wisdom of it.

I asked Bette: 'How does hearing the intimate details of my sexual encounters with another woman help Loren heal?'

She said: 'What's your alternative? That you and Lyric keep your secrets to yourselves?'

So we carried on, with Loren asking questions in a more or less obsessive way. She was particularly interested in those occasions where Lyric had 'invaded her space', by which she meant those times Lyric had come to our home, or ridden in our car. It's no exaggeration to say that Loren craved *explicit* detail about these encounters.

We had three main cars: my Porsche, which I call Middy, for Mid-Life Crisis; Loren's SUV, which the girls called the Lady Bug; and the BMW sedan that we used as a family car, which we called Beep. In one of our very early sessions with Bette, I had confessed to having had a sexual encounter with Lyric in Beep. Later that night, during what I called the 'mandatory reporting', Loren demanded details of that encounter, so I told her. I had been at a lunchtime function with Lyric at the

Bienveneda Golf Club. For some reason, I was driving Beep. Lyric jumped in the passenger seat to get a lift back to the office. At some point, I felt her hand massaging me. This was near the beginning of the relationship when I was still sex-starved, so I allowed her to unzip my trousers. Loren insisted on knowing what happened next and I had no choice other than to tell her that Lyric had performed oral sex on me while I was driving.

I relayed this episode to Loren in the starkest, plainest detail possible. She got up from the sofa, went into the garage and attacked Beep with a golf club. I remember thinking: 'This is very Tiger Woods; everyone in the street is going to know what's going on.' Also, because we were under considerable financial pressure, I couldn't get the car repaired. Unbeknown to Loren, I had by then allowed the insurance premiums on all the cars to lapse, so I had to park the car towards the back of our garage and place a cover over it so that visitors and the twins couldn't see the damage.

Another time, Loren asked if I had ever had sex with Lyric in our family home. I had been dreading the question, because Lyric visited our house twice. Our homes were actually quite close together, separated mainly by the Lemon Grove, and there had been a few occasions when I'd slipped out after Loren fell asleep, and cut through the Lemon Grove to get to Lyric's apartment. But that wasn't good enough for Lyric. She wanted to visit me in my home. My reaction, when I first heard that, was no way. Never. But I had gotten reckless, and Lyric was complaining quite a lot about feeling like a second-class citizen in our relationship.

I decided to wait for a day when I knew Loren had no staff on, and when she had plenty of appointments: committee-work, banking, manicure, and so on. My idea was to sneak Lyric into the house in something like a two-hour window. It was dangerous but doable. We drove from the office. I didn't tell her where we were going. She was amazed when I pulled into the garage. I had turned off the security cameras so there would be no evidence that she was ever there. I showed Lyric inside.

Lyric remarked how huge the place was. I suppose it was. She looked at the photographs on the mantelpiece. Pictures of Loren and our girls. She went into the master bedroom and sat on the corner of the bed and used my tie to pull me towards the bed, and although I hadn't planned on having sex with her, we ended up having sex on the bed.

When I told Loren this, she kicked me in the shins. The next day, all of our sheets – I mean, every sheet in the house, except the *Frozen* sheets from the girls' beds – were out on the lawn.

The second time I took Lyric home was obviously more serious. She stayed overnight. Loren had long been planning to take the girls to Disneyland. She went with our nanny and I took advantage of that trip to make good on a promise to Lyric to spend a night in my bed.

I don't know what I expected, but Lyric brought fresh food to my house. She was an excellent cook. I had been complaining – in a joking way – about Loren's shortage of skills in that regard, and Lyric was probably showing off. She made a lemon-and-chilli pasta. She brought wine. I'm not entirely naïve. Lyric was auditioning for the role of wife. She told me to relax and kick off my shoes. At some point, she called me into the kitchen. She was wearing only an apron and heels. I know what I was meant to feel: aroused. I felt guilty having sex in the kitchen, with the girls' purple lunchboxes on the bench.

Anyway, Lyric stayed the night, which was scary because she had long, dark hair and Loren's hair was blonde. I was terrified of Loren finding a dark hair on the pillow. Lyric also seemed in no hurry to leave. Come morning, she made breakfast and brought it to me on a tray.

I was dreading having to tell Loren these details, and I was right to be wary because as soon as I finished telling her, she went into the kitchen and emptied all of the cutlery into the trash.

From that day forward, Loren became obsessed by the idea that I had been 'test-driving' Lyric for the role of Second Wife. Which was ludicrous, by the way, and the next time I saw Bette, I again raised my objections, saying: 'How can this be good for Loren's mental health? To go over the details of this affair in excruciating detail, night after night?'

Bette was adamant that we continue. 'Lies are no good for your marriage. Marriage thrives on honesty.'

It wasn't the lies, it was the *detail* that upset Loren. Why did she need to hear all the details? Why wasn't it enough to say there was foreplay? But Loren supported the Busonne Method. She would cry out: 'But what does that even mean – foreplay? That could mean anything. I want to know, David. I want to know everything that *she* knows.'

Meaning she wanted to know everything that Lyric knew.

But there was more to the Busonne Method than honesty. I also had to accept strict monitoring of my movements, and I had to endure arbitrary checks of my iPhone and iPad that reduced me to schoolboy status – let me see your Facebook updates – which meant meekly handing my devices to an angry Loren night after night.

Flick, flick, flick.

Loren had a unique way of using her thumb to scroll through my messages. She would question me about this message, or that message. She also had Find My iPhone installed so she could keep track of my movements during the day.

She would say: 'What was this trip for? Why did you go here, at that time?' These were *nightly* questions: 'What about this missed call? What about this anonymous number? Anything you need to tell me?'

I am a grown man and occasionally took umbrage. 'Please, Loren, I implore you. Let go of the leash. I've made you a promise. I will not break it. I'm now faithful.'

Loren shot back: 'You cannot be trusted.'

Bette was completely on her side.

I said: 'Please, Loren, trust cannot be rebuilt when one partner is constantly checking up on the other.'

She said: 'Well then, you should leave. Leave, and watch us both go broke. Leave and watch the girls leave their friends at Grammar. Leave, and watch the realtor come and hammer a For Sale sign in our front lawn.'

And then, *slam.* She would slam down the phone, or slam the door.

So it was rough going, and then, after five or six sessions of Busonne Method, Bette told me that I had to initiate sex with Loren. No, I'm not kidding. She ordered me to have sex with my wife.

'You need to resume sexual relations. Energetic relations. Passionate sex,' she said.

Privately, I thought, is there something about this old pervert who just wants the details?

I said: 'I would be delighted, but shouldn't we ask Loren?' Who was in fact sitting there.

Bette folded her reading glasses and stood up as if dismissing us. 'No talking tonight,' she said. 'Only sex.'

I've never been ordered to have sex before. But did we give it a go? Sure we did. Was it awkward? Of course it was.

We started on the sofa. I put my hand on Loren's knee. She started to cry. I tried to comfort her, saying: 'This won't work if you cry.' I wiped her tears with the side of my thumb. She sat up straighter and we tried again. It was difficult. She said something like: 'You're not even aroused,' and I joked with her: 'I'm not as young as when we first met.' Which was a mistake. Because then she started with: 'I'm sure you had no trouble with your mistress.'

I put my finger against her lips. No talk. Just sex. They were our instructions. We tried again. Loren went to kiss my face – a quick peck on the cheek – and I turned quickly and she hit my lips. She laughed. So that was good. Laughing was better than crying. We were getting into the groove.

Loren said: 'This feels ridiculous,' but Bette's instructions were for Passionate Sex, so off we went.

I undressed my wife. From what I could tell, Loren had been shopping. She had new lingerie. I complimented her, and she laughed about how silly she had felt in the change room at Victoria's Secret because everyone else had been a teenager. I told her she looked great and eventually, we got things done. And afterwards, Loren said: 'That was a disaster,' and then we both looked up, and holy hell, there was Peyton!

'Honey!' said Loren. 'How long have you been there?'

Peyton was standing with her thumb in her mouth. She had a giant teddy under one arm. I grabbed a sofa cushion. My boxer shorts were still on the floor. Loren gathered up the

throw and wrapped it around herself, saying, 'What are you
doing out of bed?'

Peyton looked so sleepy. I'm quite sure she hadn't been
there all that long, but it was one of those *whoops* moments
that you have as parents.

Peyton said: 'I heard a noise … like *pigs*,' and I couldn't
help myself. I burst out laughing.

Loren smothered her own smile, saying, 'Well, there are
no pigs here,' and off she went to tuck Peyton back into bed,
turning halfway down the hall to wink at me, making me think,
Okay, wow, that worked. We've turned a corner.

* * *

They hadn't turned a corner. Less than a week after David and
Loren resumed their sex life, Loren ran into Lyric, outside the
Bienveneda Gym.

'I'd been dreading a confrontation between them,' David told
me during our interview, 'and when it happened, it was every bit
as bad as I'd feared.

'Lyric worked out at Bienveneda Gym at least four times
a week. Loren generally didn't go to the gym. It was Bette's
big idea that she start going to classes, exercise being a part
of the Busonne Method. Loren had said something like: "He
[meaning me] finds me revolting." I'd said: "I do not find you
revolting." Bette had butted in with: "But you do think Loren
is out of shape, don't you?" I'd shrugged and said: "Sure, but
aren't we all?" Bette had made some kind of mark on her
clipboard and said: "I have a new prescription for you, Loren.
Physical exercise. You are to start a gym class. Tomorrow. Not
for David. For you."

'There are three gyms on Bienveneda's High Side, and for some reason, Loren chose the gym that Lyric attends. Two days into her new program, they ran into each other. The way I understand it, Loren pulled into the car park, jumped down from the SUV and strode towards the sliding doors, apparently reading a message on her iPhone. A woman coming the other way said: "Well excuse me," because Loren had bumped her.

'Loren and Lyric had walked right into each other. And I copped it from both of them. Within seconds – literally seconds – I was getting texts from Lyric to say what a bastard I was, and calls from Loren, saying: "I hate you."

'Lyric called to accuse me: "You sent her to confront me!"

'I said: "No, Lyric, I did not. Our couples counsellor advised Loren to join a gym."

'Lyric was shouting: "And by chance she joined mine?" I had to move the phone away from my ear she was shouting so loudly.

'I left the office immediately to find Loren at home, hugging a pillow. "No wonder you liked her," she said. "She's so pretty." So we were back to square one, with Loren saying: "You love her," and me saying: "I don't even *like* her, Loren. I love *you*."

'And that was when Loren said: "I want to kill her." And I was shocked. I said: "What did you say?" And she said it again: "I just want to kill her. I mean it, David. When I saw her there, I wanted her to die."'

* * *

'Your wife and your mistress ran into each other quite by chance?'

'That's right.'

'And your affair with Lyric resumed in that same month?'

'That's right.'

David and I were well into our interview, and the time had definitely come to address the elephant in the room: his affair with Lyric was not over when Loren began planning their second honeymoon.

'Tell me how it started up again,' I said.

'Well, she basically got in touch with me at the office,' he said. 'It wasn't long after she ran into Loren at the gym. From memory, she rang me at the office.'

'And what did she say?'

'She said: "I need to talk to you." I should have said: "No." Instead, I said something like: "I will call you tomorrow."'

'But why?' I asked. 'Why did you say that you'd call Lyric? Because you knew perfectly well that you were not supposed to be in contact with her.'

'Indeed,' said David, sighing. 'And, as I said, it was a mistake. I should have said no, and yet I didn't. And the next day, I called Lyric. She wanted me to go see her. I wanted to know why. She wouldn't say. I got the very strong feeling that she expected me to turn up. Her tone was certainly not light. And so I went.'

'You went where?'

'I went to her apartment. I drove over there and shot my car into her garage, praying that nobody would see me. Lyric let me up and opened the door and she was in a very bad mood. She said there were rumours going around the town, about us, and her reputation was ruined. She hadn't been able to get a new job, and that was apparently my fault. Yet from what I could tell, she still wanted to have sex with me! And I tried to back straight out of her kitchen. But she said: "You are not leaving." And there was something about the way she looked at me that made me think she meant business. She wanted sex but she was angry. She mentioned the recordings. She mentioned my clients. And I formed the very strong opinion that if I didn't give into her demands ...'

'You mean her sexual demands?'

'Yes, her sexual demands, that she would perhaps do something to harm me, or my family ...'

'You mean, she might hurt Loren?'

'No. Well, I don't know. But I formed the very strong impression that Lyric was angry and that she had been thinking about making her recordings public. Which would be devastating for me, obviously, but it would also destroy the lives of others. Not just me. Of many people.'

'I see,' I said, bringing my hand up to my face for the classic, somewhat-sceptical-thinker pose. 'And so you agreed to have sex with her again?'

Did the cameraman guffaw? Maybe, but he was pretending that he'd coughed. David must have noticed, but he ploughed on.

'Yes, I agreed to have sex with her again. Because I felt I had no choice. I was trying to save my marriage and here was somebody who was determined to wreck my life. I had to make a decision and I obviously made a very poor one. I resumed the affair with Lyric. And that was very, very difficult, because Loren was watching me like a hawk.

'I had to source a new cell phone. I had to get it connected to a pre-paid service. I had to hide it underneath the spare tyre in the trunk of my car. And I hated myself for having to do all of that. But what choice did I have? I was under so much pressure at home, and so much pressure at work, and now Lyric was threatening some kind of blackmail. When I think about it now I can see what I was doing: I was trying to buy some time to find a solution.'

'I'm sure it was hell, David, but I'm interested, how did the resumption of your affair fit in with the Busonne Method? Total honesty?'

'Well, I had to give that away,' he said, as if that should have been obvious. 'How could I tell Loren that I had started seeing Lyric again? I couldn't. And I know that plenty of viewers will be sceptical, but seeing Lyric again wasn't fun. It felt dirty and scary. We didn't text back and forth in the same type of way we had previously. The flirtatious element was gone: Lyric's texts seemed laced with malice. And so, each time I saw her, I told myself it would be the last time.'

I tapped my pen against the clipboard. 'You did?'

'I did. And then, I guess, after a few weeks of this I decided this cannot go on; that I'm going to have to man up and face the music. I just had to find the right moment. And that moment came when Bette Busonne ordered me to take Loren away for a second honeymoon. I thought: "This is my chance. I'll tell Lyric the affair is over and I will go away with Loren. Lyric will be furious but I will be a thousand miles away and by the time I get back, maybe she will have calmed down, and maybe she'd be able to see that I had chosen Loren, and that I would always choose Loren."'

'So did you tell Lyric about this cruise?'

David seemed uncomfortable. 'Yes, I did.'

'And how did she react?'

'She absolutely blew her top. She called me a bastard and every other name under the sun. What stunned me though was that she was also adamant that it would mean the end of things between us. She told me straight that if I went on a second honeymoon with my wife, the affair would be over. I wouldn't be able to see her anymore. She said she'd tried to make me see that I was the right person for her, but that would be the end of it and she was sick of being used, and so forth. And I couldn't have been happier. Because that was exactly what I wanted to hear. I wanted the affair to be over.'

'I see,' I said, 'and so that's how you left it? With Lyric furious with you?'

'That's how I left it, with Lyric saying, "I never want to see you again."'

* * *

'David, do you know what this is?'

I had produced a document from the pile under my chair and I was holding it up.

David tilted his head as if trying to read it. His face flicked with recognition.

'It's the statement I gave to the Chief of Police after I returned from Mexico,' he said grimly.

'Could you take it from me?' I said, handing the pages to him.

David swallowed, but he took the pages.

'I'd like you to read it,' I said.

'Out loud?'

'Yes, out loud. I'd like you to read it for our audience. I'd like them to hear exactly what you told the police when you returned to Bienveneda after that cruise.'

David rubbed the top of his right cheekbone, hard. He glanced at his image consultant from Sally & Sons, took a deep breath, and began to read:

My wife Loren Wynne-Estes and I spent the evening before our planned second honeymoon to Mexico, together at our home on Mountain View Road.

Our twin daughters, Hannah and Peyton, were not at home.

Loren had arranged for them to spend the night with my parents and my sister, their Aunt Janet, as a special treat, since they would not be coming on vacation with us.

Their absence from the house would also mean that we would have the evening to pack our suitcases and the morning to get going to the airport without the two of them crying about wanting to come too.

Loren prepared a meal for the two of us and we shared a bottle of wine, having several glasses each.

Dinner concluded at around 9pm, after which I went into our home office to try to repair the wi-fi router, which had gone down for some reason.

Loren went into our bedroom to begin sorting through the various outfits she wanted to take on the cruise ship.

'Don't take too many things,' I said, 'because if I have my way, you're going to be living in a bikini.'

'But I need some nice things,' she said. 'We will be going to the Captain's Dinner.'

'So shop your heart out when you get there. There are bound to be boutiques galore.'

'Oh, don't worry. I intend to shop,' she said, not too seriously.

'Don't forget we're broke,' I said, also not too seriously because although we were facing significant financial challenges at that time, this vacation was about healing our relationship, and if Loren wanted to shop, she could shop.

About an hour after I had sat down to work on the router I heard a noise and found Loren standing in my office doorway wearing a sexy new bikini.

'What do you think of this one?' she said, striking a pose like a model, with one hand on her hip.

I could see what she was up to and since there were no children or staff in the house there was no reason not to step up to the plate. I stopped fiddling with the router and lowered Loren onto the floor of my office, where we made love.

'If that's a taste of things to come this is going to be a great vacation,' I said.

Loren laughed.

I got up off the floor and went into the en suite to freshen up. By the time I returned, Loren had left the room.

I called out: 'Hey, thank you, that was nice,' but Loren didn't respond.

I resumed fiddling with the router.

I cannot say for certain how much time passed but I don't think it was more than 30 minutes before I noticed that the house seemed to be very quiet.

I called out: 'Loren?'

I received no response.

I got up from my desk and walked down the hall to our bedroom and straightaway I noticed a cell phone on the bed. It was a secret, second phone I had purchased some weeks earlier for the purpose of communicating with my then-mistress, Lyric Morales, without my wife's knowledge.

I grabbed it up off the bed, and turned it on. There was a list of unfamiliar text messages on the screen. The first message was from me to Lyric. It said: *miss u sexy*.

My cell phone, but I had not sent that text.

I'd had the phone with me while I tried to fix the home router and it must have fallen out of my trouser pocket during the intimacy with Loren, or else Loren must have retrieved it from my pocket while I was in the en suite.

In any case, it seemed to me that Loren must have taken the phone back to our bedroom and then proceeded to text Lyric, while pretending to be me.

Lyric had replied: *miss u 2.*

Loren said: *wot you doing?*

Lyric replied: *missing you.*

Loren said: *can i come over?*

Lyric replied: *what about wifey?*

Loren texted: *just one quick one before i go.*

Lyric said: *yes good come eat me.*

That was it. There were no more messages.

My stomach was churning as it dawned on me that Loren must have left the house to confront Lyric.

I bolted towards the hooks where we kept the car keys, and that's when I saw that all the keys were still in place but the back door was open. It seemed that Loren had taken off on foot, through the Lemon Grove behind our house.

I tore out the back door, stumbling through the trails between the lemon trees. I snagged my polo shirt and scratched my face on sharp branches as I tumbled through the dark.

'Lyric was dead?'

'Right,' said David, reaching nervously for his water glass. 'She was dead. That was obvious. There was a knife on the floor. It was a shocking thing to see.'

'And what did you do? Did you take her pulse, call 911?'

'No,' said David, shaking his head, 'and that was a mistake. I panicked. I said to Loren: "We have to get out of here." And

Loren said: "Where are we going?" and I said: "We are going on our second honeymoon."'

'So, let me get this straight,' I said, tapping my pen against my clipboard. 'You've rushed into Miss Morales' home and found her bleeding on the floor, but you don't call the police? You don't call an ambulance?'

'You're thinking I'm a monster,' said David, rubbing his forehead, 'but I could see that she was dead. So my mind was just telling me: *get out, get out.* I was thinking: it will be two or three days before anybody finds Lyric here. She doesn't have family in California. She doesn't have a job. So we'll go to the airport, we'll leave the country, in a day or two, the police will find Lyric and her death will be a shock to me.'

'Excuse me, but that sounds very ... callous.'

'I know it does, but I was trying to protect Loren. If I called the police, they'd surely arrest her.'

'So you made a run for it.'

'I did,' sighed David. 'We both did. I got Loren to her feet. I took the dishcloth from its hook and wiped the door handles and anything else I could think to wipe, including the handle of the knife. I stuffed the dishcloth in my pocket. I pushed Loren back through the grove, saying: "We'll go to the airport. We'll get on the ship. We'll be miles away when Lyric is found."'

'And Loren agreed with this plan?'

'Oh, she wasn't responding, Liz,' he said, as if in dismay. 'I practically had to drag her back to our house. I had to stand her in the garden and strip her out of the clothes she had been wearing. I had to shove her into the shower ...'

'Why the shower?'

'DNA. She was worried that some of Lyric's blood or DNA had gotten on her clothes. I said, "Lyric has been in my car. I've been in her house. We're all contaminated with each other." But just to be sure, we scrubbed each other.'

'And then went to bed?'

'We did go to bed, but we didn't sleep. We were too panicked for that.'

'Alright,' I said, 'and then what happened?'

'Around nine am, I went to the office,' said David.

I let that answer hang in the air for a second, then said: 'Excuse me? With your wife a rocking mess at home, you went into the *office*?'

'I had to. I'd told my staff I'd be coming in. I didn't want to make a sudden change of plans. I raced through the things I needed to do, and raced home again, and that's when I saw Molly Franklin's car, parked on our driveway.'

'Molly's car. In your driveway?'

'Yes, and it horrified me, because I couldn't work out why Molly would be there.'

'And why was she there?'

'I still have no idea. All I know is, I found the two of them in our kitchen with two cups of tea and a box of tissues between them. I didn't want to act panicked, so I just said: "What's going on?" – like, warily. Loren said: "Oh, I forgot to tell you. I asked Molly yesterday to come over with some Mexican SIM cards, so we don't get those huge bills from roaming." I said: "Oh, good idea." And Molly said: "It's no drama. I have a bunch of them."'

'Okay,' I said, 'and then what happened?'

'I was desperate to get out of the house, so I looked at my watch and said: "Look, we have to go." Loren slid off her stool and Molly got up, and they kissed and carried on, and Molly finally left. I said something like: "What did you tell her?" because I don't trust Molly. But Loren insisted that she hadn't told her anything, and I believed her, because although Molly likes to tell people that she is close to Loren, that's not actually true.'

'Fair enough,' I said, 'and then?'

'Then we had to get moving,' said David. 'We also had to deal with the problem of what to do with the clothes Loren had been wearing. And the dishcloth. I asked her: "Didn't you pack an extra bag?" Because Loren almost always took an extra bag when she went on holidays, to stuff with new clothes, or gifts for the girls. She said yes, so I went and got her suitcase, and took out the extra bag she'd packed, which was one of those collapsible, canvas bags, with wheels on the bottom and a pull-up handle. I opened it up, and stuffed Loren's clothes into it, mixed in a few of my own, stuck the dishcloth in there, and said, you know, "We have to go."'

'With Lyric still on the floor in her kitchen?'

'Right. And trying not to think about that, obviously. Because that was unbearable. But I also had to deal with Loren. It was like she was having a nervous breakdown. I kept saying: "Loren, there are cameras in the garage. You can't get into the car crying. You have to look like a woman who is excited about going on her second honeymoon. You have to pull yourself together." She said: "I can't," and I said: "You can. You *must*. This is California, Loren. *This is a death-row state.*"'

'I see. And that focused Loren's mind?'

'It absolutely did,' said David. 'Loren took a deep breath, stood up and walked with me to the elevator. I began shoving our suitcases through. I said something like: "Cruise ship, here we come!" for the cameras. So it would look like we were a normal couple heading out on a holiday. Loren climbed into the passenger seat. We drove out of the garage, onto Mountain View

Road. And it was absolutely terrifying, driving to the airport, trying to stay in the speed limit. Every police car, I assumed was for me. But eventually we got there. And we handed in the bags. And that was terrifying, too, because I kept thinking, somebody is going to stop us, and examine what's inside. But the girl at check-in just made small talk about how light Loren's extra bag was, and how much fun she was going to have shopping. And eventually, it was time to board. So all we needed now was to get Loren onto the plane. My heart was racing as we headed towards the gate. But Loren did really well. She held it together.'

'And for viewers who perhaps don't know, how long is the flight down to Cabo?'

'It's barely three hours. A driver took us from Cabo airport to our villa. Staff came out with cold juice. The manager wanted to chat but I said: "We're tired from our early flight; I think perhaps a rest." We went straight to our room, and I put the PLEASE DO NOT DISTURB sign on the door, and Loren basically fell apart again.'

'Fell apart how?'

'She was worried about security cameras at Lyric's apartment. I said to her: "There are no cameras. Now, please, don't cry. Stop crying. There are no cameras." Then she started saying: "I can't believe I did this," and I had to say: "It was an accident, Loren. You had a moment of madness. It was a terrible accident that we have to put behind us, because if we try to go back now, if we try to explain, nobody will believe us." Which, of course, nobody does.'

Molly Franklin

'When the going gets tough,
the tough get going!'

Tweet posted by Molly Franklin

My father and I left Gail's office in an embassy car, thinking that we'd be able to inspect Loren's cabin aboard the *Silver Lining*. But by the time we reached the port, the ship had already sailed.

'But how can that be?' I said as we stood there gazing out over the sea. 'My sister is missing off that ship. Don't the police have to do an investigation? Don't they have to speak to passengers and crew?'

By my side stood a well-groomed representative of the company that owned the *Silver Lining*. According to her business card, she was Melissa Haas, Guest Relations Manager. She wore a white silk blouse that was moving gently in the breeze.

'I realise this is disappointing for you, but we had little choice other than to let the ship sail,' said Melissa in her Dutch-accented English. 'We had another cruise to get underway. Two hundred paying passengers. A whole new crew. The police examined your sister's cabin. They took statements from the captain and the crew. They spoke to Mr Wynne-Estes. I understand that you would have liked to have had an opportunity to see the cabin, too, but as difficult as this is for you personally, we do have commercial responsibilities to our guests. But I want to assure you that we will cooperate with any investigation into your sister's death.'

I turned sharply. 'Death?'

'I'm sorry,' said Melissa. 'I know it hasn't been confirmed.'

'No, it hasn't,' I said.

We walked from the port to Melissa's office, ignoring shrieks from holidaymakers on jet-skis and the hawkers selling fake Viagra.

Melissa invited us to sit, arranged for cool drinks to be brought in, and rested her pretty hands on her desk.

'We know from Mr Wynne-Estes that Mrs Wynne-Estes was extremely distressed on this cruise, for a whole range of reasons. It seems that your sister had quite a bit to drink on the night of the Captain's Dinner, both during the dinner and afterwards,' she said gently. 'The champagne bottle from the bar fridge in her cabin was empty and David agreed to blood-alcohol testing after the ship came in. He was not intoxicated.'

'David could have emptied the bottle in the sink,' said Dad. 'She's not a drinker.'

He was adamant, and why not? He was right. Loren wasn't much of a drinker. Maybe when she was younger and still living in New York. She had a bit of a thing for a while for green apple martinis. But that was when Loren was young and irresponsible. That was before Hannah. That was before Peyton. That was before Loren morphed into a High Side mom.

'She definitely wasn't a drunk,' I confirmed, 'and if somebody says they saw her drunk, can we talk to them? Because I don't really believe that.'

Melissa smiled her gentle smile. 'I can't imagine how hard this must be,' she said, 'but I'm not sure that we can just give out the passenger manifesto.'

'Forget that. What I want to know is, how far from shore was she when she was pushed?' said Dad. I could feel the desperation behind the question. 'There's no way she could swim in, I suppose? But what about a passing boat? I mean, out here today, there's a dozen cruise ships on the horizon. Isn't it possible that somebody has picked Loren up?'

Melissa turned her tender smile in his direction. 'But they would have notified us,' she said sadly, 'and as awful as this will sound, we do have some experience with this kind of thing. It's devastating for the families but when somebody decides to take their life like this ...'

'Stop,' I said. 'How do we know that nobody on board the *Silver Lining* saw anything suspicious? Like David and Loren arguing? Because you know he was having an affair, don't you?'

'We do,' said Melissa. 'He did tell us that, yes. He told the police that, too. And I can see how bad that looks for him, but the captain personally ran the data from the swipe keys through his computer, and Mr Wynne-Estes' story about his wife leaving her cabin alone checked out,' she added, patiently. 'He doesn't go near the spot where she went missing, for more than an hour, and he can be seen searching for her moments after reaching that deck. Nevertheless, the captain stopped the ship. We searched every room. We asked passengers to help us. We returned to port. The police here spoke at great length to Mr Wynne-Estes. He explained about the tension in the marriage and how difficult things have been financially, and he offered to surrender to police in the US immediately upon his return to California. We looked at all the CCTV footage, Ms Franklin. What we saw was Mrs Wynne-Estes leaving her room, and her husband frantically trying to find her. We saw her disappear around that corner; she was not seen again.'

* * *

What point was there in staying in Mexico after that? I couldn't see any point, and so, less than a day later, we were back in California.

My iPhone started beeping with messages pretty much the second our plane touched down on US soil. Mom had been calling but so had Aaron Radcliffe from the *Bugle*, saying he had a very important piece of information for me.

I'd been reluctant to speak to him and I was definitely sceptical, but I called him back. 'I have no comment,' I said.

'That's fine,' he said. 'I'm just calling to tell you something that you may not know.'

'Like what?'

'Like David arrived home this morning, and I don't know how he did this, but he shot through a side door at the airport, and we were lucky to get a picture.'

'That's it?'

'Of course that's not it. I've got big news. I'm just painting the picture. From that point, it was like the O.J. Simpson convoy down the freeway,' Aaron continued, 'until we got to the police station. The Chief of Police – Captain Sullivan – came out. I've never seen that before. He came out and shook David's hand. They went inside. Three hours we cooled our heels on the sidewalk.'

I reached towards the carousel and grabbed Dad's bag by its purple belt.

'You're not telling me anything interesting,' I said.

'No, but wait. You're not going to believe what happened next.'

'Tell me.'

'The police chief came out, saying he had news for us. We were all standing waiting, thinking, okay, they're going to charge him. But guess what he said?'

'I give up,' I said, impatiently.

'He said that David had a mistress, and guess what? She's also dead. It's just massive, Molly.'

'*What?*'

'Yes,' said Aaron. Probably in spite of himself, he started speaking in an excited voice. 'From what they said, David has told police that your sister – Loren – found out about his affair, and went to the woman's house, and killed her. She didn't mean to do it. It was an accident, or so he says. So he's been trying to cover up for her. He raced her out of the country, put her on the ship, promised to be her alibi. But she fell into despair. She kept saying she couldn't bear to come back and face a trial. She couldn't cope with what it would do to her daughters. She was terrified of going to prison. So she took her own life.'

'Outrageous.' I was so stunned I could barely speak.

'What's outrageous?' asked Dad, growing agitated beside me.

'I knew you'd say that,' said Aaron. 'So, do you still have no comment?'

'I still have no comment,' I said.

'Well, that's up to you,' said Aaron. I could imagine him shrugging. 'But just so you know, if you don't comment, all we get is David's side of the story. Because that's being leaked to everyone: how Loren was furious with him for having an affair ...'

Okay, that wasn't right.

'That is just bullshit,' I snapped. 'There cannot be a person on earth who believes that my sister would murder somebody. There's one person responsible for what's gone on here, and that person is David Wynne-Estes.'

'Murder?' said Dad.

'And I can quote you on that?' said Aaron.

'Yes you can,' I said, pulling up the handle on my suitcase. 'In fact, why don't you also quote me on this. I've heard David's version of events, and I've never heard such horseshit in my life.'

With that, I dumped my case onto Dad's trolley.

'What is going on!?' he said.

I did my best to fill him in, watching as his face contorted with the horror.

'This is just too much,' he said. 'This is just getting way out of hand.'

* * *

The press pack outside David and Loren's house the following morning had blown out to around a hundred people. I got pushed and shoved as I tried to make my way up to the gates. I was about to ring the buzzer on the stone column, but thought, *Why the hell should I? Loren gave me the code for a reason.*

I stepped quietly up to the front door and used my key to gain access. I could smell bacon frying – and I could hear children chattering away about the day ahead.

Hannah and Peyton were home.

I took a few, quiet steps down the parquetry hallway. From where I was standing, I could see into the kitchen, but I was pretty sure that David, his sister, Janet, and the girls could not see me.

I don't know what I expected – a group of people with eyes red-rimmed from crying; the girls collapsed in grief against David's shoulder – but what I actually saw was more shocking still.

Hannah and Peyton were sitting up on the pony-skin kitchen stools, with their backs to me. It was still quite early but they weren't in pyjamas. They were dressed for school.

Grey shirts under tunics. Polished shoes. Socks to the knee.

Loren had been missing less than seventy-two hours, and David was sending his girls to school?

'You've got to be kidding,' I muttered to myself.

He wasn't kidding.

I stayed out of sight, watching as David put the girls' schoolbags up on the counter and looked inside. Janet tidied Peyton's ponytail but stopped when she saw David struggling to get a lunchbox out of one of the schoolbags, and said: 'Here, let me.'

They were not whispering. I could hear every word perfectly.

'Are you okay?' Janet said, tugging the lunchbox free.

'Sure,' said David.

Janet rubbed her nose against her brother's cheek. 'And did you do it?'

Startled, David took a step back. 'Did I do what?'

'Call that police officer,' said Janet.

'Oh,' said David, visibly relieved. 'Right. No. But I will.'

Janet turned – and saw me. 'Molly,' she said.

David turned so quickly he upset a cereal box on the counter.

'Aunty Molly!' cried Peyton. She clambered off the stool so fast that it came crashing down after her. 'Did you hear? Mommy didn't come home!'

Hannah shouted over her: 'Mom's not here, Aunty Molly!'

What was that all about? Why didn't they sound upset?

Hannah said: 'We're worried, Aunty Molly.' But she didn't seem worried. What exactly had they been told?

David stepped forward. He did not seem happy to see me. 'Did you knock?' he said. 'Did you press the buzzer?'

'I have the code,' I said, as the girls gathered around my legs.

'Well hello, Aunty Molly,' said Janet coldly.

'Yes, hello,' said David, forcing a fake cheerfulness into his voice. 'We weren't expecting you.'

'So I see,' I said.

Peyton had her arms around my legs, and her face against my knees. 'Aunty Janet says Mommy was having such a good time in Mexico she decided to stay longer,' she said, 'but we miss her!'

I turned my head sharply. 'Is that right?'

'Okay now,' David said, stepping forward to peel the girls off my legs. 'That's enough. You girls are already late, and Aunty Janet has promised to take you to school.'

Peyton shook her head. 'I want to wait for Mom!' she said. 'I miss Mom.' She buried her head deeper into my knees.

I patted her hair. 'I miss her, too, baby girl.'

David was aghast. Whatever his plan was, this – my arrival on the scene – was clearly not part of it.

'Well, we can't worry about this now,' said Janet briskly. 'We have school.'

'How can they possibly go to school?' I said.

'School is fun,' said Janet sternly. 'School is distracting. Now, girls, do you have any other lunchboxes? Because these here seem to have been stuffed into your bags way too long.'

Hannah let go of my legs and went dutifully to the pantry, where she pointed to two identical pink lunchboxes stacked on the second shelf.

'Good girl, and what does Mommy – or Nanny – normally put in here?' said Janet, taking the two boxes down. 'A piece of fruit? A sandwich? A box of raisins? Something healthy, I'm sure.'

Janet had opened the fridge to begin choosing snacks and drinks. Neither of the girls answered. She turned to look at them.

Peyton had let go of my legs. Her small hands were over her face. She was crying.

'Oh, now you have to stop that,' said Janet.

'I want to stay home and wait for Mom,' said Peyton. Her face was contorted with concern.

'No, no. No. You can't do that,' said David, stepping forward to take Peyton's hands in his own. 'You need to go to school.'

'She'll be missing us,' cried Hannah.

'Of course she will,' said David, gathering her into his embrace. 'But we can't do anything about that now. And Aunty Janet has come all the way over here to take you to school. So, come on, help me pack your bags and we can go.'

Hannah opened her mouth, as if to protest. Without saying another word, David showed her the palm of his hand. I had seen that hand signal before and clearly, so had she. Hannah stopped dead.

'No arguments,' David said. 'School.'

'Do you know what?' said Janet. 'Why don't we let the girls have lunch from the canteen today? Special treat?' Then, more firmly: 'You'd enjoy that wouldn't you, girls? No lunchbox. Canteen? So come now, let's get in the car.'

She began to guide the girls towards the elevator that led down to the garage.

'I'll take the SUV,' she said.

'Thank you so much,' said David, sounding grateful.

The elevator came and went. Quiet descended upon the kitchen. David stood staring at me. I wasn't scared of him. I stared right back.

'So,' I said.

'So?' he said, like I had no right to be there, asking questions.

'You haven't told them.'

'I don't know what to tell them,' he said.

'You don't think it's going to come out in the playground? You don't think the media is going to follow them down the street? You've got an army of press parked in the street. How can you even think of doing this? Can't you see what's going to happen? Every parent in the drop-off lane is going to be staring. Every kid is going to want to blurt something out.'

'The principal said she could handle that,' said David, but even as he said it, I could see the reality dawning on him.

'Handle it how?'

'She said the parents have been told to tell their children not to say anything,' he said, with real doubt in his voice.

'Like they can police every five-year-old?'

'Well, I don't get what you want me to do,' said David. He had started taking plates off the bench and was rinsing them. 'At some point, they're going to have to face up to what's happened. We all are.'

I stepped further into his kitchen, surprised to find my heart pounding.

'You included?' I said. 'You're going to face up to what you've done, are you?'

David put a plate back down on the bench and strode towards me. Would I describe his expression as menacing? Yes, I think I would.

'Molly, I'm as horrified by this as anyone …'

'I doubt that,' I said, 'after all, this has all worked out rather well for you. Your blackmailing mistress is dead and you say your wife must have done it. How convenient.'

'I went there that night, Molly,' said David. 'I saw what Loren did. She was angry. She had not been thinking clearly for a long time. She lost her mind that night. And now ... Well, I'm not sure what else to say, Molly.'

'So, what are you going to tell the girls?'

'The truth,' said David.

'The truth?' I repeated. 'I don't think so, David.'

David took another step towards me. For a split second, I was frightened. We were alone in that big house. Then I remembered: the press was outside. They knew I was there. David wouldn't dare.

'I'll tell the girls that it was an accident,' he said. 'Their mom didn't mean to do it.'

'And then what?' I said. 'She accidentally fell off the boat, as well? She accidentally took her own life? Or did you accidentally push her after she accidentally got rid of the biggest problem in your life?

'Don't insult me,' I continued. 'You did this. You killed your mistress, and then your wife. You think it's a perfect crime, but everyone can see through you, David. This is not a perfect crime. Do you think you're going to get away with this? There is just no way.'

David stepped closer still. 'I'm telling you now, you've got the wrong end of the stick, Molly. The police have the footage from the ship. I'm not a suspect. This is not what you think it is.'

Fearlessly, maybe even ferociously, I said: 'It's exactly what I think it is.'

David was by now standing less than an inch away from my face. 'No, it isn't,' he said. 'I'm telling you now: just back off, Molly.'

Did that sound like a threat to you? Because it sure sounded like a threat to me.

* * *

'I want to speak to the Chief of Police.'

'Who is speaking?'

'My name is Molly Franklin. I'm Loren Wynne-Estes's sister.'

'One moment please.'

It had been six weeks since Loren had gone missing. After the initial flurry of interest – police cars at my house, at Dad's house, at David's house, TV anchors taking up all the rooms at the Bonsall – the heat had well and truly gone out of the story, yet no charges had been laid against David, and every time anyone from my family tried to ask Captain Sullivan about it, he said the investigation was 'ongoing'.

What did that even mean?

'This is a very complicated and difficult case,' Captain Sullivan said, the last time I'd managed to reach him. 'And we want to make sure we have all our ducks in place before we charge like a wounded bull into a china shop.'

I'd asked Aaron from the *Bugle* to interpret the delay, if not the metaphor. He said: 'On one hand, he's already got these crimes solved. David says he saw Loren at Lyric's house on the night she was killed and he helped get her out of there. Then Loren disappeared from the ship and David was nowhere near her when she walked out of her cabin. The Chief could pretty much leave it there. He's got to charge David with being an accessory of course. Maybe that's what's taking time. Maybe David wants to do a deal.'

'But that story is rubbish,' I said.

'Maybe it is; maybe it's not,' said Aaron. 'I guess that's what they're trying to determine.'

In the meantime, David was still living in the big house on Mountain View Road. The nannies and gardeners were gone – some had been sacked; some had been scared away – but Janet seemed to be staying in the guest house, probably because David had no idea when it came to the girls. As far as I could tell, he still had his Porsche, and Hannah and Peyton were still at Grammar, so life was going on pretty much like normal for him, except that Loren – his needy, miserable wife – was gone.

I wanted David charged. Why hadn't he been charged?

'Captain Sullivan can't speak to you right now,' said the receptionist, coming back to the phone, 'but I have a message for you. He says he'll be in touch when there's something to report.'

'Oh no he won't! I've been waiting for a call from him for a month. I want to speak to him now.'

'Well, he can't speak to you now.'

I said evenly: 'Then how about this. You tell him that if he won't speak to me now, I will come to the station. I will come to the station and I will sit on your pretty little porch. I will come with fifty coloured balloons and a giant sign that says Justice for Loren. I will sit there – and I will be well within my civil rights to do so – making balloon toys for passing children until he comes out.'

The receptionist paused. 'One moment please,' she said.

The phone went quiet, then crackled to life.

'Hello?' said Captain Sullivan. 'Who is this?'

'You know perfectly well who it is. This is Loren Wynne-Estes' sister, Molly Franklin. I've been calling you every other day since I got back from Mexico. I dropped in a file of information into your office about David's affair and his money troubles and I have not heard a peep.'

'You dropped an unauthorised file of information based on a journal that you were not authorised to remove from Mr Wynne-Estes' house,' said Captain Sullivan.

'I dropped a detailed and very interesting file of information that proves that my sister was not suicidal, and nor is she the kind of person who could kill anyone. David's story is not credible. You know it and I know it, and I'm now insisting on a meeting with you to find out where your investigation is at. If you don't meet me, I'm going to call the *Bugle* and tell them that you're refusing to meet with Loren's family.'

Captain Sullivan sighed. 'There isn't anything to tell you. I'm trying not to waste your time. If you want to come in, come at ten tomorrow, but I won't be able to tell you anything more than I've already told you. The ducks have to be lined up before we draw a circle around them.'

I arrived fifteen minutes early. From my seat in the waiting area, I could see Captain Sullivan working in his office. Whatever he was doing – scratching notes onto the pad in front of him, and turning occasionally to look at his computer screen – didn't seem all that urgent. Finally, he got up and came to the counter. Bienveneda's police station is old. It has one of those counters that lift up to let people through.

'Come in,' he said.

I took a seat opposite his desk.

'I'll go get us some coffee,' he said.

In his absence, I had a good look around his office. It was incredibly crowded. There was his desk, strewn with manila folders, pen holders, paperclip holders, a scorpion caught under Perspex, a stars-and-stripes football on a stand; there were framed certificates and medals on the wall; there were framed drawings of the old Bienveneda's city lines; an old, box-style computer, with a printer on the short filing cabinet standing next to the desk. There was a hat stand for Captain Sullivan's hat and jacket, and there was a fancy armoire with leather-bound books inside. Also a Derek Jeter–signed baseball in a Perspex box.

Captain Sullivan returned with two old-style coffee mugs. He leaned back in his chair, which went very far back under his weight.

'I'm trying to figure out how I can help you,' he said.

'I'd like to know where things stand with my sister's murder,' I said calmly.

Captain Sullivan put his mug on a coaster, and his elbows on his desk. 'I know you think it's murder, but David has given us a very different account of what happened on that boat.'

He picked up his mug and gulped some coffee, before quickly putting it down again.

'And you know, even if I accepted that David did in fact commit a crime on the ship, there isn't much we can do about it,' he added. 'You know as well as I do about the jurisdiction. That ship was off the coast of Mexico. And it's owned by a company in Holland. So ...'

'So it's not your business?'

'You make it sound harsh, but you're not wrong. Technically speaking, it's none of my business.'

'My brother-in-law also told you that Loren killed his mistress, didn't he?'

Captain Sullivan looked uncomfortable. 'You know he did, it's been in all the newspapers.'

'Don't you find that a little bit too convenient?' I said calmly.

'No, I don't, and the reason I don't is that he has a good explanation for what happened there. He says Loren found text messages on his phone, and went over there in a rage.'

'You don't believe that,' I said.

'As it happens, I do believe that,' said Captain Sullivan, gulping more coffee.

My own mug sat undisturbed on the desk. The silence between us stretched out to several seconds.

'Besides,' said Captain Sullivan eventually, 'what's his motive for killing Miss Morales? Why not just break up with her?'

'Well, tell me this,' I said, 'does Loren have life insurance?'

Captain Sullivan gazed through the window of his office. There was nothing going on out there. He just didn't want to look me in the eye.

'You know perfectly well she does,' he said. 'It's been in the *Bugle.*'

'I don't necessarily believe everything I read in the *Bugle*,' I said, 'but I'm guessing from what you're saying the answer is yes?'

'The answer is yes, but here's something that maybe you don't know. Loren's life insurance doesn't cover suicide. You can't take your own life and still get your life insurance,' he said, shaking his head in a manner that suggested that he understood these things far better than I did. 'So if you're thinking David's done this for money, you're wrong. There will be no money.'

Leaning forward on the desk, he added: 'So you can understand why I don't see a motive. Plus there seems to be no reason for David to murder his mistress.

'What I do see is Loren's motive. Her husband isn't supposed to be seeing Miss Morales anymore. He's supposed to be concentrating on his marriage. Getting back together with his wife. But that's not what's happening. He's still seeing his mistress, and on the eve of the so-called second honeymoon his wife finds out that the affair's not over. Her husband isn't giving up his mistress, and it looks like he's still pretty keen on his mistress. Now, I don't know how much training you have, Miss Franklin, but in my book, that's motive. Not for David. For Loren.'

* * *

'Molly Franklin?'

'That's me.'

I had gone from the frustrating interview with Captain Sullivan back to Mom's house, with no real news to report. I hadn't been there more than half an hour when my cell phone rang.

'This is Officer Callie Croft. I just saw you in Captain Sullivan's office.'

My heart skipped a beat. 'Yes,' I said, 'that was me. What's happened?'

'I'd actually like to come and see you.' Callie wasn't talking so much as whispering. 'Are you at home now?'

'I'm at Mom's,' I said.

'Would you mind if I dropped by?'

'Do you have news?'

'I'll come this evening. Now I have to go.'

Impatiently, we waited out the day. Mom made like she was busy clipping leaves off plants. Dad paced the patio. I did my best not to behave like a cat on a hot tin roof. It was after dark when Callie finally arrived in her own car. I barely recognised her out of uniform.

We sat down in the kitchen.

'I'm breaking all the rules just being here,' said Callie.

Dad nodded. 'That's a good strategy in this life. I'd encourage you to keep doing that for as long as you can. Please tell us what you know.'

'Well, the news isn't good,' said Callie. 'From what the captain was saying after Molly left – and he was like a bear with a sore head, by the way – you're sitting around expecting David to be charged with your sister's murder, but I can tell you now, that isn't going to happen.'

'But why not?' I said, indignantly. 'Surely nobody believes the story he's telling?'

Callie looked uncomfortable. 'I don't believe David's story,' she said, 'but what Captain Sullivan told you about jurisdiction is right. Loren is a US citizen, but she wasn't in the US when the ... accident, incident, whatever you want to call it, happened.'

'Let's call it murder,' I said.

'This is outrageous,' said Mom. 'We're talking about a man who killed his mistress, then dumped his wife off a ship. They're not going to let him get away with it, surely?'

Callie took a deep breath. 'I need to tell you something. I have to get it off my conscience. And I realise that once I give you this information, I'll have no control over what you do with it. But I can't keep it in anymore.'

'Tell us, Callie,' said Dad.

'David's mistress, Lyric Morales ...'

'Yes?'

'Well, it seems like she wasn't just *David's* mistress.'

'What?'

'She was having sex with some of his clients, too. It seems like she was doing it to stop these clients from taking money out of David's business, to kind of protect the business. So you can see the problem?'

I looked around the table. Poor old Mom seemed absolutely stunned.

'He was offering her up to his clients?' said Dad. No question he was thinking about the mistake we'd all made in welcoming David into our family. 'What kind of man are we talking about here? What was he doing? Running a brothel? Is he a monster?'

'I wouldn't necessarily disagree with that description,' said Callie, 'but from what he's saying, Lyric was having sex with these guys willingly. He says she really enjoyed it. The power. But if she's having sex with different people, then we suddenly have a whole lot of suspects. Because when a woman has not one but two, three different lovers, there's a lot of potential jealousies and rivalries and secrets.'

I gulped in a breath. 'So, that's why it's taking so long for him to be charged? They're ruling out all the other suspects?'

'Not exactly,' said Callie, 'because there's more.'

Dad's eyes widened. 'There's more?'

'Right. It seems like Lyric has quite a few of these men on tape,' Callie said.

'Oh my goodness,' said Mom. 'You mean … sex tapes?'

'Right,' said Callie. 'Sex tapes. I don't know who's on them. Nobody does. That's been kept tightly under wraps. Because David's clients, they're a pretty big deal. My guess is, they're businessmen, politicians, people from the golf club.'

Dad put his hand over Mom's. Neither of them seemed to know what to say.

'So, let me get this straight,' I said. 'Are you telling me that the reason Captain Sullivan is prepared to accept David's explanation – that he walked in on Loren after she had killed Lyric – is because they don't want those tapes to come out?'

'Right,' said Callie miserably, 'and it seems like David is willing to plead guilty to being an accessory after the fact. He's admitting to helping Loren get out of Lyric's kitchen. He's admitting to disposing of her clothes and offering her an alibi. He's admitting to getting her out of the country the day after Lyric's death. There're quite a few of us at the station who disagree with the captain's decision. We'd like to see a proper investigation but that seems like something the Chief is a bit too keen to avoid.'

* * *

Callie left Mom's house the same way she came, under the cover of darkness.

'What do we do now?' I asked.

Mom – still in shock – didn't answer. She kept her gaze down as she cleared away the cups.

'We bust this scandal right open,' said Dad, slamming down his fist. 'We go straight to the media and say this is a cover-up.'

I still had Aaron Radcliffe's number on my phone. He called once a week but I never had anything to tell him. I wanted David charged with Loren's murder, or even Lyric's murder, but it seemed like the police weren't convinced, and in the absence of any new developments in the story, the *Bugle* had taken to running shameful articles about David's new life without Loren. One photograph showed him guiding the girls into an SUV outside the Grammar school. The headline said: GRIEVING DAD SHOULDERS HIS NEW RESPONSIBILITIES.

Furious, I'd texted Aaron: How can you publish this rubbish?

He'd texted back: We're not taking sides, Molly. Call me if you want a chat.

I fished my iPhone out of my pocket and put it on the kitchen table.

Aaron picked up after just one ring. 'Hello, Molly. How can I help you?'

'I have some information.'

'Great! I'll be there in five minutes, or as soon as I can get across the bridge, anyway.'

Aaron arrived in an old car, dark jeans, and old Vans sneakers.

'I hope you don't mind but I brought my dinner with me,' he said, dragging a bag of corn chips and a tub of hummus out of his satchel. 'With the newspaper online, they never give me time to eat.'

Mom watched as Aaron tore open the bag and began crunching through the chips. 'Why don't you let me fix you something proper?' she said, but Aaron replied, 'This will do me, Mrs Franklin.'

Keeping Callie's name out of it, we told him what she had told us: that David's mistress had sex tapes, featuring what she'd described as 'Important People' and maybe that explained why the investigation was moving so slowly.

'Sex tapes! That's amazing,' Aaron said, wiping his hands on his jeans. 'And how many lovers are we talking about?'

'We don't know for certain,' I said. 'Do you think you can write a story about it? That might get the wheels of justice turning.'

'I can try,' he said, scooping up some dip. 'The question is, will my boss believe me? Because I'm going to have to tell her where this information came from. And she's going to say that you're not a good source because you weren't even that close to Loren.'

'Who says we weren't that close?'

'David says.'

'You're still talking to David?' I was incredulous.

'I'm a reporter,' said Aaron. 'I talk to everyone.'

'Do you tell him what I tell you?'

'Don't complain. I'm sitting here now, telling you what he told me,' said Aaron, crunching through another handful of chips. 'He says you weren't close. You're not Loren's sister, you're her stepsister. He makes the point: where did Loren leave the girls when she went away? Not with you. With Janet.'

'And what about me?' said Dad, closing his fists on the table in front of him. 'Am I not close to my own daughter? Am I not close to my own grandchildren?'

Aaron didn't respond.

'Listen to me Aaron,' I said, stabbing at the cover of his notebook with my finger. 'I've known Loren since she was eight years old. That is far, far longer than she knew David.'

'I'm just telling you what he told me.' Aaron wiped the back of his hand across his mouth. To Dad, he said, 'And to answer your question, yes, David is saying that Loren wasn't close with you. Because, you know, you left her mom for another woman.'

Mom's face was scarlet.

'Why, you—' Dad rose from his chair.

'Everyone settle down,' I jumped in. I had my hands out, trying to calm the situation. 'Dad, sit. Mom, don't you worry what David says. Aaron, you are wrong. Loren loved Dad. She loved Mom! She loved all of us.'

* * *

It was late at night and I'd been pacing the garden, trying to think.

'There must be a way to get the police to lay charges,' I said, coming to sit beside Dad on the patio.

'We've had no luck so far,' he replied.

It had been at least a fortnight since Aaron had gotten permission to publish his big SEX! LIES! VIDEOTAPE! story, and while there had been plenty of outrage and speculation as to who might be on the tapes, still nothing had happened.

'It's like, he's High Side, so he has all the power,' I said. 'We're Low Side, so we just get ignored. It's not right. Who can we appeal to? We must know somebody who can speak up for us.'

Dad was looking skyward, deep in thought.

'Well, there is that pretty lady who's always in her underpants,' he said suddenly.

'The who?'

'The pretty lady who gets photographed in her underpants,' said Dad, 'the one who played the blind girl. The actress. The one who's in Loren's journal. Nadine what's-her-name. The famous one.'

The blind girl? What was Dad on about …? Oh my goodness, yes. *Yes.*

'Dad, you're a genius!'

'I am?'

'You are. You're right! You're so right! We need to rope in Nadine Perez.'

Because that's the kind of world we live in, right? Small people like Dad and me can't get anything done; famous people like Nadine, they can get the whole country's media to turn up to watch them try on a new pair of shoes.

'But how are we going to get her attention?' asked Dad. 'She's a famous person. And she might not even remember Loren.'

'Well, let's find out.'

I got right to it. Like every megastar, Nadine has a massive online presence. She is on Facebook, Twitter, Instagram and Pinterest and probably a few others I'd never heard about.

'How does it all work?' Dad said, peering over my shoulder.

'I'll leave a message on her page,' I said, tapping away at the keyboard. 'I can write: "Please get in touch, it's regarding your old friend Loren Franklin."'

From the look of her page, Nadine was having a busy year. She had one big movie out – people were saying she might even win the Academy Award for playing a blind girl marked by the Nazis for extermination – where she had to wear white cups, like the backs of spoons, over her eyes. She had been skiing in Switzerland, and then sailed to the French Riviera on a rap star's yacht. She was in Dubai, promoting an airline; she was in Milan, endorsing a watch; she was in New York as a guest on a talk show; she was in Australia, holding a koala.

'I bet she doesn't even read her messages,' I said, scrolling through page upon page of Nadine at different points on the globe in various states of undress. 'What we need to do is approach her in person, so she can't just ignore us.'

Dad scoffed. 'And how are you going to do that? You're not planning on flying first class anytime soon.'

'You could go to her star ceremony,' said Mom. She had come onto the patio in her dressing gown and slippers.

'Her what?'

'Her star ceremony,' she said. 'I read about it last week, Nadine Perez is getting a star on Hollywood's Walk of Fame.'

'They do those in public?'

'Yes they do. I went to one for Vince Vaughn,' said Mom, clutching the neck of her nightie to her throat, 'now I get updates.'

I turned back to the computer and entered the relevant search terms into Google, and there it was: 'Nadine Perez gets Star on Walk of Fame.' The event wasn't scheduled for several weeks, but that was fine; I could keep trying to email, tweet and message my sister's star friend in the meantime.

'Mom, you're the best,' I said.

'Anything for Loren.'

* * *

'You guys must be big fans!'

The security guard was even larger than Dad and what he said thrilled me because Dad and I had gone to some lengths to make sure we looked like fans of Nadine Perez. I had a poster of her from an old *US Weekly* stuck on an old school ruler. Dad had a framed photograph from *Fancy* magazine and he was carrying a gold permanent marker. Aaron, who had insisted on coming along for a possible story, looked like Aaron: poor and scruffy.

We took three seats in the front row of bleacher seats. The red carpet was directly in front of us. We were easily the first ones to arrive, but as the hours went by, a small crowd – intrigued by the red carpet, the velvet rope and the light stands – began to gather.

We passed the time people-watching. At some point, a Jack Sparrow lookalike came by, chanting: 'One dollar, photographs are one dollar.'

Then along came Marilyn Monroe (not the real one, obviously, but a woman – or maybe a man? – in a copy of the white dress Marilyn had been wearing when she stood on the grate). 'Who's on today?' she purred.

'It's Nadine Perez,' said Aaron, drawing doodles on his notepad.

'Oh, she'll get a crowd,' said Marilyn, taking up a new position near the red carpet.

The seats around us began to fill. There were Australian tourists in blindingly bright, outlet-centre sneakers; American tourists with fanny packs and water bottles; photographers with Canon lenses.

I waved my poster. Aaron took a thousand calls from the newspaper's editor wanting to know if anything had happened yet. Dad sweated in the heat.

Eventually, an MC turned up in a Hollywood-style, velvet tuxedo. I couldn't help but feel sorry for him, sweltering out there under the Californian sun.

'Are we all ready to cheer?' he cried.

I warned Dad against getting carried away. 'Don't do anything that might get us in trouble. Don't get in her face.'

'What are they going to do?' he said. 'Arrest me? They don't arrest anyone in this town.'

'Well, get ready, ladies and gentlemen, because we're about to induct the beautiful, the gorgeous, the talented Nadine Perez into our Walk of Fame,' cried the MC.

The crowd around us got to their feet. They were cheering and clapping. We got up with them. A bodyguard was leading Nadine into the arena. He was even bigger than the bodyguard who had greeted us earlier that day.

'Oh my God, she's tiny,' I said, shouting a bit so Dad could hear me over the racket.

'I heard Tom Cruise is tiny,' Dad shouted back, as he clapped.

'He is tiny,' confirmed Aaron.

'Hello, everyone!' cooed Nadine, blowing kisses towards the crowd. 'Oh goodness, did you all come here for me? And I was late? I hope you can forgive me.'

The crowd cheered their forgiveness.

Nadine beamed. 'Now, where do I go?'

A harried woman with a face microphone took her gently by the elbow and directed her towards a card table covered with a red velvet cloth.

'I'm going to put my hands in here, am I?' said Nadine, surveying what looked to be a tray filled with freshly poured plaster of Paris.

Her assistant handed over a pair of silicone gloves.

'Ooh, I put these on, do I?' said Nadine, holding them all floppy like flesh-coloured condoms.

The crowd roared. Nadine winked back and drew the gloves slowly onto her hands. She positioned herself over the wet cement and pressed.

The MC was ecstatic: 'Yes, yes, ladies and gentlemen, Nadine Perez, look at her go ... Walk of Fame ... What a moment!'

'Oh wow,' Nadine said, 'this is fun!'

With the formal part of the ceremony over, reporters began shouting questions.

Nadine cupped a hand to her ear.

'What was it like playing Robert Redford's love interest?' shouted a man next to me. 'He's old enough to be your grandfather! That scene in the steam room, we haven't seen female nudity like that since *Basic Instinct*. How was it, shooting that scene?'

Nadine peeled off her gloves, winked and smiled. 'What is it you really want to know? What exactly are you asking me? Did they see my coochie? Is that what you want to know?'

The reporter turned scarlet. My father whispered to me: 'Coochie? That's the word now?'

The MC laughed and shouted back to the crowd, 'Come on now, a serious question for Nadine if we've got one?'

This was our moment. I dug an elbow into Dad's side. He stood up and, in the front row of the bleachers, he could hardly be missed.

The MC came running with the microphone. 'Here we go, we have a question here,' he cried. 'What's your name, sir?'

'I'm Danny Franklin.'

The microphone screamed. The MC snatched it back, tapped it, and handed it back to Dad, nodding with encouragement.

'Nadine, I'm Loren's dad,' said Dad, his voice now booming. 'Your old roommate, Loren Franklin. I'm her dad.'

Nadine had been standing in her pretty high heels, patiently listening to Dad's question. Her head was tilted slightly to the right, and the diamonds in her left ear were cascading down her neck. Now she straightened and seemed to frown. The MC glared at Dad, and then glanced back at Nadine, waiting for the signal to snatch the mic away. Sensing this, Dad gripped it tighter.

'I'm Loren's dad ... Loren was your friend in New York. We need your help.'

Reporters turned in their seats to stare. By the look of things, we had maybe seconds for Nadine to respond. The security guard who had seemed so friendly was now moving in a menacing way in our direction. Any minute now, Dad would have his arm twisted up behind his back – but no, because Nadine put a pale and elegant hand up and said: 'Wait, wait, wait. No, no, no, wait. Did you say Loren Franklin? You're her father?'

'I am,' said Dad, relieved. He was still standing, so I stood up, too.

'You know she's missing?' said Dad.

'I didn't know that,' said Nadine. 'What happened to her?'

The security guard stepped back. Dad had the floor. He cleared his throat.

'She married David Wynne-Estes. You know, from Book-IT. The guy you warned her about.'

The crowd laughed and Nadine laughed, too.

'And you said she's missing?' she said, head tilted as if to hear us better.

'She disappeared from a ship,' said Dad. 'This was off the coast of Mexico, so the police are saying it's outside their jurisdiction. We think her husband did it and he killed his mistress, too. It's a big story in our town, but the police won't lay any charges. We need your help to put some pressure on.'

The crowd was hushed, expectant.

'Well,' said Nadine carefully, 'I don't know all the details, so I probably shouldn't comment, but if Loren is missing, and you think something terrible has happened to her, of course you have my support for a full and complete investigation.' The crowd started clapping. 'And I'll probably get in trouble for this, but for what it's worth, I don't mind telling you, I never liked that man. David, I mean. I always thought Loren deserved better ... and now everyone, I've got to go! Thank you all so much for coming! Bye! Byeeeee! Bye-bye!'

And with a wave of her pale hand, she was gone.

* * *

Who are you?

What's your name?

Who is the missing lady?

Nadine had left the stage and the media transferred its white-hot focus to poor old Dad. He was still standing in the bleachers, with his hands over his ears. Aaron, determined to be first, had run off to file his story: Nadine Perez wants an investigation into the deaths of a Bienveneda businessman's wife and mistress!

I was doing my best to sort one question from the next, when one of Nadine's people – her name was Myah, although I wouldn't learn that until later – pushed through the crowd.

'Come with me,' she said, gripping my arm with a firmness I didn't expect from such a tiny girl. 'You need to do this properly.'

I put my head down and allowed Myah to drag us towards the Chinese theatre, squinting at the camera bulbs flashing in my face.

'Look at the storm you've created,' she said approvingly, once we got inside and had a chance to sit down. 'But listen, there's a way to go about getting publicity for your cause, and this is so not it. Why didn't you just write to us?'

'I did,' I complained, 'but nobody answered. And Loren's husband, David, he's got all the power where we come from. It's like everyone just believes his side of the story because he's rich, he belongs to the right clubs, he knows all the right people.'

'He can't be that powerful,' said Myah, 'because I've never heard of him. Vaguely, vaguely I remember this story. A woman missing off a cruise ship, but there's more to it, am I right? There's a mistress? The wife killed the mistress?'

'She didn't kill the mistress! See, that's what I mean. That's what David is saying. And at the rate we're going, that's what Loren's daughters are going to grow up believing.'

'Alright, alright,' said Myah. 'Well, this is well outside my remit, but Nadine wants to help you, so ...'

She took a tiny notepad out of her purse and began scribbling down a name and number. 'This here is the name of a friend of mine who is an agent. Do you know what an agent is? She can arrange a deal for you with one of the big networks. You call this number and you tell them Myah sent you. Tell them you want to do a deal to tell the whole story properly. A calm, professional interview. Because an hour from now? This is going to be a massive story, and you want to be prepared. You want to be able to say no, we've signed an exclusive deal with whomever. And then they'll report that. Believe me when I tell you there is a science to turning a small-town story into national news.'

She wasn't wrong.

Already, the headlines were starting to appear online.

MY SECRET SORROW! SEXY NADINE SPEAKS OF HEARTACHE OVER FRIEND'S MYSTERY DEATH!

WHERE IS LOREN? NADINE PEREZ CRIES OUT FOR HELP FOR HER MISSING FRIEND!

The story was on Facebook, in *People*, on *Huffpo*. My phone went into meltdown as I tried to deal with all the calls.

'How do you know Nadine Perez?'

'What do you believe happened to your sister?'

'Where is the investigation at?'

'I'm sorry,' I said. 'We have no comment. We have signed an exclusive agreement with *RealNews*.'

And so we had. Myah's friend, the agent, did that deal for us in less than an hour. Then Dad, Aaron and I headed back to Bienveneda. A paparazzo photographer followed us for a while, on a motorbike, snapping away with one hand, clinging onto his driver with the other.

'Imagine living like this,' I said.

'You don't ever want the spotlight of fame to fall on you,' said Aaron, shaking his head. 'People like Michael Jackson – he couldn't leave the house without being photographed. It's torture.'

'People like the Kardashians – they seem to love it,' I said, as the bike finally fell away.

We arrived at Mom's to find another photographer camped on the lawn. The producer from *RealNews*, Sunday Dow, was also already there, and she tried to get the photographer to go away when we arrived, but he remained defiant, saying, 'This is America. I can stand on whatever sidewalk I want.'

'Well, make sure you stay on the sidewalk, then,' she said, shooing him off Mom's lawn.

'Don't let anyone photograph you,' Sunday said.

'Why would anyone want to photograph me?' Dad asked, lumbering towards the door.

'Because they know we've paid for your story,' said Sunday, 'meaning your story has value. Meaning, they'll want to get it free. So let's get down to it. Where shall we go to discuss?'

We took her into the kitchen, where Sunday moved her chair so close to mine that our knees were almost touching.

'As I understand it, the police can't investigate your sister's disappearance,' she said to me, reading from notes she had brought to the house, 'because of problems with the jurisdiction?'

'That's right,' Dad and I said in unison.

'Okay. And you'd like us to help you get around that by forcing an investigation into the death of Lyric Morales? Because you think David killed her and has blamed the death on Loren?'

I nodded.

'And so, if he can't be charged with the death of his wife, you're hoping to get him for the death of his mistress? That's great. I really like this,' Sunday said, 'and tell me, when David goes to prison for Lyric's murder, who's going to look after the girls? Your family, surely? Not his family. So this is about getting those girls away from a monster, too.'

I would be lying if I said I didn't want the girls. David had stopped all contact when I told him that I wanted to see him charged, and I guess I can't blame him for that, but it made me sick when I thought about what he might be telling them.

That we didn't love them.

That we didn't care.

That their mom was a crazy lady who disappeared from their lives.

'Well, you know, this is a little off-topic, but what we heard was that David encourages the girls to think that their mom is still alive,' Sunday said, leafing slowly through the notes on her lap. 'Not more than half an hour ago, we were offered a picture, like a crayon drawing, by a teacher at the Grammar school they attend. Teachers don't earn much so I suppose you can't blame her for trying to sell it. Apparently it was something that Peyton drew. That's her name, isn't it? Peyton? And we were intrigued, because it was a picture of her mom, Loren, resting under a palm tree on a desert island. The way it was described to us, Peyton thinks her mom got shipwrecked and is maybe coming back to her one day.'

'Please say you didn't buy it.'

'Oh no,' said Sunday gently. 'We definitely said no.'

'I should hope so,' I said. 'I can't believe a Grammar teacher would do that.'

Putting the girls in Grammar was a big part of what Loren loved about having moved to the High Side. She was always going on about it. 'Such a beautiful school,' she used to say. 'The grounds! The teachers! They have music. They have drama. They have debating. They organise field trips to places like Peru.'

Now they're selling pictures by her children?

'Well,' said Sunday. 'Let's help you get those children away from there, shall we?'

The interview started with Dad and me sitting opposite the reporter, Christina Alley, who arrived an hour after Sunday, looking like a skeleton. I know what the gossip magazines are saying: anorexia. I'm not sure, but she was certainly all knuckles and cheekbones.

'Tell me about that suit, Mr Franklin,' she said, as Dad sat waiting for the cameras to roll. He had been tugging on the sleeves of his jacket since Christina sat down. 'Did wardrobe supply that? Do we need to get you a larger size?'

'I got this suit for Loren's wedding,' said Dad. 'It's only the second time I've worn it, and I put it on for today. I want to feel close to her.'

Christina looked up from her notes. 'Now, make sure you say that on air.'

We didn't get a room at the Bonsall for our interview. The producers wanted what they called 'a feel for what's real' and Mom's house was apparently 'just perfect'.

Mom was aghast. 'You don't want people to see all this,' she said, waving her hand around the sitting room with its worn armchairs and the window-mounted air-conditioner and the no-brand TV screen.

'We definitely do,' murmured Sunday. 'And we are going to compare it to some footage from David's house. In fact, I just did a little helicopter ride over that property with a cameraman in tow. Do you know they have a leaping dolphin statue in their pool?'

It was a surreal experience, walking through Mom's home to my old bedroom, being followed by a man with a furry microphone and another with a camera, talking to Christina Alley in a way that was supposed to sound spontaneous although it was all rehearsed.

'So this is where Loren slept when she was a little girl?' asked Christina.

'It is,' I said, moving towards the small white bookshelf to extract an old photo album, 'and I have some photographs here of when she was a kid.'

The photographs showed Loren as she was at age nine: pretty and blonde with a blue ribbon in her hair. The *RealNews* team also took photographs from Loren's Facebook – how they did that after David took it down, I do not know – showing Peyton wearing a pair of dotty plastic sunglasses; and of Hannah learning to ride a red trike; and of Hannah racing ahead of Peyton in an egg-and-spoon race; and of Loren holding both girls as babies in her arms.

They took the footage of Dad and me standing in the bleachers at the Walk of Fame ceremony, pleading with Nadine; and the footage of Nadine in all her diamond splendour, agreeing to help.

'Do you think she'll agree to an on-camera interview?' I asked.

'We asked, and her people said no,' said Sunday, clearly despondent. 'Apparently, her people decided it's too risky, especially if there's going to be a trial … but she has given us a statement, and a photograph of herself at age nineteen,' she added, brightening. 'You should see it, she's sitting on the fire escape in the apartment she shared with Loren, in underwear and black toenail paint. It's amazing. We're going to show the picture, and have the statement rolling down the screen.'

The statement wasn't very long. Basically, it said: 'Loren Franklin paid my rent for six months when I first moved to New York … I would be nowhere without her.'

'And maybe you can use bits and pieces from Loren's journal?'

'Her journal?' said Sunday.

'Well, it's not strictly a journal,' I said, 'but her marriage counsellor, Bette Busonne, had her writing down all her thoughts and feelings after she found out that David was having an affair.'

'And can I see this journal?'

I fetched a printout of a scan I'd made, and handed it to Sunday, who did not even bother to sit before opening the cover and beginning to read.

'Oh my,' she said. 'Juicy!'

'Pardon?' said Dad.

'Heartbreaking,' said Sunday, recovering herself, 'but very, very difficult to get across on screen. I mean, so many words.' She fanned the pages, thinking. 'But do you know what might work,' she said. 'How would you feel, Molly, if we had somebody transcribe this journal completely and we published it online? Unedited. Untouched! So everyone can get to know Loren, in her own words.'

It seemed to make sense. The footage would show me handing the diary over to Christina, saying: 'I'm giving this to you because I want the world to know my sister. She was a lovely person. She loved her husband. She loved her children and I will fight until my last day to find out what happened to her.'

* * *

You have made a BIG mistake.

Those were the first words I heard from David after the *RealNews* interview went to air. Not face to face, or on the phone. He sent a text.

It went on:

Molly, you have made a SERIOUS mistake. Loren would be so ANGRY with you. All this attention is NOT what Loren would have wanted. Our girls have already lost their mother. Do you want them to lose their father, too?

I didn't respond. Honestly, by then, I had nothing left to say to David. Except maybe: 'See you in court.'

Three days after the *RealNews* program went to air, reporters were called to a press conference at the office of Bienveneda's Chief of Police, Captain Sullivan.

I wasn't allowed to go. Media only. But Aaron went.

You won't believe it, he texted me from the venue. Fifty people have turned up. There's enough pancake makeup in here to cover a chorus line.

I texted back: What are people saying?

Everyone's impressed with you, Aaron responded, getting your Hollywood movie-star friend to intervene.

I was pretty pleased with myself as well. The full glare of attention was finally upon David.

I have to go, wrote Aaron.

I'm watching from home, I replied.

'Which network will have it?' asked Dad, pointing his remote control at the TV.

'Looks like all of them,' I said.

We settled on Fox9. For a long time, there was nothing to see. The cameras were aimed at a rostrum, behind which stood the flags of California and the United States.

By my count, Captain Sullivan kept viewers and reporters in the room waiting about twenty minutes before marching up to the rostrum in his dress uniform, complete with braiding and medals.

A team of detectives followed him.

'Gee, none of them look happy,' I said.

Captain Sullivan, in particular, looked grim.

'It's because they don't want all the tapes to come out,' said Dad, pointing his remote to turn up the volume.

I felt some sympathy, not necessarily for the people who had been coaxed into having sex with Lyric, but for the people who were likely to become collateral damage.

How many marriages were about to end?

How many children were about to find themselves the butt of jokes at school?

'Thank you all for coming,' said Captain Sullivan, rustling the papers on the rostrum. 'As you probably know, we're here to announce the fact that we have today issued a warrant for the arrest of local businessman David Wynne-Estes.'

Camera shutters went wild.

'And, contrary to some of the reports that have gone to air, this development hasn't just come out of the blue,' Captain Sullivan added, 'and it most certainly hasn't come as a result of intervention by some Hollywood movie star.'

Some of the reporters tittered.

'We've actually been working on this case for a while,' the captain continued. 'Obviously, I can't say much more than that, other than to say that David Wynne-Estes has been informed that he will be arrested; his lawyers have been informed; we're expecting him at the station this afternoon so we can lay the charges formally. He's not resisting that. He's coming in. And beyond that, I'm not sure what else we can say, although our advice to you media is as always, to let the law take its course. So, without further ado, does anyone have any questions?'

A reporter in the front row raised her hand to half-height. 'Carrie Freeman from CBN,' she said. 'You said that this arrest has nothing to do with the intervention of the Hollywood movie star Nadine Perez, but surely ...'

Captain Sullivan looked annoyed. 'That's right. This isn't a soap opera. Police work is a serious business. We don't go around arresting people because stars tell us to,' he said.

A second reporter raised her hand. 'But, in fairness, Chief, it does seem like a coincidence that it wasn't until ...' she began, but Captain Sullivan wasn't having it.

'I've just said, I don't need movie stars to tell me how to do my job,' he said grumpily. 'So unless anyone else has a different question ...'

An older reporter – he was still using a paper notebook – raised his hand. 'Hello there, Chief,' he said in a velvety voice. 'If I could just put the Hollywood nonsense aside for a moment ...'

Captain Sullivan picked up his water glass, and took a satisfied sip. 'Yes?'

'What I'd like to know is, at what point did you decide that David needed to face a murder charge, and have you informed the family of Lyric Morales?'

The camera shifted back towards the captain, who seemed positively flustered.

'Oh, you misunderstand,' he said. 'No. This is my mistake. I'm sorry for the confusion. David Wynne-Estes isn't being charged with the murder of Lyric Morales. No. No. No. We are doing what Loren's family wanted. The warrant we are issuing today, it's for the murder of his wife.'

Judge L. Samuel Pettit

'They say the truth will set you free –
but I have faith in juries, too!'

Tweet posted by David Wynne-Estes

'Oh my goodness, this is going to be the easiest ten million dollars Dick van Nispen has ever made.'

Cecile was seated in the atrium adjacent to our kitchen. I was doing my duty in the kitchen: squeezing oranges, boiling the fresh brown eggs and lightly buttering the toast.

'Samuel, have you seen this?' Cecile asked, a little louder this time. 'There's a story in the *Bugle*. It says Dick van Nispen will be representing that awful man, David Wynne-Estes, in court.'

I went into the atrium, bearing the juice, toast, eggs and of course the French coffee press.

'So I've heard,' I said, lowering the tray onto the timber table. 'In fact, he told me personally, yesterday.'

'What an appalling client to take on,' said Cecile, placing her tablet back on its stand. 'David Wynne-Estes is obviously as guilty as sin.'

'He's still entitled to a defence,' I said, lowering myself onto the bentwood chair, 'although, given he's engaged Dick, it's probably going to end up costing him whatever money he has left.'

'And they say crime doesn't pay,' said Cecile disapprovingly. 'It certainly pays for lawyers.'

I flicked open my hardcopy of the *Bugle*, and cracked the top of my egg.

'Why was Dick talking to you about David Wynne-Estes?' said Cecile.

'He's scheduled to be in court with me this morning. He wants to move a motion to have the case against David struck out.'

'On what grounds?'

'On a tricky point of international law.'

Cecile had put down her spoon and glared at me, as if to say: 'Are you being condescending?'

'Forgive me,' I said. 'Dick says I have no right to hear the case, on the grounds that David's wife went missing in international waters.'

'And therefore you don't have jurisdiction?'

'Correct. Dick intends to argue that this case is outside my jurisdiction.'

'And what do you say?'

'Well, I don't know yet, do I? As I say, Dick's due in court in an hour. I'll hear him out, I suppose, and I guess I'll decide then.'

* * *

Tap-tap.

Tap-tap-tap.

'Order,' I said. 'Order in the court.'

The room fell silent. I put down the gavel and directed my gaze towards a young man with a septum piercing, in the courthouse media seats.

'Now, I'm going to say this once,' I said in my sternest voice. 'This is an open court and there is no question of whether you, as members of what we still call "the press", are entitled to be here. What you're not entitled to do is make an unholy racket. One more peep or ping or bling or zing out of any of you bloggers or tweeters or Instagrammers or whatever you call yourselves … you'll be out on the street.'

The young man with the piercing glared back at me, as if to say: 'And who exactly are you, old man?'

Who am I?

He had not actually asked the question, yet I was tempted to answer: I am Judge L. Samuel Pettit, and I have been presiding over this court since you were in diapers.

I've seen it all, including the decline of the mainstream media. Now, I have no objection to the New Media. I don't tend to put a ban on devices in court. I have no real objection to your ribald headlines like DIRTY DAVID DOES HIS BUSINESS ON THE KITCHEN FLOOR.

It's all good, as my grandson would say. What is not good is the noise you make while you tweet and post and gram in my court.

'I'm sitting here trying to listen to the evidence, and all I can hear is ping, ping, ping. It has to stop,' I said. 'So please, put your devices on silent. Now, Mr Van Nispen, you may go on.'

Dick van Nispen is one of the oldest lawyers still working in the Bienveneda justice system, not that I can talk. I'm one of the oldest judges working at the Bienveneda Courthouse.

Between us, we've probably seen every conceivable human failing – and its comeuppance – on display.

Dick had been standing by the defence table, waiting for me to finish.

'Thank you, Judge Pettit,' he said in his sonorous voice. 'As I was saying …'

What had Dick been saying?

Essentially, that David Wynne-Estes couldn't come to trial in Bienveneda. Never mind that David was a prominent Bienveneda businessman, never mind that his wife grew up here (although not in the same neighbourhood, obviously), and never mind that he had two little girls born at Bienveneda Private.

Apparently he was untouchable.

As most people know, David's wife disappeared off a luxury cruise ship. Less than a day later, his mistress, Lyric Morales, was found dead in the kitchen of her apartment in an affordable housing development, behind the Lemon Grove.

Two deaths in two days? It never looks good, yet there was no shortage of lawyers in Bienveneda willing to bet that David would walk free.

Why?

Three reasons.

First, the case against him – that he murdered his wife – was entirely (and I do mean entirely) circumstantial. I would hope that everyone understands what that means? The police had no direct evidence of David's guilt. They had precisely no witnesses.

Second, the police didn't have a body, or indeed a murder weapon, and therefore they had no cause of death. If you can't say how somebody died or even where, how can you say she was murdered?

Perhaps Loren Wynne-Estes got washed overboard.

Perhaps she tripped and fell.

On the other hand, maybe she was feeling desperate – David was claiming that she had flown into a rage before the cruise and killed his mistress – and didn't want to live anymore.

Also, even if the police or the District Attorney could prove that David tipped Loren over the edge of the ship, did he do so deliberately? Maybe she went over trying to escape him?

Third, there was the question of jurisdiction. Loren disappeared from a ship and that's always tricky. By rights, jurisdiction lay with Holland. The *Silver Lining* had been in international waters when Loren left her cabin, which was about as close as anyone was going to get to the time that she disappeared, which let Mexico off the hook. Holland was not remotely interested in prosecuting the case and had eagerly offered the brief to the District Attorney in Bienveneda. David's team was of course going to object to the merry handing over of a murder trial, and I was the judge sent to sort the mess out.

David wouldn't have to be in court; the press had still turned up in droves.

Dick was there to argue the negative and it pleased me to see him, for I do love Dick's face. The deep lines. The worried forehead. The wisps of grey hair greased over the sunspots on his balding head. We greeted each other warmly. I've known Dick for nigh on thirty years. We're members of Bienveneda Golf, Sail and Tennis.

The Bienveneda District Attorney's Office had gone with a newcomer, Sandy Ruiz, to argue the affirmative. I can't say I know Sandy all that well. Like me, she is not from Bienveneda – one can live in this town thirty-odd years and not be considered a local – although she does live Low Side, which is interesting.

I say that only because it's a fair commute from the Low Side to the Bienveneda Courthouse, as most of the people who appear before me already know, and I don't mean the lawyers.

My wife, Cecile, is a fan of Sandy's. I'm not convinced she – Cecile – has ever seen her in action in the courtroom, but she's impressed by the idea that Sandy is Low Side.

'How tenacious must she be to rise to the DA's office in a place like Bienveneda,' she mused, when news of Sandy's appointment broke in the *Bugle*.

Innocently and maybe stupidly, I said: 'Maybe she came through on a diversity program?'

That earned me a glare.

'You should show more respect,' said Cecile. 'Men in your position – you have no idea how difficult it is for a woman trying to rise. Sandy has no rapport with you, the way somebody like Dick does. You won't be playing golf with her after hours, will you?'

'She's very welcome at the club.'

'Her name is Ruiz,' said Cecile. 'She can't join the club.'

'I don't see why not.'

'Then you don't see anything.'

For the record, my wife is from Bienveneda. Cecile was born at Bienveneda Private and schooled at Bienveneda Grammar. Her father, Brennan Chambliss, served as a judge of the Superior Court in the 1970s; her mother, Stacey Chambliss, was a founding president of Booster Club. There is no royal blood in this country, but that makes her Bienveneda royalty.

My own background is more mutt than pedigree: I was educated in the LAUSD elementary school before I got the scholarship into a private school, and then another scholarship into law school, where I met Cecile.

Our son, Brandon, likes to say Cecile's my Uptown Girl, like the Billy Joel song. We graduated on the same day and got married a week later, with Judge Chambliss presiding.

Cecile's affection for Sandy may stem from the fact that Cecile hadn't pursued her intended career, mainly because we had three children, including Edith, who gave us some trouble, and that slowed Cecile down.

By the time she was ready to return to the workforce, a career in law was out of the question. Cecile could do the work – she's far smarter than me – but not the hours. She went into social work, instead; for a while there, she worked at Grammar, work she characterised as 'the lonely and the rich, crying on my shoulder'.

'Sandy Ruiz will give that Dick van Nispen a run for his money,' Cecile told me.

I couldn't disagree.

'Maritime law is very clear,' Dick said, tapping his cane ever so lightly on the court's smooth, cement floors. 'This vessel – the *Silver Lining* – was registered in Holland. As such, the flag state is Holland ...'

I listened. Dick has a soothing baritone. I was going to say that I could listen to that voice for days except that with Dick, that's a real possibility. He charges by the hour; he can indeed go on for days.

I've developed a few tricks over the years to keep myself awake when he's in court. I'll pinch the skin on the outside of my left thumb, or else I'll turn my feet in their shoes, ten times clockwise, ten times anti-clockwise. I'll point my toes up towards the ceiling, and then down towards the floor. But at some point, even those tricks stop working.

'Now, Mr Van Nispen,' I said, 'I'm sure you'll agree that you've been on this point for quite a while. I get your drift. I really do. And now I'd like you to wrap this up.'

'We can indeed wrap this thing up right now, Judge Pettit,' said Dick, spreading his arms wide. 'My argument is a simple one. This court does not have the jurisdiction to hear this case. Loren Wynne-Estes is a person overboard, but she's not overboard in Bienveneda. She's not overboard in California. She's not overboard in the United States of America. She's overboard in places unknown. Where exactly, we don't know, but she certainly isn't here. And this, therefore, has nothing to do with you, Judge Pettit. Much as you'd like to claim the case, much as the press would like to hear it, it's got nothing to do with you, or me, or with any of us. We have no right to be here, even discussing it. Jurisdiction for this matter lies elsewhere.'

'Very well,' I said. 'Ms Ruiz?'

Sandy rose. She has a reputation for plain speaking that Grammar girls do not as a rule enjoy.

'We have every right to be here,' she said. 'Holland has formally relinquished its jurisdiction over this matter and my office has accepted the brief. This trial should be heard in the United States.'

Looking directly at Dick, she added, 'Forgive me, Mr van Nispen, but your client is using you – or this action, anyway – to try to get away with murder.'

The bloggers and tweeters in the back seats tittered their approval.

Sandy resumed her seat.

Dick rose, and smiled. 'Oh really?' he said. 'That's quite a big call. You're assuming that we all know what happened on that ship, which strikes me as rather odd. I, for one, don't know what happened, and unless you have some powers of insight unavailable to the rest of us, you don't know either. You can speculate. You can point the finger. You can gossip. But you can't know for certain.'

Sandy snorted. It was only a little snort, but it was definitely there.

'Oh yes, you can do that. You can snort. You can roll your eyes,' said Dick in his big voice, 'but let's examine this courtroom, shall we? Who don't you see? Loren's own family. Her father. Her stepsister. They've been making a song and dance about David being responsible for her death, but look around you.'

Dick spread one arm around the court in a movement that was almost ballet-like.

'So, come on. We've all seen cases like this on the TV. Where does the victim's family sit? They sit right here, don't they?' he continued, pointing his cane towards the front row of seats. 'Right here, in the front, that's where they sit.'

Dick turned to the people in those seats – a middle-aged man, his wife, and her sister – saying: 'But let's see … you're not Loren's family, are you?'

The family giggled and shook their heads.

'No, you're not. You are seated where Loren's family should be sitting, but you're not her family,' said Dick. 'Loren's father, he's not here. Loren's stepsister, Molly – where's she? Not here. So, where are they? At home, watching television? Walking the dog? We don't know, do we? All we know is they aren't here. Which is odd, because it's not like they don't know about the case. They've been talking about this case to the media. Not just telling their story but also selling their story. And if we consider some of the things they've said in their interviews, we can quickly figure out why they're not here. Loren's family told the media that they would not come and sit in court because they think my client is going to get off. That's a quote! That's a direct quote. They think that David is going to get off and they can't bear to watch. How about that? Not even Loren's family think there's enough evidence to convict my client.'

I smiled to myself. Not for nothing is Dick van Nispen known as Tricky Dick. Loren's family had sold their story to *RealNews*, but that was in an effort to get the police to take some action. To my knowledge, they haven't sold a story since then. The quote that Dick was talking about came from some comments Molly had given the *Bugle* after Dick had announced his intention to move a motion to have the whole case thrown out.

'If it comes to trial – and it should – we will be there every day,' Molly had said. Like Loren, she's only little, and her face was pretty much hidden by the forest of microphones. 'But we absolutely won't sit there and watch David get off on a technicality.'

She meant, during this preliminary stage.

She meant, while they're all so busy arguing about the jurisdiction.

Tricky Dick!

'Okay,' I said, banging my gavel. 'I think we've heard enough of that, Mr Van Nispen. Let's get back to the main point, shall we? You say that we can't hear this case. Who do you say can?'

'Well, if it's anyone, it's Holland,' said Dick.

Sandy rose, saying: 'The government of The Netherlands – which is the correct term – has transferred this matter back to the United States.'

Dick moved his head slowly from side to side, like a big old bull. 'As they say in the South, that don't matter.' (Dick's not from the South; he lives seven doors up from Cecile and me.)

'Why doesn't it matter?' I said. 'Ms Ruiz is right. The Dutch aren't interested. And who can blame them? This happened in international waters. What are they going to do, send a team of investigators from Holland to the Baja Peninsula? It's not practical. It's not logical. So what would you have me do? Charge over there and put a clog up their behind?'

The bloggers liked that.

Dick wasn't amused. 'You know, Judge Pettit, you don't actually have to do that,' he said. 'In point of fact, you don't have to do anything. That's precisely my point. You don't have to do anything. Under maritime law – some of the oldest law in the world – this is not our business. You know it, and I know it, and my friend from the DA's office also knows it.'

Sandy made to rise.

'It's alright,' I said, moving my hand so that she sat down again. 'I've heard enough. Mr Van Nispen, I don't want you to worry. I'm not going to scold you for insubordination, although you probably deserve it with a remark like that. I respect you. You've put up a good fight, but now it's time for me to put you out of your misery.'

Dick resumed his seat, with his cane lying flat over his white trousers.

'Let's consider the facts here. The Dutch have jurisdiction, but they don't want it, and I don't blame them,' I said. 'They've handed the case to us. You say we shouldn't take it, and you're relying on ancient maritime law to make your case. Good for you, Mr Van Nispen, but let me tell you what I'm relying on. I'm relying on decency. This young woman, Loren Wynne-Estes, was born in Bienveneda. She was born in this town. Raised in this town. She went to school here, she married here, and she had those little girls here. They're Grammar girls! You're on the Grammar board aren't you, Mr Van Nispen? It doesn't matter. The point is, Loren Wynne-Estes is missing. She's a local woman and she's missing. How can you, in good conscience, say that it's none of our business? Of course it's our business. Who else's business could it possibly be?'

Dick began swinging his big head from side to side again, as if to say 'no, no, no', but he knew what was coming.

'Of course it's our business,' I said. 'It's not only our business, it's our responsibility. What happened to this woman? We need to know. Her girls need to know. I'd go so far as to say that your client needs to know if, as you say, he has no idea what happened. So the answer is yes. Yes,' I said, banging my gavel again, 'in the matter of *The People* v *David Wynne-Estes*, this court claims jurisdiction. Let's bring the matter to trial.'

* * *

'You did good,' said Cecile.

She was seated in the far corner of the floral sofa doing the *Times* crossword. She hadn't looked up when I entered the room, but a smile played on her face.

'Why thank you,' I said, moving towards the bar, 'and now it's over, and so is my career.'

'Tosh.' Cecile put the folded newspaper aside and removed her reading glasses. 'You're leaving the bench. You can still work in the law.'

'Ah, but can I?' I said, holding a seventieth birthday bottle of whisky up towards the light to see what remained. 'I'm only saying I would've liked to have seen this one through to the end,' I continued, taking a glass down from shelves built at eye level over the bar, 'and instead I have to hand the matter to a girl who wasn't born when I graduated from law school.'

'She isn't a girl,' said Cecile. 'She's a lawyer. A grown woman. Now, stop moping and turn on the TV so we can watch David Wynne-Estes bury his wife.'

Bury his wife?

Yes, indeed. While I'd been in court, David had been at home, preparing to bury Loren. If that sounds macabre, it absolutely was, because it wasn't like they had a body.

About a week earlier, David had given a short press conference to explain his motivation.

'My lawyer, Dick van Nispen,' he'd said, 'intends to move a motion saying Bienveneda court has no jurisdiction in this matter. He has, however, advised me that we have a no better than fifty-fifty chance of winning, and as such, it seems that I must prepare myself for what is likely to be a long, drawn-out trial.'

David paused. 'I'm also advised that if we lose the motion – and we might – I will be taken into custody. Now, as most of you know, I have two small children. Girls. Twins. Hannah and Peyton.'

David paused again, to touch the corner of his right eye. 'Night after night, my girls ask me, when is Mommy coming home? I have dodged and weaved because I just haven't wanted to answer, but now it seems I have no choice. I'm to be charged with murder. As such, anyone can conclude that my wife – Loren – must be dead. And if she's dead, then the time must have come to bury her.'

'Why is he doing this?' Cecile had asked. 'Is this part of some plan to soften up the jury?'

I had no idea.

'Given that I have only a fifty-fifty chance of the motion to dismiss being granted, I propose to hold Loren's funeral on the day that my lawyer is in court. We will wait for the judge's decision, and then proceed.'

Cecile couldn't wait to watch.

* * *

'You two look like a couple of rap stars.'

I'm quoting our son. That is what he said the first time he saw the black leather viewing chairs with the extended foot rest, the walnut panelling and drinks holders I got to go with the mega-widescreen I got for Cecile's seventieth birthday.

'Your mother likes to binge-watch,' I said.

And it's true. She does. We both do. We like it more than reading books in the evening, mainly because neither of us can see the text anymore. We like it more than crosswords, because, ditto. We got into it with *Breaking Bad* and *Mad Men*, before moving on to *House of Cards* and *Orange is the New Black* (a very realistic look at a female prison, I thought). We haven't watched *Game of Thrones* (too much violence).

In any case, we meandered from the sitting room into what Cecile now calls the Viewing Room. I took my whisky; Cecile prefers gin-and-tonic, but usually only after four pm.

'But I guess I can make an exception,' she said, 'for your last day on the bench.'

I settled down with my footstool right up, and the chair reclined.

'How can you even see?' said Cecile. 'You're nearly horizontal.'

'I can see fine,' I said, putting the chair back up a little.

The funeral hadn't yet started but Fox9 was running what it called 'exclusive, uncut footage' from Liz Moss's earlier interview with David – bits and pieces that maybe hadn't made it to air the first time, including what they described as a 'dramatic revelation', so we settled back to watch that. I do like Liz. She's got what they call the Voice of Experience.

'How old would she be?' I asked. Because I mean, Liz was an ABC war correspondent during the first Gulf War. That's, what, forever ago. Yet her show still starts with shots of Liz in tight cammo pants and a press vest.

'She'd be a fair age, now,' said Cecile, 'not that you'd ever be able to tell. She's holding up okay, don't you think?'

Me? No, and I wasn't just saying that because Cecile was there. Living in Bienveneda, I see a fair bit of plastic surgery. Mainly boobs. Big melon boobs. Whatever floats your boat, but in my opinion, women ought not to touch their faces. They're trying to stay young, but they don't. No, in my considered opinion, most women who have their faces stretched just look scared.

The promo finished, and David came onto the screen.

'Look at his hand,' cried Cecile, pointing. 'Is that his wedding ring?'

'Good spot,' I said.

David was wearing his wedding ring. I'd heard on the grapevine – it starts and ends at Bienveneda Golf Club – that he'd employed image makers for the interview. The ring was undoubtedly part of that, and they'd had it buffed to make it gleam before the camera.

'Good touch or bad touch?' asked Cecile.

'Hmmm ... good touch?'

'Yes, I think so,' said Cecile. 'A wedding ring says: "I'm a family man. Never in a million years would I kill my wife."'

I'd already been warned that Liz didn't have her combat boots on for the interview. She started by saying, 'This is a crime that has received a lot of attention. It seems that everyone has an opinion. We all think we know what happened. But now, in your own words, David Wynne-Estes, please tell us what you think happened.'

David paused, and said: 'I can't believe I'm even saying this, but I think that my wife decided to take her own life.'

He was not crying exactly, but his lip trembled.

I glanced at Cecile. She was not buying it.

Liz pressed on. 'And why do you think that?'

David rubbed his forehead. 'This is hard for me.'

'Take your time.'

'I suppose the reason is obvious,' he said. 'She wasn't thinking straight. Not before the cruise, and not during the cruise. But it's still hard for me to face up to the fact that she didn't want to be with me or with her children anymore because, whatever anyone thinks, Loren and I loved each other.'

'The hide of him!' said Cecile, sipping her gin.

David dabbed at his eyes. 'Loren's family has been flinging mud at me. Loren's stepsister, Molly, and her father, Danny Franklin ... they're wanting revenge and I suppose I can understand that.'

I looked over at Cecile. 'How's he doing?'

'He's doing okay,' she said, shrugging.

Liz said: 'Loren's father has told the world he doesn't believe a word that comes out of your mouth. So I guess I have to ask you ... are you a liar?'

The question seemed to hang for only a second.

'Yes, I am,' said David. 'I lied to Loren about my affair with Lyric Morales. I told her it was over when it wasn't.'

Cecile scoffed. 'She's under his spell.'

'And just for the record,' said Liz, 'what else have you been lying about?'

'Nothing else,' said David adamantly. 'I promise you, Liz, I've given up telling lies. Lying gets you nowhere. It has cost me everything. So no, I'm not lying now. I'm telling the truth: I did not kill my wife.'

'That can't be it?' said Cecile, eyes wild. 'He got off pretty easy.'

'That's not the whole interview,' I said.

'No, but it's all we get to see before the funeral, which I can't wait to watch,' said Cecile, rattling the ice in her glass.

I rose to get her a refill.

'Shame on you,' I said. 'I've never known you to be so ghoulish.'

'Everyone will be watching!' she protested, and she wasn't wrong.

Everyone would be watching, and tomorrow they'd be gossiping. Bienveneda had the Wynne-Estes bug and why not? The case had everything: David was rich and Loren was beautiful. The mistress was a siren and the girls were angelic.

Here was evidence that awful things could happen to beautiful people; that the big house and the expensive cars can be that old cliché, the glittering façade.

Plus, sex tapes!

Let's not forget the sex tapes. Ever since David's interview, all of Bienveneda had been abuzz with gossip about the sex tapes.

'I can't believe that the police were reluctant to investigate Lyric's death lest the tapes got out,' I said, returning to the room with Cecile's gin-and-tonic. 'It seems to me that the police believed David's story. Why wouldn't they? He was ready to plead guilty to being an accessory. That carries jail time, or at least, it might. Does David strike you as the kind of person willing to go to jail to protect the reputation of Fat Pete Evans?'

'So Pete *is* on the tapes,' said Cecile.

'I didn't say that. I have no idea. That's just what people say. But anyway, are you sure you want to watch the funeral?' I added, even while settling into my extravagant chair to watch it. 'Burying an empty coffin for the theatre of it? That seems wrong to me.'

'I want to see the empty coffin,' said Cecile. 'I want to see David bend over the flowers on top of the coffin and whisper something, and I want the microphone hidden in the flowers to pick up what he says.'

'What makes you think the police will bug the flowers? I'm not sure that would even be admissible.'

'Well, if they don't, they should,' she said, taking a satisfied sip of her drink.

A Fox9 logo zoomed across the screen along with a photograph of Loren. The funeral was about to start.

'We're coming to you live from the little church in Bienveneda where Loren Wynne-Estes was married,' said Liz.

'Oh look,' said Cecile. 'It's Liz again!'

'Shhhh ...'

'And you can see here, a centrepiece inside the church is a photograph of Loren on her wedding day,' Liz continued in a reverential tone.

'She's so pretty,' Cecile murmured.

The Fox9 cameras zoomed back to show different pictures of Loren, including one in which she was wearing Breton stripes – I know what they are because every woman at Bienveneda Sail owns a boat-neck top with Breton stripes, Cecile included – with her hair swept up in a ponytail, and David's arm wrapped protectively around her shoulders.

'He's so creepy,' said Cecile.

The cameras zoomed away from the photographs, and back into the church. It seems that David's team – I'm guessing it was his team – had been busy all morning, tying yellow balloons to the posts at the end of each pew.

'What's with all the yellow?' said Cecile, because the casket was likewise laden with yellow flowers.

I had no idea.

'We'll just do a sweep over the guests,' whispered Liz, 'and I think we'll find that Loren's father and stepsister are not here.'

The cameras swooped, and Liz was correct: Daniel and Molly were not there.

'But we can see here, David's parents, Belle and Garrett Wynne-Estes,' whispered Liz. The camera lingered. Loren's parents-in-law sat stiffly near their son. They wore dark suits, and their lips were drawn thin.

'Are you sure we don't know them?' I asked.

'I wouldn't think so,' Cecile said immediately. 'They aren't from here.'

'They live on this road,' I said.

'It's a long road,' she replied dryly.

David's regal sister, Janet, was next to fall into Fox9's all-seeing viewfinder.

'Is that really a pillbox hat?' said Cecile. 'She's like something out of *The Godfather.*'

'And now, here, we see the little girls,' said Liz, her voice more hushed than ever.

Hannah and Peyton were seated near the very front, to the right and to the left of their father.

'Now, they've been dressed by somebody who knows what they're doing,' said Cecile approvingly. From what I could tell, the girls had come as flower girls. Their dresses were white satin; they had wide yellow sashes, short socks, and polished black shoes.

'Why all the yellow?' Cecile said again.

Liz must have heard. Quietly, she said, 'And notice there, Hannah and Peyton also have the yellow in their sashes ... yellow being Loren's favourite colour.'

'He made that up,' said Cecile.

You can probably guess what colour David had chosen for his tie. Red. No, I jest. More yellow. The camera did another swoop over the audience, pausing here and there to pick up other bits of yellow.

'Ooh, the Grammar girls have yellow ribbons in their hair,' said Cecile. The Grammar moms hadn't let the side down. They'd come with sunflowers.

'Not one of them supports David,' said Cecile confidently. 'He's become an absolute pariah. They're there for Loren.'

David's team had placed a simple rostrum on the stage, near Loren's coffin. There were a number of speakers. Liz's voice came on during breaks in speeches, reminding the audience at home that the matter of jurisdiction had been decided just hours earlier, meaning David would face trial.

'Oh, come on,' said Cecile. 'I only want to see the murdering bastard.'

The Fox9 cameraman seemed to get that. He spent much of the service with his lens trained on David, who sat with his arms around his daughters, who took turns resting on his chest and weeping.

'Such a scene!' said Cecile.

When time came for David to speak, he rose, kissed each of the girls on the parting of their hair, and whispered something to each of them. Behind the rostrum, he heaved a heavy sigh. 'I don't want to be here,' he said. 'Burying my wife ... it's wrong.'

'Of course he doesn't want to be there,' said Cecile, 'if she wasn't *dead*, he wouldn't be charged with murder.'

'The fact that we all have so many unanswered questions just makes things so much harder,' David continued. He looked up to the ceiling. 'But somebody knows the answer,' he said, pointing upward. 'Our awesome God knows the answer.'

Fox9 had been carrying tweets from home along the bottom of the screen, and Twitter at this point exploded: tweets like '#spareme' were typical.

Looking out towards his daughters, David continued. 'Hannah and Peyton, I'm speaking directly to you now. Whatever gossip you might hear, your mom loved you. She really did. She loved you from the bottom of her heart. When she found out she was pregnant with the two of you – that was the happiest I had ever seen her. And the joy when you arrived ... oh, yes, she loved you to the moon and back.'

Cecile's expression was priceless.

'What do you think?' I asked, amused.

'I'm thinking: lucky I'm not there, I'd pick up a cucumber sandwich and hurl it in his face. Now shush.'

David was still speaking. 'My darling girls, I know you're finding it hard to accept that Mom is gone. But she is gone, and we have to accept it.'

The Fox9 cameraman did a sweep back across the audience. The twins were weeping uncontrollably. Janet had taken up David's seat between them. She mopped their tears with yellow tissues.

'Now I'm going to show you some photographs to help you remember your mom,' said David, stepping back to allow viewers to see photographs rolling along the big screens in both corners of the church. There were pictures of Loren and David on their wedding day; photographs of Loren in a lopsided tiara, seated on the now famous gold throne; photographs of Loren pregnant, with a delighted David pressing his hand against her belly; of Loren cradling the two babies at once; of David and Loren boarding the *Silver Lining* with champagne glasses in their hands.

'Oh, he's so gross,' said Cecile.

The photographs faded to black. A pastor stepped up, hands folded gently in front of white robes. Pallbearers – David included – got to their feet.

'They're not going to need eight men to carry the coffin,' cried Cecile, 'it's empty!'

They assembled nonetheless. Dolly Parton's version of 'I Will Always Love You' began to play.

'Look at them, look at them,' said Cecile, 'the coffin is so light it's wobbling everywhere.'

The cameras zoomed in on David's face. He was to the right-side front of the coffin, with tears streaming down his cheeks. Behind him came the girls, also weeping. Aunt Janet stepped forward with her hard face, using her handbag to usher them towards a waiting limousine.

David did not join them. He waited for their car to be halfway down the hill before clearing his throat, a signal that he wanted to speak. Reporters gathered round with iPhones and microphones.

'You've no doubt heard the news,' he said. 'Our motion in court this morning – it failed. I won't be able to speak to you again before the trial, so I'm using this – my last few moments of freedom – to make it plain: I did not kill my wife. Loren did a dreadful thing in killing Ms Morales, but I would've continued to support her for as long as I was able. Instead, I stand accused of doing my wife harm. Never in a million years did I expect to be here, saying, "I'm looking forward to my day in court." But I am. I'm looking forward to clearing my name and returning to my family.'

The camera watched as David got into a second limousine and went down the hill. He didn't get far. Sandy Ruiz had done a deal with Dick van Nispen in my courtroom to take David into custody immediately following the funeral. The police waited for the limousine to pass the corner down the hill before flipping the lights atop the patrol car. David's limousine stopped. The driver got out and opened a rear door. David stepped out and put his wrists together, on went the cuffs, and off David went, into custody, to await his day in court.

* * *

The original, domed Bienveneda Courthouse was destroyed by fire in 1998. The new building is modern. I would say stark, but that is a cliché. My chambers are adjacent. By chance, I was there when the telephone rang. It was my clerk, Ben Tandberg, saying, 'I've got San Francisco on the line.'

San Francisco?

The California Superior Courts are headquartered in San Francisco. Judges sit in fifty-eight locations across the state, Bienveneda being one of them. I'd sent my letter of resignation to San Francisco on the day of my seventieth birthday as required by Californian law and, as per tradition, I was due to leave on 30 December of the year in which I turned seventy.

Dick van Nispen's motion to dismiss was to have been my last day in court, and the last of my responsibilities as a judge. I was in the process of placing books into boxes and googling the best way to store my robes when the call came in. Could I stay?

To say that I was flummoxed would be to understate it. The judge who had been announced as my replacement, Rebecca Buckley, had become ensnared in a scandal involving her domestic staff. An investigation by the *Bugle* had revealed that her nanny and housekeeper were undocumented. According to the *Bugle*, Rebecca had also failed to pay their health insurance and withhold their taxes.

That's one, two, three offences right there. She couldn't take the appointment.

I put down the phone and called Cecile.

She sympathised with Rebecca. 'Maybe they had fake papers. How was she to know?' she said.

'Judges are held to higher standards.'

'The rules work against women. If Rebecca was a man, she'd have a wife. But wives don't get wives.'

'The question is, do I stay on?' I said. The decision would mean taking on the Wynne-Estes matter.

'Oh dear,' said Cecile, 'although it'll certainly be satisfying, seeing David go to prison.'

I wasn't so sure he would go to prison. The case was as flimsy as it had been when Dick's motion came to court: there was still no body, no witnesses, and no cause of death. Not that it mattered what I thought. Judges don't decide the outcome of murder trials; juries do.

Judges preside. Juries decide. That's my mantra.

I accepted the appointment and soon after accepted another call from my clerk. The *Bugle*'s editor-in-chief, Marguerite Herrera, had an idea.

'I feel we almost missed an opportunity, and now we're saved. This will be your last big case,' Marguerite said.

'It will.'

'I've always wanted to ask a judge to chronicle their experience. It's difficult because nobody wants to do it while they're still sitting. But you're retiring. So I'm asking you. Take daily notes. We'll turn them into a special for *Bugle* readers – INSIDE THE MIND OF THE JUDGE.'

I sat, contemplating. 'It's rather unorthodox,' I said.

'That's what will make it readable. The judge sits through the whole trial yet we rarely get to hear what he or she thinks. I'm not asking you to say whether you think the jury reached the right verdict …'

'I should hope not,' I said.

'But I am asking you to comment on the process. Take us into the mind of the person who has to sit there, presiding over the circus.'

I laughed. Marguerite wasn't wrong. A trial can be a circus.

And so it was agreed. I would take notes.

'Maybe start by saying how you feel about being asked to take notes,' Marguerite suggested. Very well.

Twenty-seven years I have been a judge in Bienveneda. Never before have I been asked for my opinion on the justice system. So why now? The *Bugle* says it's because I'm retiring and therefore I can speak freely. That may well be right. But the truth is that few trials have excited our town like the Wynne-Estes murder trial.

And why is that?

I say it's because we live in a town divided. Literally and figuratively. Our town is divided by the Bienveneda River, but that's not all that divides us. Income divides us. Race divides us. How many African-Americans live on the High Side? Not many. How many of my neighbours turn up as defendants in my courtroom? Hardly any. Who do I see in court? Mainly people from the Low Side of town. Why is that? We kid ourselves that we're better over here: better parents, with kids in better schools. Can that really be the reason? The Low Side lives much closer to the poverty line than we do. People ask me if race plays a role. Of course it plays a role. Sit in court every day for years, and you'd be forgiven for thinking that African-Americans commit more crime than white folk, but it's not so. African-Americans are more likely to be charged and brought to court; less likely to get off with a warning. It's a subtle but important difference.

Besides being African-American, most of the offenders I see are in poor health. The circumstances in which they live – poverty, mental illness, alcoholism and illiteracy – are ugly. Occasionally, I'll say: 'How do you plead?' The defendant might say: 'Why does that matter?' None come with lawyers. We have to give them lawyers. The press isn't interested; the *Bugle* occasionally sends a junior reporter into court to file some brief items for the CRIME AND PUNISHMENT page. I can count on the fingers of one hand the number of times I've seen a TV camera in the back of the court.

This case is different. It involves beautiful people with a great deal of money. The defendant is – or was – a successful businessman. He presents well. The crime of which he stands accused is ugly, but he's not. He's white. He's fit. He's handsome. His parents are upstanding members of our community. They have a fine home on the same road I live on with my wife, Cecile.

Will the outcome be different for him? A number of people are betting that it will. I've seen the odds that the bookies are giving: three-to-one, David Wynne-Estes walks. I can understand that. The case against him is weak and that is certainly one of the factors that we need to take into account, but what else is different? Mr Wynne-Estes has top-class representation. He has a team of people working on his public image. He doesn't look like the kind of man who belongs in prison. Will he end up there regardless? Time will tell.

* * *

DID HE DO IT?

That was the headline on the first page of the *Bugle* website on the first morning of the first day of the Wynne-Estes trial.

Cecile, sitting opposite in our atrium with her egg and her juice, asked: 'Who wrote that? And come on, what's his or her verdict?'

My eyes scanned the page for a by-line. They're not always easy to find on the web.

'Aaron Radcliffe,' I said, 'he's only been at the *Bugle* about a year, but he's broken some good stories on this one.'

'Must have a good source,' said Cecile, winking and biting into her toast.

Gossip around town was that he had struck up a friendship with Molly Franklin. He'd been spotted, by a rival publication, helping one of Loren's girls out of Molly's car in the Kiss-and-Go at Grammar. The Department of Child Services in Bienveneda had granted Molly temporary custody of Hannah and Peyton when David went to prison. Janet had protested, saying, 'Their mother left the girls with me when she went to Mexico, which must surely be taken as a signal of Loren's intentions, should anything ever happen to her.'

The problem with that argument was that Loren had signed a legal document back when the girls were born, saying Molly should have custody of the girls in the event that neither she nor David were capable of taking care of them (one imagines that she hadn't figured prison time for Dad into the equation).

Janet's counsel – Dick van Nispen – argued that note was signed when Loren was new to marriage and motherhood – and to the High Side.

'Loren was still getting used to her new situation when she signed that note,' said Dick. 'These girls have spent their whole lives on the High Side. They'd be able to stay in their own home on the High Side if they stay with their Aunt Janet. She has the means to take care of them.'

Buried in that argument was the idea that Loren had grown apart from her family after she married David. Her life – and the girls' lives – was conducted entirely on the High Side, with occasional visits to her father on the Low Side. The High Side was where Loren shopped and socialised, and it was where the girls went to school. Molly occasionally visited Loren at home, but did Loren visit Molly in her condo? Not all that often.

As arguments go, it wasn't a bad one, but Dick still lost. ('I'm not having much luck, am I?' he said, over rattling ice cubes at the Nineteenth Hole, after court that day.) The document Loren signed when the girls were born was legally binding; had she wanted her girls to grow up on the High Side with Janet, she needed to have said so.

As I understood it, Molly hadn't moved to accommodate the twins. They were all squeezed into her little condo, with Grandpa around the corner. Not fancy, not flash, but in all the circumstances, probably not a bad outcome.

What she'd told them about their dad, I couldn't say. No question, Grammar would be doing its best to shield the girls from gossip, but there's only so much a school can do.

'So, come on, what does Aaron Radcliffe say?' asked Cecile.

I cleared my throat and began to read aloud from the newspaper: 'There is one person who knows for certain whether

Bienveneda businessman David Wynne-Estes murdered his wife.'

'Oh, really?!' said Cecile.

'That person is David Wynne-Estes.'

'Ah,' said Cecile, disappointed. 'I see. I thought they were going to reveal some super new witness. Do they predict an outcome?'

'Not overtly,' I said, skimming the text. The tone of the article clearly suggested that David was guilty, but the *Bugle* had been leaning that way for a while.

'There's a quote from me,' I said.

'Oh yes?' said Cecile. 'What do you say?'

I took a quick sip of coffee and began to read again: 'This will be the last trial in the long and distinguished career of the judge, L. Samuel Pettit, who has agreed to keep a journal for the *Bugle*.

'"I will go into court with an open mind," Judge Pettit says. "There has been a great deal of publicity and gossip surrounding this case, but everyone is entitled to a fair trial and I will be working to ensure that's what happens for Mr Wynne-Estes."'

'Very good,' said Cecile, nodding approvingly. 'Now, off you go and get yourself to court.'

I rose from the breakfast table. It's a timber table, built long and narrow, and able to seat ten, although it hardly ever seats more than two these days. In rising, I lowered my head to place a light kiss on Cecile's raised hand. It's one of our traditions.

As a judge, I'm entitled to a car and driver, but my habit has long been to drive my own car to the courthouse. The new building sits above an underground car park; I can glide right in and make my way up in the elevator. The building is, as I've said, quite modern. There are seven courtrooms, all identical in their furnishings – the walls are blonde wood; the seats are pale blue – but Court Five is extra large, for cases like this one.

Ben was standing ready to help me into my robes. The clerk's job is also to ensure that all my notes are in order. Court goes into session at ten am, but anyone who wants to be inside should be seated before that.

'Is the public gallery full?'

'Yes, Your Honour,' said Ben. 'Some people have been waiting since before dawn.'

'Are the families here?'

'Yes, Your Honour.'

'His and hers?'

'Yes, Your Honour.'

'And they have reserved seating?'

'Yes, Your Honour.'

'And the press seats? Are they full?'

'Yes, Your Honour.'

'Well then, please go in and remind them to turn off their phones.'

'Yes, Your Honour.'

I waited for Ben to return before striding down the corridor to the courtroom. I won't shy from this, it's a magical feeling, having everyone rise and fall silent upon the clerk's opening the door to announce my arrival.

I've been at pains over the years to ensure that power – I'm the most important person in the room – hasn't gone to my head. Cecile had been generous in her desire to assist in this regard (now, where do I find one of those winky emoticons?).

I gathered my robes around myself, and settled into the high-backed chair.

'Court is in session,' said Ben.

The court manager – his identity changes from one day to the next, depending on rosters – strode across the courtroom and opened a side door for David.

David Wynne-Estes has been described in the *Bugle* – and online – as tall and handsome too many times to count. He is indeed tall and handsome. I knew him slightly; we are – or were – members of many of the same clubs. Flanked by burly armed security, he did not look particularly tall. Nevertheless, he was the star attraction, so all heads turned to watch as he made his way not to the front but to the back of the courtroom. In Bienveneda, the defendant sits at the back of the court, directly facing me. His chair – an ergonomic chair like mine, although not as high in the back – sits within a three-sided, bulletproof Perspex box. The box is open at the front, so the defendant can see and hear (and, I suppose, breathe). He sits behind a desk, made of the same blonde wood as the table for the attorneys, with a modern microphone – thin, like a black straw – screwed into the top.

David reached out and bent and tapped the microphone, as if to see whether it was working – it was – but thereafter he left it alone.

David seemed to be doing extremely well, given the circumstances. He hadn't been in prison all that long and he hadn't yet put on, or taken off, any weight (either is possible, depending on whether one can stomach the food; also depending on how much use one makes of the gym). He was wearing a terrifically expensive suit, but who besides those who routinely wear terrifically expensive suits would have known that? To most people, the suit would simply have said: 'I accept that this is a serious situation, and I am taking it seriously.'

Predictably enough, his tie was yellow.

There was no sign of David's daughters, for which I felt grateful. Little girls should not under any circumstances have to sit through their father's murder trial, and doubly so when the victim is their mother. Then again, it's amazing what some image makers put up as ideas to win the jury's sympathy.

The defendant's sister-in-law, Molly Franklin, was there with Loren's father. David's new girlfriend was also there, sitting right in the front row, with Janet, and David's parents.

His new girlfriend? Yes, the *Bugle* had already outed David for having a new squeeze. Cecile assures me that Cody Kim is her real name. Cody had platinum-blonde hair. Her cardigan was pink. Her bosom swelled perfectly. The first time Cecile saw her picture in the paper, she said: 'She looks like Betty Draper. Where did they find her? She's so perfect.'

'Perhaps she comes from Sally & Sons?'

'I'd put nothing past them,' said Cecile. 'They could well have a closet full of girls who look exactly like that for occasions exactly like this.'

I must admit to being perplexed as to why David would want a new girlfriend.

'Isn't that a bad idea?' I asked.

'Oh no,' said Cecile. 'It's a fine idea. It's a subliminal message to the jury: "Look at this lovely lady. She believes me. Why not you?"'

I glanced over at the jury. They were six men and six women, all suitably, sombrely attired. At least one of the six men was indeed focused on Cody, and not in a bad way.

I turned my attention back to the court. Besides the girlfriend, it seemed that we were to be blessed with a daily performance by David's new lawyer, Tucker the Texan (after losing on the maritime argument, poor old Dick had been given the shove).

Tucker's real name is J. Tucker Bingham, III. Is he Texan? I heard a rumour he was from Tennessee. I guess it doesn't matter.

As he himself says on his website, Tucker is about the best defence that High Side money can buy. There are people within the Bienveneda legal community who will tell you that Tucker is a tool, but I quite like him. No, I do. I like him. He looks the part, if the part is that of the Texan. He has a good head of white hair. He brings his hat into court. He isn't allowed to wear it, yet he still brings it in and lays it on the table. He wears a suit built around the idea of a safari suit, with boots. The boots have amethyst detailing.

With court in session, I read out the charge – first-degree murder – and I asked David: 'How do you plead?'

David leaned forward. 'Not guilty,' he said.

The bloggers and tweeters in the back row tapped hurriedly at their screens: David Wynne-Estes has entered a not-guilty plea ...

'Very well,' I said. 'Let's begin.'

* * *

'Well, I don't think I've ever seen such an attractive jury.'

Tucker the Texan was standing in the middle of the courtroom with his thumbs in his pockets and his hat on the table.

'No, I'm serious. Look at you folks,' he said, looking directly into the eyes of each of the twelve jurors. 'What an attractive bunch you are.'

The jurors grinned. Probably they knew better than to be seduced and yet couldn't help themselves, not with Tucker standing there like Colonel Sanders, grinning right back at them. Tucker's strategy – and I've seen him do this more than once – is to appeal not to me, not to the noisy press in the back row, but directly to the jury. To their intelligence, their better natures, their collective maturity, and to their sophistication. It's a clever move.

I've seen plenty of defence lawyers – especially the younger ones – go the other way. They address the jury, but in doing so, they bore the jury. Worse, they badger the jury.

Tucker the Texan, he flatters the jury. And why not? It's their vote he needs, not mine. It's the jury he needs to win over, not me, and not you, following on Facebook. He doesn't need you. He needs the vote of every single person on the jury. As such, he goes after them like a presidential candidate.

'Now, I want you to know that we screened you people pretty well,' Tucker said. 'And not only for your looks. We need you for your brains. I mean, maybe there's been a more attractive jury put together in Bienveneda, but I don't think so. No, I'm messing with you! Don't let me mess with you. What I mean to say is, you're good people. I know that. You wouldn't be here if you weren't. You're interested in justice. That's obvious. And you already know quite a bit about this case. You can't help that. You're smart people: you read the newspapers, you watch the news. You've heard this and you've heard that, and maybe you've already got an idea in your mind about whether or not my client here is guilty.

'Well, I'm here to tell you, he's not. He's not guilty. Yes, yes, the media says otherwise, or implies otherwise, but you're not going to subject this man to a trial by media. That's not part of our Constitution. We're going to try him on the basis of the facts. We're going to try him in accordance with the law. And you're going to come to a verdict based not on what you've seen or heard to date, but on the basis of the evidence presented to you in this court. So, thank you for coming. I mean that. Thank you. It's a big job you've got in front of you, but we know you're up for it. We screened you just right.' Tucker took his seat.

Sandy rose from hers. 'Yes, ladies and gentlemen of the jury, welcome,' she said briskly. 'My name is Sandy Ruiz and I hope you're all comfortable. We may be here for several weeks. I'm not going to try to flatter you. I would prefer to simply lay down some facts: the victim in this case is Loren Wynne-Estes. Loren was thirty-five years old when she went missing from the cruise ship, the *Silver Lining*. She was married, with five-year-old daughters that she adored. Their names are Hannah and Peyton. They aren't with us today. They are in the care of Loren's sister, Molly. Before she disappeared, Loren was living what many of you will recognise as a High Side life. She had a large home on Mountain View Road, with Pacific Ocean views from every room. There was a fleet of luxury cars in the garage. Loren was luckier than most of us, in that she didn't have to work ...'

I was beginning to wonder where all this was going, when Sandy turned suddenly to the jury and said, 'Why would Loren give all that up? My argument will be that she wouldn't, and she didn't. Her husband, who was intent on blaming Loren for his own heinous crimes, pushed her to her death. Now it's your job to make sure he pays for that crime. Thank you very much.'

How long did it take Tucker to demolish that argument? About thirty seconds.

'Why would Loren give all that up?' he asked, pacing the courtroom. 'Why would she step deliberately off that boat? What was her alternative? Life in prison?'

Sandy got to her feet. 'Objection,' she said.

'I know, I know,' said Tucker. 'I know what you're objecting to. I'm not supposed to say that Loren is responsible for the death of her husband's mistress. I'm not supposed to say that, because she's never been found guilty of that crime and she never will be. And that's fine. Let me make it clear to the good folk on this jury that Loren isn't guilty of that crime. You'll hear her husband saying that he came across her committing the crime, and you'll hear Ms Ruiz here move to strike that, and you might even hear Ms Ruiz say that Loren didn't do it because the defendant did, and he's in fact guilty of not one but two murders, but you don't have to make a decision about any of that. All you have to decide is whether David killed his wife. He says he didn't and I believe him and when all is said and done, I'm confident that you'll believe him, too.'

'Very good,' said Sandy, 'but Judge Pettit, I really think we should state the rules ... Loren hasn't been found guilty of any crimes. She's an innocent woman missing from a ship. I'd like the jury to understand that.'

'Yes, I agree. You need to cut that out, Mr Bingham. You're not going to stand in my court and flat-out call the victim a murderer.'

Tucker was chastened, but soon brightened. 'Well, maybe I'll just say that Loren had quite a bit going on when she boarded that ship,' Tucker said cheekily. 'Is that acceptable, Judge Pettit? May I say that? Loren's marriage was a mess. Can I say that? Her husband had been having an affair. Oh, come on! We all know that, don't we? It's been in all the papers. He was having one hell of an affair with a younger woman. Not only that, Loren had just found out that her husband – this man here, in the witness box – was not only an adulterer, he was broke. Hard to believe, looking at him, that he's broke, but that's what my people tell me. They warned me, before I took his case: "Tucker, he's broke."'

One of the jurors laughed, and I admonished him with a frown.

'Forget what you've just heard from my esteemed colleague. Loren didn't have it all. On the surface, yes, on the surface, she was a pretty lady with a High Side home and an upcoming tennis lesson. Beneath it all, she was a woman on the edge of despair.'

The jury looked interested. No more or less than that. I glanced at my iPad. The tweeters in the back of the court were doing a running commentary under the hashtag #wynneestes and readers were joining in. I scrolled through some tweets. As far as I could tell, public opinion was still running firmly against David.

One tweet said: YES she had two beautiful children. Why would she kill herself? He obviously DID it.

Another said: Disgraceful … killed his mistress blames his wife and is trying to get away with it.

But there was also this, from an anonymous user: Is David Wynne-Estes guilty of murder? No. I know David, and it simply isn't possible.

I stored that one to my favourites. It wouldn't be the first tweet ever written and sent by a PR company, but I hadn't yet seen one quite as lame.

* * *

There isn't space in the kind of account I'm giving to go over what each and every witness said. Suffice it to say that the first part of the trial – after the two opening statements – were taken up with expert testimony of the type that never makes the newspapers. Dry stuff, like what constitutes an expert in Man Overboard surveillance systems, and what constitutes an expert in the tides and currents in that particular part of the world.

The rest of the trial would be what I call speculation.

Did David have a motive? Well, sure, if he'd already killed Lyric and was planning to blame Loren, of course he did.

Was David the last person to see Loren alive? Presumably yes, since nobody else had come forward to say they had seen her on the deck.

Was David on the lower deck long enough to locate Loren, push her over and then carry on as if he was searching for her?

Sure, of course he was, because how long does it take to push somebody? Seconds, but then again aren't we pre-supposing that Loren was standing at the railing?

Did she see David rushing towards her? We don't know. And if she did see him, why didn't she scream?

You see what I mean, I'm sure, about it all being speculation. Nobody had a clue what had happened to Loren after she reached the end of that corridor and disappeared.

It was Sandy's job to make the jury believe that David had been involved in her death.

She seemed to believe it, passionately.

* * *

Many times in that first week, my attention wandered to the jury, comprised of six men and six women. All were white; most were middle-aged, although one of the women had turned eighteen just four months before the trial began. She had not yet started college. The middle-aged women tended towards cotton trousers and polo shirts; the young woman wore fitness gear, and had a stripe of purple through her hair.

On Monday of the second week, I started to see one of the middle-aged men enter the court kneeling on one of those brilliant new wheelchairs for people with ankle injuries. He had twisted his ankle during weekend sports. It was painful, but if the court could provide him with a chair to rest it on, he would be happy to continue his duty.

The second week mostly comprised witnesses able to set the scene for the jury. This included lessons in geography (the *Silver Lining* set sail from Cabo San Lucas, a resort village on the southern tip of Mexico's Baja Peninsula at latitude 22 degrees, 53' 23" north and longitude 109 degrees, 54' 56" west, and so on) and physics (it takes at least thirty minutes to slow and then stop a ship the size of the *Silver Lining*, by which time, any object – a body included – may have drifted at least as far again in the opposite direction).

From my vantage point on the bench, I saw jurors stretch and yawn and flex their feet. Some witnesses were better than others, in terms of holding their attention. Some topics were more interesting than others. Questions as to why Loren's body wasn't found were addressed to a marine scientist who noted the sharks.

One of the jurors shuddered.

'Oh, I know it's horrific,' said Tucker, 'but that's the truth of it.'

It's all very necessary, in terms of clarifying what happened and where, but in truth, the jury snoozed – not literally – through most of it, as they patiently waited for each side to put its case.

By the third week of David's trial, I found myself living in a house divided. Cecile – following mostly on Twitter – remained convinced of David's guilt.

'I sit and watch him every day,' I said. 'I don't see him through the filter of television or social media. I see him in the flesh. He seems to be in agony. He's under pressure. But he never looks guilty. I know the difference. It's compelling to watch.'

Cecile snorted. 'You've been snowed. You're a victim of the charm offensive,' she said.

'Now you're being unfair,' I said.

David struck me simply as one of those men raised with towering expectations by parents who gave him every opportunity and never let him forget it: the money we spent on your education ... we expect you to make the most of the opportunities you've been given ... we sacrificed so much for you ...

The bulk of Cecile's work as a school counsellor at Grammar had been with teens wilting under precisely that kind of parental pressure. They grow up driven to succeed at almost any cost. David's whole life had been about demonstrating how well he was doing.

You won't be surprised to hear that Cecile did not agree with me.

'Loren was a lovely young mom trying to hold her marriage together,' she said briskly, 'and David would do anything to get out of a fix.'

Our breakfasts – which for so long had been pleasant in the pretty atrium by the kitchen – grew tense.

* * *

'How many of David's witnesses are being paid to be there?'

Cecile had wandered away from our breakfast table to peel the skin off a mandarin. We were deep into week four of the trial. Fatigue had set in: how long would this go on?

There is an urgency in the community that cannot be allowed to infiltrate the courtroom. I felt the public's hunger for a verdict. To many, the outcome seemed obvious, but it is neither right nor fair to rush.

David Wynne-Estes was entitled to his day in court; each and every witness is entitled to be heard in a thoughtful way.

Tucker the Texan had spent the previous day quizzing psychologists. Cecile was quite right, most of them were paid by David's team to be there.

'It's quite proper and legal,' I said.

'But does the jury understand that they're paid?' asked Cecile.

'Indeed they do,' I said. The District Attorney, Sandy Ruiz, had pointed it out for them.

'Could a man who planned this type of vacation for his wife – a soothing, romantic vacation – also be planning to kill her?' Tucker had said, resting his hand on his hat.

'Oh, no, I wouldn't think so,' the psychologist had replied.

'You know he's paid to say that?' Sandy had asked the jury.

'Objection,' Tucker had said wearily. 'He's not paid to say that. He's paid to be here. Big difference. He's a professional, being paid for his time. He's here giving an honest, professional opinion.'

'I think we're done with psychologists,' I told Cecile, 'and we're moving on to people who were on the ship.'

The press seemed relieved. Paid witnesses don't make for good copy. The ship's captain would surely be more interesting? And so it proved but only to a point. The captain came to court in a white uniform with gold on the shoulders and a chest of medals. What those medals were for, I couldn't say.

What had he seen? Precisely nothing.

'But weren't you there on the night of the Captain's Dinner?' asked Sandy, vexed.

'The Captain's Dinner is a dinner for two hundred people,' he replied. 'I remember Mrs Wynne-Estes because she was beautiful. She wore blue. I remember that. I can't remember how much she had to drink. I can't remember seeing her leave. I can't say more than that. This is a tragedy for her family.'

The ship's surveillance expert came to the stand. He explained that the *Silver Lining* didn't have a Man Overboard detection system. Such systems have been developed, but they are far from perfect and very few ships have them.

'A bird can set them off,' the expert said, 'as can anything tossed from a balcony or deck.'

'But isn't that the point?' said Sandy, prowling the court. 'To know when something has gone overboard?'

'The cruise industry has twenty million customers a year worldwide,' he said. 'We lose maybe fifteen people to Man Overboard events. It's a tiny percentage. And it's almost always deliberate.'

'Almost always?' repeated Sandy.

'Tragically, yes.'

The same expert explained that it was not possible to have every inch of the ship covered by security cameras.

'There are cameras in elevators, the hallways, and in the disco area; there are cameras in the gaming room, to deter card counters. But you can't have them covering every inch of every deck.'

The jury saw footage from the corridor outside David and Loren's cabin. It was black-and-white and grainy. Loren came out of their cabin with her hands in the back pockets of her white jeans, palms facing outward. She went down the corridor without looking back.

'Does she look like a woman about to take her own life?' asked Sandy.

It seemed an odd line of questioning. The jury could not see Loren's face. The footage had been shot from behind. Then came David, moving at speed.

'Does he look like a man about to kill his wife?' asked Tucker, but again, who could tell?

* * *

Day two of week five, Molly took the stand.

'If you could please state your name?'

'Melinda Franklin, but people call me Molly. I'm Molly Franklin.'

'Welcome, Molly,' said Sandy warmly. 'And if you could describe your relationship to the deceased?'

'I'm Loren's sister,' said Molly. 'Technically, her stepsister. But we were very close. Loren's girls – they live with me now.'

I glanced at the jurors. Having endured the expert-witness testimony – currents, camera angles and so forth – they were warming to Molly as a real person with much at stake.

'That must be difficult?'

'Oh, no,' said Molly quickly. 'They're wonderful. And they're a wonderful reminder of Loren. It's like seeing Loren when she was a girl. They're pretty and kind. Loren had them at Grammar and that's expensive, but together with my dad, I'm doing what I can to keep them there.'

'You're trying to pay the fees yourself?'

'Yes, and it's not easy,' said Molly. Wryly, she added: 'The school say they're "all about the child", but in my experience, so far, anyway, they're "all about the money".'

Several of the jurors exchanged knowing smiles.

'All right,' said Sandy. 'Now, Miss Franklin, I understand that you booked this vacation for Loren, is that right? You booked the flight, the villa, the cruise ship that Loren was on when she went missing?'

'I did,' said Molly ruefully.

'And I'm wondering, Molly, what did Loren tell you about this particular vacation? Did she explain what it was for?'

'She said it was a second honeymoon.'

'And did Loren say why she was going away on a second honeymoon?'

'She didn't,' said Molly, 'but I realise now that it was because David had been cheating. She was trying to save her marriage. Why she'd want to do that is beyond me, and it's beyond Dad, too. David didn't deserve somebody like Loren.'

Tucker rose from his seat. He had different boots on: these ones were Cuban-heeled with pewter toecaps.

'Now, let's just cool down,' he said. 'That's some pretty tasty opinion you're offering the court, but just so the jury understands the context here, your relationship with my client, even before his wife went missing, it's never been warm, has it?'

'David treats anyone from the Low Side like they're a piece of gum stuck to the bottom of his shoe,' said Molly indignantly. 'He's a snob. The whole family are snobs, like they don't have to sit down and poo.'

A juror laughed before stopping himself.

Tucker didn't object.

'So you're not much of a fan of Mr Wynne-Estes,' said Sandy.

'Me? No,' said Molly. 'I don't like him, not at all.'

She was looking at David with real distaste. David, seated behind the blonde-wood desk, didn't take the bait. His expression stayed neutral.

'And why is that?' asked Sandy. 'Why don't you like him?'

'Why would I like him? He was horrible to my sister,' said Molly.

Tucker rose. 'Careful,' he said, flashing a smile that seemed to come with a diamond ping.

'Oh, I'll be careful,' said Sandy. Collecting herself at her table for a moment, she said: 'Miss Franklin, we're talking now about the time before Loren went missing. What I'm trying to get from you is a sense of what their relationship was like.'

'I would say terrible,' said Molly. 'David's big thing was to call Loren fat. We were sitting by her pool in our bikinis this one time. She pulled two handfuls of her tummy up over her bikini bottom, saying: "David says it's disgusting." It wasn't disgusting. Her skin was loose because she'd carried twins. I said, "Don't be so hard on yourself. Those gorgeous girls came out of that body." She said: "That was two years ago and I've still got a stomach like a hundred-year-old woman. Isn't it supposed to bounce back? David wants to know when I'm going to get back into my sexy underwear." I said: "Tell him to shut up," because I just don't think a husband should harass his wife about how she looks after she's had his babies for him.'

One of the jurors – a woman about Molly's age – smiled at her.

Encouraged, Molly went on, 'People think Loren had everything. The nice house, the nice cars ... but being married to David ... I can't see how anyone would enjoy being married to somebody who didn't take care of them when they were pregnant, didn't help with the children, didn't try to boost their self-esteem, and who cheated with a woman in his office.'

'Thank you,' said Sandy. 'Thank you very much, Miss Franklin.'

Tucker got to his feet. He took a few steps this way, and then a few steps that way, before launching into his defence.

'Now, I mean no disrespect, Miss Molly, but when Loren went to Mexico, did she leave her girls with you?'

'Well, I wanted to take them ...'

'No, no, no,' said Tucker, gently shaking his head. 'No, it's a simple question. Did she leave the girls with you? Yes or no?'

'No.'

'No? Then who did she leave them with?'

'With their Aunt Janet.'

'With their Aunt Janet. I see. Not with their Aunt Molly but with their Aunt Janet. Who is my client's sister, am I right?'

'That's right.'

'Well, I have to say, that surprises me,' said Tucker. 'That surprises me because you've just finished telling us how close you were to Loren and yet she didn't leave her daughters with you when she went away. She left them with her husband's sister, Janet.'

'Yes, but that was because ...'

'No, wait,' said Tucker. He stopped pacing and spoke firmly but gently. 'I ask the questions, and you answer them. That's how things work in the good ol' Bienveneda Courthouse. I ask, you answer. And I didn't ask you a question. But I'll ask you one now. David's sister, Janet ... she lives much closer to Loren than you do, am I right?'

Molly said: 'Yes, and that's why ...'

'No, see, here we go again,' said Tucker, smiling (ping!). 'We don't want "and" and we don't want "ifs" or "buts". We want "yes" and "no". That's all. "Yes" and "no". Loren Wynne-Estes's sister-in-law, Janet Wynne-Estes, lives close by to Loren on what we locals call the High Side?'

'Yes,' said Molly, grumpy at being restrained.

'And you live Low Side. So, over that bridge,' said Tucker, waving an arm in that direction, 'a fair way from where Loren lived?'

'Right, and that's why ...'

'No,' said Tucker. 'No. The point I'm making is that you say that you're close to Loren, and that's what you'd like the jury to believe, but how can they believe that? You don't live near her. She didn't leave her daughters with you when she went away. You had to go to court to get custody of them because they were actually in their Aunt Janet's care when Loren went missing, isn't that right?'

Molly looked peeved. 'That's not right—'

'I'm sorry, Miss Molly?' replied Tucker. 'That's not right?'

'No, I mean, they were, but—'

'No buts,' said Tucker. 'They were in Aunt Janet's care when Loren went missing because that's where Loren left them. With their Aunt Janet. Not with you. And one more thing, you've testified that David was awful, and David was dreadful, but the fact that David was having an affair – that wasn't something you had any idea about before Loren went missing, was it?'

'The fact that I didn't know about it doesn't make him any less horrible,' said Molly.

'No, it doesn't,' said Tucker, 'but the fact that you didn't know about it shows us that Loren didn't confide in you about it. You say you're close, but when Loren was having problems in her marriage, she didn't come to you, did she?'

'No, because she knew what I would say,' cried Molly. 'I'd say leave him. I'd say you deserve so much better.'

'Forget that. That's not the point,' said Tucker, very cross now. 'You carry on like you're close. You're not close. You didn't know anything about Loren's life. You weren't the person that

Loren trusted with her children when she went away. Loren told
you nothing about the trouble she was having on the home front.
You're sitting here, pretending to have insight into this marriage,
and into your sister's state of mind, but let's be honest. You have
no idea.'

* * *

Molly turned to the bench. 'Could I have some water, please?'

'Of course,' I said, signalling. The court manager came
running with a pitcher.

'Do you feel alright?' I asked.

Molly had been seated in the witness box for about an hour.

'I'm fine,' she said, 'I just needed some water.'

Tucker seemed pleased. His point had been to rattle Molly's
belief in the closeness of her relationship with Loren, and he had
perhaps succeeded, but Sandy wasn't done with Molly.

'I'd like to talk to you about an evening that you spent at
your sister's house a couple of days before she left for Mexico,'
she said.

'Stepsister,' said Tucker, rising.

'Yes. Stepsister. Now, may I go on?' said Sandy, vexed.

'Please,' said Tucker, sweeping into a bow.

'Yes,' said Molly. 'That was the night we got the takeout
chicken.'

Sandy stepped back to the District Attorney's table, where
she ran her hand over an open binder.

'Yes. I'd like to talk to you about the night you got chicken.
That was three or four days before Loren was due to fly out
of LAX?'

'That's right,' said Molly, taking another small sip of water.

'You went to Loren's house?'

'Yes. She was making out a schedule for the girls: what time they had to leave for school, and so on. And the girls were anxious saying, "Why do you have to go, Mom?" And Loren was doing her best to make the whole thing seem like an adventure for them, too. She said: "You know what we're going to do? We're going to have takeout!" And the girls couldn't believe it. Takeout was a no-no at Loren's house,' Molly said, wagging her finger to stress the point. 'Loren was a very healthy person. A farmers' market person. She and the girls mostly ate all organic. So takeout was a big treat.'

Sandy nodded. 'And Peyton and Hannah – they perked up after that?'

'A little,' said Molly. 'Peyton was given the job of finding the takeout menus in the kitchen drawers, and she seemed excited about that, but then she put the menus down and looked a bit sulky and said, "No, because I don't want you to go." Loren took her by the shoulders and said: "Listen to me. It's only a few days. And we can Skype." And Peyton perked up again, saying: "They have wi-fi on the ship?" And it was so cute, because you know, the girls are not that old, but they know how to connect to wi-fi. It all comes naturally to them.'

Sandy put a hand down on the binder on her desk. 'And then Loren told the girls that they could have takeout?'

'Yes,' said Molly. 'Fried chicken, potatoes and salad. Hannah was rapt but Peyton couldn't, or wouldn't, decide what salad she'd like. She kept saying: "Can I come with you? Can I decide when we get there?" and "Can I sit in front?" Like she needed to be with her mom every second. Loren said to me: "Are you okay here, if I go with Peyton?" I said, sure, and I would set the table, so Loren scooped up her keys, and David ...'

'You mean the defendant?' asked Sandy.

'Yes, the defendant, David. He was sitting on the sofa with his back to us, reading his iPad, which frankly wasn't that unusual because he was never not reading his iPad. That is all I ever saw him do. Loren said something like, "Hey, babe, we're going to get some fried chicken." She had her hand on David's shoulder, but as far as I could tell, he didn't even respond. She had to ask him again – something like: "Anything else I can get you?" – because David didn't respond. He was tapping and swiping at the iPad. I remember thinking if he was my husband, I'd whack him one.'

One of the jurors – middle-aged and probably married or divorced herself – laughed. Not loudly, but in my view, that was a bad sign for Tucker. Or, I guess, more accurately, for David.

Molly seemed buoyed. She sat a little higher in the witness box. 'David had that glazed look people get when they've been dragged away from their computer screen. He was like: "Fried chicken?" Loren had to repeat herself again, saying, "Yes. Special treat. Would you like anything else?" David was annoyed, like, you interrupted me to talk about chicken? And then – and I will never forget this – he just said: "Whatever."'

'So, this is not quite a picture of domestic bliss?' said Sandy.

'Oh no,' said Molly, 'no, no, no. But then it was often like that. David was often mean to Loren. Really mean. Rude. Disrespectful ...'

Tucker got to his feet. 'My oh my, are we going to go through this again?' he said. 'We are not interested in your opinions, Miss Molly.'

'You know, Mr Bingham, I think you'll find that the witness's name is Miss Franklin.'

Twitter exploded with **Woo hoos!** and **Go yous!** and so on.

Tucker smiled and sat down.

Sandy turned her attention back to Molly. 'I'm sorry. Please go on.'

'Well, I'm not sure what else to say,' said Molly, shrugging. 'Loren took Peyton to the store to get dinner. I guess they were gone around half an hour. And now that I think of it, I don't recall David speaking to me at all during that time. He was swiping away on his iPad but not offering to help with setting the table or anything like that.'

David rolled his eyes at the jury. I thought: *Bad move, bad move, bad move.*

Sandy seemed delighted. 'Please go on, Molly,' she said.

'Well, Loren came home with enough food for an army. The girls crowded around and Loren hadn't got the fried chicken, she had got a whole chicken. That was more like Loren. She started to carve and oh, I remember! She extracted the wishbone, and that was exciting. Loren told Peyton, "You can have it. Now, close your eyes and make your wish." And they were both silent for a bit, while they each made a wish, and Loren said: "Okay, now, pull." And they pulled, and Peyton tugged hard and Loren, being the mom, didn't really tug at all. That was Loren's theory: when you play games with the children, they should win. Not like David, who would smash them at Scrabble and then laugh about beating five-year-olds. So the bone broke, and the big part was Peyton's. She was ecstatic. She was saying, "I won! I won!" And Loren was so happy, saying: "Good girl. Did you make your wish?" and Peyton said: "I did," and Loren said: "Well, don't tell anyone or it won't come true," and I said: "Make sure you keep that safe, and your mom can take her part on the ship, and when she gets back you can put them together again," and Peyton said: "Maybe not," and Loren said: "What do you mean, maybe not?" and Peyton didn't say anything, but looking at her, I knew exactly what she meant. Her wish had been for her mom not to go.'

* * *

There is a turning point in every trial, and with David's trial, it came when District Attorney Sandy Ruiz wheeled two empty suitcases into the court.

Tucker the Texan stood up. 'Objection,' he said.

I waved at him to sit down. 'You knew this was coming,' I said.

'I want my objection on the record,' he said, wagging a bent, white finger in the direction of the court stenographer.

'It's on the record. Now sit.'

Tucker sat. Sandy wheeled the two suitcases into the centre of the courtroom. I stretched up in my seat and peered over the bench. One of the suitcases was a black Samsonite, 100 per cent polycarbonate with a scratch-resistant, micro-diamond finish, guaranteed for life. It had four spinners – wheels that turn the full 360 degrees – and a brushed metal, side-mounted combination lock.

The other suitcase – well, was it even a suitcase? More like a travel bag. It had four sturdy wheels on the base, but it was collapsible, with zips that would allow somebody to make it bigger and then bigger again.

'Ladies and gentlemen of the jury,' Sandy said, 'you have been sitting in court for a long time. I thank you for your patience and your attention. I need a little more of the latter because these suitcases are an important part of our case. Please take a good look.'

Some of the jurors shuffled forward in their seats.

'Now, with this big one, some of you can probably tell that this is an expensive case. In fact, it retails for nine hundred and eighty dollars,' said Sandy.

A couple of the jurors raised their eyebrows at each other, as if to say: '*Woo-wee, that's expensive.*'

'Yep, that's a lot of suitcase,' said Sandy, reading their minds, 'and that's a lot of money. Although, probably not to the defendant ...'

'Objection,' said Tucker, rising slightly from his seat.

'Withdrawn,' said Sandy. 'Still, you get a lot for that money. For example, look how light this case is,' she said, using the top handle to turn the case a full 360 degrees, 'especially when it's empty. But is this case empty? Let's see, shall we?'

Sandy's junior got up behind the defence table and helped her place the suitcase gently on its side. The jury watched, transfixed, as the two of them got onto their knees and unzipped it, leaving it open like a clam on the floor.

'Yes. Here we go,' said Sandy. 'This case is definitely empty.'

One of the jurors stretched up in his chair. As far as I or anyone else could tell, there was nothing in the case but elastic cross-straps, and silky lining, billowing up like clouds.

'Now look at this second case,' Sandy continued. 'It is much smaller, but hey presto, when you start undoing these zips' – she began doing just that – 'it expands and expands, and by the time you're done, why you could almost fit a whole person in here.'

'Oh, objection,' said Tucker, exasperated.

'How can you object to *that*?' said Sandy. 'That's just a fact.'

Tucker glared, as if to say, 'Why *wouldn't* I object to that?'

'That's leading the jury,' he said.

'Well, fair enough,' said Sandy, putting a hand on her knee for balance as she got shakily to her feet, 'fair enough. I'd be objecting to this case being in court if I were you, too.'

She smiled. Tucker was in no mood to smile back. Sandy looked up at me, and said: 'May I?'

'You may,' I said.

Sandy turned to her junior, who left the court through a side door. The jurors seemed curious. What was happening? The junior was wheeling old-fashioned medical scales into the courtroom.

'Thank you,' said Sandy. How much she knew about medical scales before the trial of David Wynne-Estes, I don't know, but she set about balancing the weights and a steel hook. She picked up the Samsonite with both hands, and hung it from the hook, and moved the weights again.

David, in the witness box, couldn't take his eyes off the scales.

'Let's see,' Sandy said, thoughtfully. 'I make that ... five pounds. Tucker, if you could confirm that?'

Tucker got up, sulkily. He strode towards the scale and gave it a cursory glance.

'You agree?' asked Sandy.

'Sure,' he said, all surly.

'We're agreed,' said Sandy, happily. 'Lovely. We are agreed on something. That's so nice. This empty case weighs five pounds. Now, if I could just ask the jury to again examine the footage of the defendant – David – and his beautiful young wife, Loren, leaving their house to go to the airport ...'

The jurors turned to look at the big screens. There, again, was footage they had seen a dozen times of David rolling their suitcases towards the car that would take them to LAX for the flight to Cabo.

'We've seen this a dozen times. My friend Mr Bingham has already explained to you why Loren looks so happy. It's not because she's heading out on a much-needed second honeymoon with her husband, who she's forgiven for his affair. It's not because she believes that her marriage is back on track. It's because she's just killed a woman and she's trying to cover it up by pretending to be happy. Ridiculous, in my opinion, but never mind that – how many cases do they have?' asked Sandy.

One juror lifted a finger and began to point and count, silently.

'By my count, they have three cases between them,' said Sandy, 'but let's count them together, shall we?' She moved her red laser pointer onto the image. 'Here we are. Loren has one – and it's a big black Samsonite, just like this one here – and here David has two, and one of them is a blue Samsonite, pretty much like the one we have here in court today, and the other ... well, it's like this collapsible bag, isn't it? It's like this bag, opened up to about half its possible size, would you all agree with that?'

The jurors reacted cautiously. Were they supposed to answer?

'No, don't answer,' said Sandy, reading their minds, 'all I need is for you to see what I see, which is Loren with one big black case, and David with one big blue case, and then David with his computer bag strapped around his body, and then this third case – a collapsible, canvas case – out on its wheels, too. And now, Your Honour, I'd like to call Naomi Linden.'

'Very well,' I said.

'Ms Linden, what is your occupation?' said Sandy. The question hardly seemed necessary. Naomi was wearing a flight-attendant's uniform, complete with a silky, corporate neckerchief.

'I work for North-South Airlines,' she said.

'Of course you do,' said Sandy. From there, she took the jury through the basics: Naomi had been on duty when David and Loren Wynne-Estes had approached her counter to check in their bags for the flight to Cabo San Lucas; and yes, one of the cases that David checked in was a blue Samsonite; another was a black Samsonite; and the third case was a collapsible case, with four wheels and canvas sides, and a steel, retractable handle on the top; and yes, Naomi was able to confirm for the jury that David's blue case had weighed fifty pounds, while Loren's black case weighed only twenty-two pounds, and as for the collapsible case, it seemed to have almost nothing in it, for it weighed only fifteen pounds.

'So that collapsible case wasn't quite empty, but it was pretty much empty when David checked it in?' suggested Sandy.

'It was.'

'And how commonly do you see people checking in almost-empty cases?'

'Oh, it's not *uncommon*,' said Naomi. 'Many people take half-empty cases when they travel. Shopping is a big part of the vacation experience for them. They know they're going to be buying things. A light case like that isn't something I'd normally be concerned about.'

'And so you weren't concerned?'

'I wasn't. In fact, I remember joking with his – the defendant's – wife: "Oh, you're going to have fun filling these up," and she said, "Yes, yes, yes."'

'Lovely,' said Sandy, and Naomi was dismissed.

Sandy turned to the jury. 'Now I'd like to show you some more footage,' she said, using the clicker to change the images on the screen. 'You've seen the defendant and his wife getting into their car with three cases. You've heard Ms Naomi Linden saying she checked in three cases. Now you see David and Loren boarding the ship. Up the gangplank they go. There's Loren, with a little frangipani behind her ear. There's David with his glass of champagne. And look here, behind them; that's one of the ship's porters, and how many cases does he have? Two! One of them is the tall black Samsonite, and one of them is a tall blue Samsonite.'

A couple of the jurors nodded. Yes, okay, the porter had only two cases, and both were Samsonite.

'So, where is the third case?' asked Sandy.

The jury didn't answer. They weren't supposed to answer. Also, how were they to know?

'Well, our side say it's inside that black Samsonite,' said Sandy, 'which was of course where it started its journey. You all remember that, don't you? David says that Loren had this case inside her big black case, ready to do some shopping, and he took it out and stuffed her clothes into it, right? The clothes she wore on the night she killed Lyric. Which, if he had them, would help to prove that she did indeed kill Lyric. Because maybe they'd have a fleck of blood or something on them. But he doesn't have those clothes. Why not? He says that when he got to Cabo, he threw them out. Why? Because he was helping Loren cover up her crime. That's what he says. What I say is that David did no such thing. I say he simply told Loren that he was going to make three cases two cases, by folding this collapsible case back into her Samsonite before they got on board the ship. And I say that we can prove that, because these suitcases were weighed going onto the plane, and they were weighed again going onto the ship, and Loren's case, when it goes onto the ship, is no longer twenty-two pounds, it's actually almost forty pounds, so it seems to me that the collapsible case is now inside this bigger case.'

Some of the jurors nodded. That seemed to make sense.

'And now, if it pleases the court, I'd like to recall Melissa Haas,' said Sandy.

A door at the back of the courtroom opened. The Guest Relations Manager of the company that owns the *Silver Lining* wasn't happy to be recalled. She had previously asked the court for permission to give all her testimony at once, rather than having to make multiple trips to the States, but that didn't suit Sandy.

'I realise this is your second time here, and I do apologise for the inconvenience,' said Sandy.

'It's fine,' said Ms Haas, smiling weakly.

'The reason I've called you back is, I need you to confirm something for me. How many suitcases did David and Loren have when they boarded?'

'Two,' said Ms Haas.

'And how many suitcases did your porters carry off the ship for David after Loren disappeared?'

'Two,' said Melissa, her lips in a thin line.

'Two.'

'That's correct. Two.'

'So two went on, and two went off?'

'Correct.'

'And, Ms Haas, just while I've got you there,' Sandy continued, 'you testified to this earlier, but just to be sure, you have checked every inch of the surveillance tapes, haven't you?'

'We have.'

'And it goes without saying that you found no footage of anyone lobbing a suitcase over the edge of your ship?'

One juror gasped.

'We most certainly did not,' said Ms Haas.

'You're sure? You've checked all the tapes? All the cameras? Every inch of every one? That's got to be a big job. A labour-intensive, time-consuming task, checking all those tapes. Maybe you missed it?'

Ms Haas shook her blonde head. 'We have examined every inch of every tape,' she said, firmly, 'as have your police here in Bienveneda, as have police in Holland. That's not the kind of thing we – or anyone – would be likely to miss. Had one of our cameras captured that, we'd have seen it.'

'Okay, but just to be doubly sure that I understand the situation correctly, you don't have Man Overboard technology that would detect an item of that size going over, do you?'

'No,' said Ms Haas.

'And you don't have security cameras aimed ...'

'At every balcony? On every deck? Into all corners and on all levels? No. Of course we don't. Nobody does.'

Ms Haas was getting cross. Sandy could sense it, too.

'Please don't misunderstand me,' she said, 'I'm not accusing you of anything, but for the jury's sake, I need this point to be extremely clear. A suitcase – an expandable case, like the one we've all been looking at here in the courtroom today – could go overboard, and you'd never know?'

'It's possible,' Ms Haas conceded.

'What did you say?'

'I said, it's possible.'

'Oh, but it's not possible,' said Sandy, smiling. 'It's much more than *possible*. Because we say that's what *happened*. A case like this one went on your ship but it did not come off.'

'I can't see how you'd say that,' said Ms Haas. 'Mr and Mrs Wynne-Estes took two cases onto the ship and Mr Wynne-Estes took two cases off. The collapsible case could still be inside the big case.'

'Absolutely true,' said Sandy. 'They took two cases on, but they left the US with three cases. We saw them do that! And we say that David took that third case onto the ship, inside one of those Samsonites. And that third case is now missing. And I think I know what happened to it. I think this man' – here, she swung around, to point a finger at David – 'put this beautiful woman' – Sandy swung back to point dramatically at the large photograph of Loren on the easel in the courtroom – 'inside a case just like this one,' she said, swinging her arm back towards the collapsible case, 'and then ...'

'Objection!' said Tucker, nearly falling over his own boots as he pushed back from the defence table.

'And then,' said Sandy, ignoring the banging of my gavel, 'he threw the third case over the edge of your ship, and watched while it sank to the bottom of the deep blue sea.'

* * *

'Your Honour, I call David Wynne-Estes.'

David got to his feet and moved towards the witness box. Every eye in the courtroom followed him.

From my position up high on the bench, I said: 'Are you a Christian, Mr Wynne-Estes?'

David said: 'I most certainly am.'

The clerk of the court rushed forward with a Bible. David closed his eyes and clutched the book to his chest, before placing his palm flat upon it, and taking the oath.

'Thank you,' I said.

'Thank you,' he replied.

I took careful note of David's stance. His shoulders were back. He stared straight ahead, towards where Tucker was standing. His hands were clasped loosely in front of his groin.

'The first thing I'd like to do is to thank you for being here, David,' said Tucker warmly. 'I know in my heart that the jury will be pleased to meet you, and to get to know you. You know, and I know, and I guess everyone knows that you don't have to be here, in the witness box. You don't have to testify. Our friend, the District Attorney, has to convince these good folk on the jury of your guilt, and to my mind, while she's made a big old song about this, that and the other, she's well short of producing any evidence that you did anything wrong. And you don't have to help her. You're innocent until that jury there says you're not, and I don't believe they can do that, not with the evidence – or lack thereof – that we've heard to date. So I thank you for stepping up. You don't have to be here, but as I understand it, you have something that you'd like to say?'

'I do,' said David. He was speaking far more softly, with much less cockiness than he had done in his TV interview with Liz Moss. He looked directly at the jury, and continued: 'I'm charged with the murder of my wife,' he said gently, 'but I'm not guilty.'

Tucker stepped forward so aggressively that at least one juror jumped. 'You did cheat on her, though,' he said gruffly.

David hung his head. 'Yes, I did,' he said, his face full of remorse. 'I did, and I'm sorry for that. I ... well, I guess I was weak. I was tempted, and I gave into my temptation, and that was sinful, and that was wrong. I prayed for strength, and yet I was weak. I should've prayed harder, been stronger.'

I could just imagine Cecile's response to that. She would be maddened that Lyric Morales was twenty-five years old yet apparently capable of bringing not only David but many a rich, grown man to his knees with desire.

'The way they paint this woman, it's disturbing,' Cecile would say. 'Like she's a temptress. A tigress. A vixen! Why don't they just say she gets on all fours and waves her hindquarters about and that's the end of any commitment that any man has made to his wedding vows. Why don't you just say she had the power to make men crumble before the power of her coochie-hoo-ha, and that she had to be stopped!'

I must say, it disturbed me, too.

'Very well,' said Tucker, 'now, I won't keep you here for long. But one thing I thought we should deal with straightaway is the matter of these suitcases. Let's talk about them. What can you tell us about the suitcases?'

David rubbed his forehead. It was exactly the gesture he had employed on television.

'My wife, Loren, she loved to *shop*,' he said. 'She was excited by the idea of bringing exotic presents home for our girls. She had promised them the world, of course. It wasn't uncommon for her to take an extra case when she went on holidays for shopping, and she'd normally fold it up and stick it inside her big case. That's the point of having one of those collapsible suitcases: you can fold them up when you don't need them and you can expand them after you've been shopping.'

Tucker said: 'So she put that collapsible case in her Samsonite, for shopping?'

'Yes. And then, after the ... the ... incident with Lyric, I dragged the collapsible case out of the closet and threw Loren's clothes she had been wearing at Lyric's into the collapsible case, and checked it onto the flight.'

'And yet, when you boarded the *Silver Lining*, you had only two cases?'

'Right,' said David, rubbing his forehead again, 'because by then I'd gotten rid of Loren's clothes.'

'And where did you do that?'

'In Cabo.'

'Where exactly?'

'I can't even remember. I walked through the heat until I found a dumpster and I threw them in there, and I watched until a guy from a restaurant came out and flung more stuff on top of it, and that's the truth of the matter.'

'And, just to be clear, you didn't dispose of those stained clothes in the collapsible case that my colleague, Ms Ruiz, has been going on about?'

'No I did not.'

'Although it would be very easy for you to say that you did, because that of course would explain why that case was missing when you boarded the *Silver Lining*.'

'Yes, but I'm not going to say something that's not true.'

'And – just so as we don't insult the good people of the jury – that's not because you don't like telling lies. Because you are a bit of a liar by nature aren't you, Mr Wynne-Estes?'

'I have lied,' said David, sighing deeply, 'and I'm paying for that now. I'm paying for that in that people don't believe me when I'm telling the truth. But I am telling the truth. I didn't throw that collapsible suitcase away, and the reason I'm not saying I did – although that would be handy – is because when the police said the case was missing, I thought, oh, sure. And they want me to come up with some wild explanation for what happened to it, so they can say, "Well, actually, we found it," and it was somewhere that I couldn't explain, so then they could say, "Why did you lie? And what else are you lying about?" So I won't lie. I didn't throw out that suitcase, and I don't know where it is.'

'If you didn't throw it away at the villa, you must have put it into one of these two Samsonite cases – the blue, or the black.'

'That's what I thought. But when the police here in Bienveneda asked me to give them that third case, well, I couldn't find it.'

'You couldn't find it?'

'No.'

'And you didn't notice that it was missing when you got off the ship?'

'I didn't notice anything. I searched Loren's things, for a note. I didn't find one. Then police in Mexico asked me to leave my cases – to take what I needed and to leave my cases – so they could continue their investigation. Maybe this was foolish, but I agreed. I had no choice. I had to get home to my children.'

'And it was two weeks before the cases came back to the US?'

'Correct. And I was still grieving. Distraught at losing Loren. Horrified by what had happened to Lyric. I opened Loren's case, and to be honest, I still didn't notice that the collapsible case was missing. I had so much to contend with, what with trying to shield the girls and with Loren's family making accusations. It wasn't until after I got charged that I was asked about it. And I can see how it looks. There's a missing case. That's bad for me. There's no note from Loren, and there's a missing case.'

'So you never mentioned to police that one case was missing?'

'No, because I didn't notice. They brought it up, as part of the investigation.'

Sandy stood up. 'I'm sorry to interrupt,' she said, 'you just said, you can see how it looks?'

'That's right,' said David.

'Just checking,' said Sandy.

Tucker resumed, saying: 'This is not great for you. This is in fact terrible for you. But it is what it is, and we need to move on. What I'd like you to do now, David, if you could, is explain in your words, how Loren was when you last saw her.'

David cleared his throat. 'Publicly or privately?' he asked. 'Because her two faces were very different. Privately, she was a complete wreck. She trembled so badly on our first night in the villa at Cabo ... it was like she was freezing cold and she could not get warm.'

Tucker said: 'And yet, on the last night of her life, she got all dressed up and went out with you to the Captain's Dinner?'

David blanched. 'Yes, because Loren was doing her absolute best to keep up our charade,' he said. 'We couldn't stay locked up in our cabin the whole time. That would have looked very suspicious. So we did our best to get amongst it, like two people enjoying their second honeymoon. And Loren was keeping up appearances, but behind the scenes she was a wreck. Yes, you can find photographs of her sipping champagne on the ship. What people couldn't see was what was going on behind closed doors. Every second of every day, we dreaded getting a call about Lyric. It was no secret that I'd had an affair with her. I was sure that the police would call as soon as she was found. We were anxious. We were frightened.

'We returned to the stateroom after the Captain's Dinner, and Loren began to drink. I urged her not to drink too much. She had been drinking every night, and she was already distressed. The alcohol made everything worse. She kept saying: "What does it matter? It's not like you love me." I was on my knees – in my suit, on my knees – pleading with her, saying: "Please, please, Loren, we have to hold it together." She drank and drank, and

her head began to loll on her shoulders. I picked her up – gently –
and put her into the bed.

'At some point, I must have fallen asleep. I was exhausted. I
had been exhausted for days. I reached out—' here, David spread
his fingers to mimic his hand feeling the bed next to him '—and
Loren was not there. Instantly, I sprang from the bed. I can't say
how or why, but I knew that something was wrong. I checked
the en suite. I went out onto our balcony. I looked over the
balcony, which I think shows that I was already dreading what
might have happened. I pulled on loose pants, a loose shirt. I did
up one button, and I hurried out of our cabin. And I searched. I
searched everywhere.

'I was in such a panic. But from the moment that I couldn't
find her,' David said, 'I knew. I just knew.'

* * *

Which way would the jury go? That was the question on
everyone's mind on the final day of the trial. The *Bugle* had a
long piece, ending with a prediction: not guilty. To my mind,
they'd have done just as well to flip a coin. Heads for guilty.
Tails for not guilty. There was no way to know. It was too close
to call.

I spent the morning speaking directly to the jury about the
responsibility that lay before them. I summarised some of the
evidence, such as it was, and I made the point that nobody could
say for certain what had happened to Loren, or to Lyric for that
matter.

I went over some of the more obvious points: an adulterer
was not necessarily a murderer. David was missing from the
surveillance tapes for only a matter of minutes. David had

nothing to gain from making Loren's death look like a suicide, because the policy would not pay out.

The foreman and his fellow jurors nodded, and retreated.

I retired to my chambers to wait. Bored, I went for a wander in the courtyard, outside the main court building. I saw Loren's family sitting at a picnic table, each wearing a splash of yellow: a ribbon, a blouse, a set of earrings.

I hurried past, not wanting them to see me.

The press had gathered in an opposite corner of the same courtyard. They were starting to get twitchy. I have developed a good relationship with some of the older, regular court reporters over the years. They feel free to speak frankly when I pass by.

'What's happening, Judge Pettit?'

'I have no more information than you do.'

'I wish they'd hurry up. We need a verdict by four pm to make the evening news.'

'I'm sure that's at the forefront of their minds,' I said.

'They'll definitely find him guilty. Definitely. There's no other verdict they can reach.'

He had no idea. Hardly anyone ever does. What the jury can or will or might or should do – it's all a mystery, until they come back. I returned to chambers. Some of the shelves were empty from when I'd packed up the books in anticipation of Rebecca Buckley's arrival. Her replacement had been announced. Brett Wagner. He's from Bienveneda. He'll do a good job.

I stood and stretched my back. I reached into my top drawer for my wallet, thinking that a bagel or Starbucks might be in order, and then the phone on my desk rang, and it was Cecile, saying: 'Are they back yet?'

'No.'

'Which way do you think it will go?'

'I wouldn't want to speculate.'

'Do not think I'm crazy,' she said evenly. 'Do not think I'm old. Do not think I have dementia. Do not judge me, but I think he's innocent!'

'I'm not sure I can direct the jury to acquit on the grounds that my wife has changed her mind.'

'Don't be stupid, Samuel! I'm being serious.'

'I'm sorry, Cecile,' I said, 'but I don't see what you want me to do?'

'You can't do anything. It's up to the jury now, isn't it?'

'Of course it is,' I said, 'it's been their decision all along.'

* * *

There is a special telephone in my chambers that rings only to tell me when the jury has returned its verdict.

'They're back, Your Honour,' said Ben.

'Thank you,' I said, putting down the phone.

I adjusted my robes over my collar and tie and made my way down to Court Five.

David Wynne-Estes came into the court flanked by two security guards. I asked him to remain standing in the Perspex box and he did. He was nervous and pale, and although doing his best to keep his hands lightly clasped in front of him, I could see that his hands were shaking.

'Ladies and gentlemen of the jury, have you reached your verdict?'

'We have, Your Honour.'

The foreman passed a small piece of paper to the court manager, who passed it up to me. It's no small matter, the business of keeping one's expression – be it surprise, or resignation – to oneself at such moments, but I like to think that I have, over the years, done my level best to betray nothing of the outcome to the accused.

Did the verdict surprise me? No. Two women were dead in horrible circumstances. David was a liar and a cheat. That was probably enough for the jury. The trial itself may even have been beside the point.

'And what is your verdict?' I said, handing back the note.

The foreman did not look at David, and that alone should have told David all he needed to know.

I did look at David, just long enough to see his knees collapse a little against the base of his chair. 'No,' he said, 'you don't understand.'

Tucker stepped in. 'It's fine, David,' he said. 'We'll be appealing.'

'Appealing?' exclaimed David. 'You said ...'

Yes, Tucker, you said this was a lay-down misère. You said they have no body, no weapon, no cause of death and no chance in hell.

The sentence?

I got through that quickly. It was life without parole. It had to be; for all their theatrics in the courtroom, Tucker and Sandy had agreed before the trial to take the death penalty off the table, leaving only life in prison.

I returned to my chambers and I was in the process of placing the last of my law books – the ones I'd needed for the trial – into a cardboard box when Ben knocked.

'Come in,' I said.

'May I assist?' he said, taking the robes from my shoulders.

'Don't hang them,' I said, 'send them out. Get them cleaned. There's a place on Main that will box them up like a wedding dress. You never know, some descendant of mine might want them one day.'

Ben bowed his head. Breaking with protocol, I stepped forward and shook his hand.

I left the courthouse as I'd arrived, behind the wheel of my own car, and as I eased the wheels from the underground garage onto the gravel drive, I was surprised to find Molly waiting for me.

'Miss Franklin,' I said, having brought down the tinted window. 'How may I help?'

Molly gripped the windowsill. Loren's girls – Peyton and Hannah – were standing behind Molly, with yellow ribbons in their hair.

'We wanted to thank you,' Molly said. She had ducked down and her face was so close to mine, I could smell her toothpaste.

'No, no, the verdict had nothing to do with me,' I said. 'I am the judge. Judges preside. The jury decides.'

Molly didn't seem to hear. 'Can you wait?' she said. 'Dad's coming. He wants to thank you, too.'

'It's not necessary …' I said.

'Please? I'll just run and get him.'

Molly released her grip on the car and ran to assist her father, who was lumbering slowly across the driveway in my direction.

I waited, trying hard not to stare at the two blonde girls with their stoic faces and their cascading curls.

'Here he is,' said Molly, returning to my window breathless, holding her red-faced father by the hand.

'Yes, we just wanted to thank you,' he puffed.

'We do,' said Molly.

Like a bumbling fool, I repeated my mantra: 'This has nothing to do with me. Judges preside. The jury decides. If you've got anyone to thank, Ms Franklin, it's the jury.'

'Well, we still wanted to say thank you,' she said, 'so, thank you. Okay. Girls, come on.' She took Peyton and Hannah by their hands, and the girls went with her.

I watched as they became specks on the landscape, and I thought to myself: has justice been served? I had no way of knowing. Was the outcome a good one? Again, that's not a question for me.

Judges preside. Juries – you, the people – must decide. I pressed the button to bring my driver's side window up, and drove towards home.

Molly Franklin

'You get justice in the next world.
In this world, we have the law ... that
is now my favourite saying!'

Observation by Molly Franklin in her personal journal

I would hate for anyone to take this the wrong way but it turns out Loren was right, it isn't at all difficult to adapt to the High Side life.

This morning was typical.

I was lying out by the pool. I had on a blue-and-white striped bikini and big sunglasses. Loren's old housekeeper – now my housekeeper – came out with juice on a tray.

Peyton came running with her foam noodle. 'Come and play, Molly,' she cried. Water dripped in a circle around her feet.

'No, no, you finish your juice, then you play with Hannah,' I said, gently.

Hannah's nanny – and you do need two – knows a cue when she hears one. She took the glass from Peyton, placed it on a side table and said, 'Come on, let's get those kickboards out!'

With that, they were off.

I leaned back on the sun-lounger, and observed them through my sunglasses. The girls are doing well. Everyone who sees them says so. They look great. They hardly cry.

The business of asking why Mom and Dad can't come home has basically stopped.

The period immediately after the trial was difficult, with Long Tall Janet wanting to push for a greater role for her family in the girls' upbringing but, as I'm their legal guardian, that is now well and truly behind us. Also, Loren's insurance has paid out and the way I've set up Loren's estate ... well, it's at my discretion.

I decided that the girls should stay at Grammar. They do look sweet in those boaters.

I decided that we should all move back into their home on Mountain View Road.

Has the odd person raised an eyebrow about that? I can't see why they would. Where are we supposed to live? In my old apartment? I don't think so.

Aaron from the *Bugle* gets on my case from time to time. His latest report was all about how I used some of the money from Loren's estate to make my gran more comfortable, which was something Loren didn't do.

My gran wasn't her gran, I guess was the excuse.

Yes, it's true that I moved her out of the state-funded Low Side place that smelled like death and moved her to The Manor, which people over here describe as 'the last stop on the High Side road to Heaven'.

Gran deserves no less, and it's not true that she's not family.

Aaron's report also had Janet complaining that my mom and dad had taken up residence in one of the guest houses here on Loren's property. Where is Mom supposed to live? She's married to Dad, who is still grieving for Loren. It's good for him to be here with the girls. It's good for the girls to have him here. He's a different influence. He can do things like keep a fire pit going.

All our lives were changed by what happened to Loren, mine included.

I had to give up the business. Yes I have the nannies for the girls but apparently heading down to Cabo four times a year so Low Side penny-pinchers can get fake boobs isn't the kind of thing a Grammar mom is supposed to do.

Also, with the staff and the house and the Grammar Booster Club board position, it's not like I don't have plenty to keep me occupied, and I won't deny that a lot of my new life is fun.

I have to remind myself not to feel guilty.

To that end, there are things that I allow myself to think about and there are things that I don't allow myself to think about.

I do allow myself to think about the desperate, garbled call I got from Loren, the day after Lyric died.

It was nine am, or thereabouts. She was calling from a number I didn't recognise. Later I found out that she still had David's secret cell phone, and just as well because imagine if the police had found that at the scene of her crime?

'Come over,' she said, 'please, Molly, come now.'

My instinct was to say: 'Oh, okay, so when you need me, that's when I get a call?' But I was always a sucker for Loren, so over I went, wondering what little job she'd have for me this time.

Holy moly, it was a doozy.

The story that Loren told me that morning was very different from the story David told the jury. He said it was an accident. I think David and I both know that's not true.

In Loren's version of the story, there was no love-making.

Loren told me that she went to bed early that night, suffering a migraine, wondering at the wisdom of trying to save her marriage.

She woke to find David gone and knew exactly where he'd be.

David's midnight trips out the back door and down through the Lemon Grove to Lyric's house were a well-established pattern, and one that he'd revealed in those stupid sessions with Bette Busonne.

Loren found him in Lyric's kitchen: David had his pants around his ankles and Lyric was bent over the kitchen bench.

Loren said she picked up the nearest implement – a kinfe – and lunged towards them. Who did she want to kill? Maybe both of them, but David sprang away and it was Lyric who ended up in a pool of blood.

'Holy hell,' I said. 'Is she *dead*?'

'She's dead.'

'Oh my God. And what did you do? Don't tell me you left her there?'

'We had to, Molly.'

'But why? Why didn't you call someone? Maybe you could have saved her.'

'I wanted to call the police,' said Loren. 'I wanted to explain. But David refused. He kept saying nobody would believe it was an accident. He'd get the blame. He'd go to prison. Or we both would, because Lyric had so much dirt on David. He talked me out of it. He wanted to get out of there. He wants us to just get on the plane and deny we were ever at Lyric's last night.'

'And what if you were seen? What if there's a camera? What if the neighbours heard something?'

'David says he'll think of something.'

'Something like what?'

'I don't know. He wants to help me.' Loren was distraught.

'Oh, come on, Loren. If David wanted to help you, he'd have a lawyer here by now. Can't you see what he's doing?'

'What is he doing?'

'He's making sure you can't say it was an accident. He's making you look like somebody who is running away!'

'David wouldn't do that.'

'How do you know? Do you really trust him to protect you when the police come calling? Because what if the police think it was him? He's definitely going to say it was you!'

She didn't answer.

I told Loren: 'Believe me, you cannot go along with David's plan. I don't trust David not to tell the police what you've done. This is a death-penalty state. You have to save yourself.'

'But how?'

I had no idea how. All I knew was that I had to step in. 'I booked you onto that ship, and I can get you off.'

'I don't get it,' she said.

'I don't either,' I said. 'But I'll figure something out. Just do as I say: get on the ship and let me think about how to get you off.'

'But what about the girls?' she asked, anguished.

'I'll figure that out. I know people in Mexico who can help us. I will get the girls to you. The main thing is to get off that ship before police come to arrest you.'

We did not formalise the details. For one thing, there was no time. For another, I hadn't worked them out myself yet. Loren would have to get off the ship. It would have to look like David had pushed her. He would have to go to prison because if not him, then her.

It was the only way.

I told Loren to make sure she kept her cell phone with her at all times. I had some Mexican SIM cards I could give her, so that we could communicate without anyone knowing.

'You don't think he's gone to the police, do you?' she said.

'What now? I don't know,' I said, 'but that's not a bad point. If you accept his help now, you will have to live the rest of your life wondering when he's going to turn you in.'

'But he loves me,' cried Loren.

I'd never believed that.

The hours and days that followed were frantic. Loren and David left for Cabo. I went back to my apartment and began making calls. I'm lucky I have contacts. The guy I hired ... let's call him Vincent. He lives in Mexico and he's good in a crisis. That's all I'll say.

I'd previously used him to help a client who went to Mexico to get new teeth and ended up in a car accident that killed the son of one of Mexico's most prominent politicians.

Sorting that out had cost a pretty penny. Not me, her. But still, Vincent had gotten it done.

Another time, he helped a client get out of prison, after the guy got caught smoking pot on the beach, two days after having penis-fattening surgery.

'What crisis do you have for me now?' he said.

I refused to say more than I needed to. Vincent didn't need to know the details. I simply told him: 'You need to get on this ship, and you need to get one of my clients off.'

'The first bit will be no problem,' he said, 'the second might take some doing.'

He wasn't wrong. Vincent was easily able to board the ship as a porter, taking a job from someone who was happy not to have to work for five days. We had this idea that he should take onto the ship an extra suitcase, not unlike the one Loren had taken for her shopping, and maybe wheel Loren off in it.

We had been watching too many movies, obviously.

'I just can't see how,' he told me, in one of his calls from the ship. 'They have cameras on this boat. I've found a few places on the deck where it's dark' – meaning, where there was no coverage – 'but how am I supposed to get her into a suitcase on the deck? People are going to see me wheeling it onto the deck, and they're going to question me. And how long is she going to be in the case before I can get it off the ship?'

Also, where would he hide the case – with panicky Loren inside – while police searched the ship?

'Your plan is full of holes,' he said.

I didn't disagree. The plan was full of holes. We thought up a few alternatives. Could Loren duck out of camera range, scurry down into the bowels of the ship, and hide among the laundry, for example?

I could practically see Vincent shaking his head, no, no, no, it was impossible.

'The biggest blind spot is on the deck. That's where she has to go missing. But your plan – to carry her off – is impossible,' he said, 'because what if this woman's husband doesn't wake early and doesn't go looking for her? She could be in that case for hours.'

'I don't have all the answers,' I said, exasperated. 'All I know is, we have to fix this.'

'Then let me fix it,' he said. Then, after a pause: 'Tell me, Miss Molly, who is this person to you?'

Who was Loren to me? That was a good question.

She was the girl who hated me as a child for reasons I couldn't fathom.

She was the teenager who grew up slimmer and prettier, who escaped the Low Side, and moved to New York City.

She was the stepsister who married rich.

She was a person bound to call on me in a crisis, but not when time came to take care of her little girls while she went on vacation.

'No, no, it's just easier for them to stay in their own home ...' she'd said.

Vincent broke the silence between us.

'You want me to fix it, Miss Molly?'

'Fix it,' I said.

'You know that's a different price?'

'I understand.'

I don't allow myself to think about what happened next. I think only of how I retreated to my apartment, put my bare feet up on the balcony rail and waited for my father to call and say: 'Molly? Can you come over? Please. Just come now.'